AN A1
FIL
CRAWLING TERROR...

Moran cut apart the yard-long monstrosity with a slash of flame. The thing presumably died, but it continued to writhe senselessly. He turned to see other horrors crawling toward him. Then he knew he was being marooned on a planet of endless terrors…

Here is a gripping tale of deep space horror about a doomed spaceship that has the misfortune of landing on a weird planet filled with marauding alien monstrosities, hell bent on murdering everything in their paths. Penned by one of the master story tellers of science fiction, Murray Leinster.

FOR A COMPLETE SECOND NOVEL, TURN TO PAGE 75

CAST OF CHARACTERS

MORAN

He had two choices…to be tried and executed for murder, or be marooned on a planet filled with giant insect monstrosities.

BURLEIGH

He was the captain of the spaceship Nadine, and therefore the only man with the power to spare Moran's life.

CAROL

Even a revolutionist can have a heart. And hers belonged to a man who was about to die in the most horrifying manner imaginable.

HALLET

Another revolutionist, but he was not so much dedicated to any great cause as he was to himself. What were his secret plans?

HARPER

A crewmember on the Nadine—his life had been saved by the man he must now help condemn to death.

BRAWN

He helped salvage limitless treasure out of the crumbling hull of a wrecked spaceship—lost for over a hundred and fifty years!

PLANET OF DREAD

By
MURRAY LEINSTER

ARMCHAIR FICTION
PO Box 4369, Medford, Oregon 97504

*For more information about Armchair Books and products, visit our
website at…*

www.armchairfiction.com

Or email us at…

armchairfiction@yahoo.com

CHAPTER ONE

MORAN, naturally, did not mean to help in the carrying out of the plans that would mean his destruction one way or another. The plans were thrashed out very painstakingly, in formal conference on the space yacht *Nadine*, with Moran present and allowed to take part in the discussion. From the viewpoint of the *Nadine's* ship's company, it was simply necessary to get rid of Moran. In their predicament he might have come to the same conclusion; but he was not at all enthusiastic about their decision. He would die of it.

The *Nadine* was out of overdrive and all the uncountable suns of the galaxy shone steadily, remotely, as infinitesimal specks of light of every color of the rainbow. Two hours since, the sun of this solar system had been a vast glaring disk off to port, with streamers and prominences erupting about its edges. Now it lay astern, and Moran could see the planet that had been chosen for his marooning. It was a cloudy world. There were some dim markings near one lighted limb, but nowhere else. There was an icecap in view. The rest was—clouds.

THE icecap, by its existence and circular shape, proved that the planet rotated at a not unreasonable rate. The fact that it was water-ice told much. A water-ice icecap said that there were no poisonous gases in the planet's atmosphere. Sulfur dioxide or chlorine, for example, would not allow the formation of water-ice. It would have to be sulfuric acid or hydrochloric acid ice. But the icecap was simple snow. Its size, too, told about temperature-distribution on the planet. A large cap would have meant a large area with arctic and sub-arctic temperatures, with small temperate and tropical climate-belts. A small one like this meant wide tropical and sub-tropical zones. The fact

PLANET of DREAD

By MURRAY LEINSTER

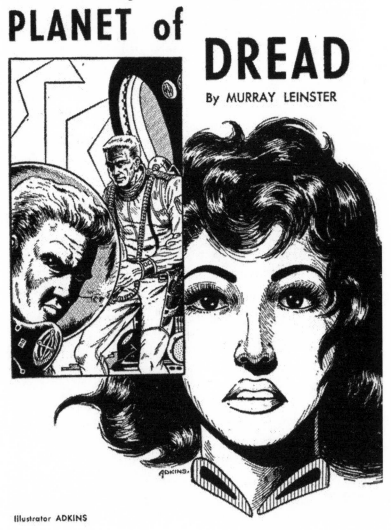

Illustrator ADKINS

was verified by the thick, dense cloud masses that covered most of the surface—all the surface, in fact, outside of the

Moran cut apart the yard-long monstrosity with a slash of flame. The thing presumably died, but it continued to writhe senselessly. He turned to see other horrors crawling toward him. Then he knew he was being marooned on a planet of endless terrors.

icecap. But since there were icecaps there would be temperate regions. In short, the icecap proved that a man could endure the air and temperature conditions he would find.

MORAN observed these things from the control room of the *Nadine*, then approaching the world on planetary drive. He was to be left here, with no reason ever to expect rescue. Two of the *Nadine's* four-man crew watched out the same ports as the planet seemed to approach.

Burleigh said encouragingly, "It doesn't look too bad, Moran."

Moran disagreed, but he did not answer. He cocked an ear instead. He heard something. It was a thin, wabbling, keening whine. No natural radiation sounds like that. Moran nodded toward the all-band speaker.

"Do you hear what I do?" he asked sardonically.

Burleigh listened. A distinctly artificial signal came out of the speaker. It wasn't a voice signal. It wasn't an identification beacon, such as are placed on certain worlds for the convenience of interstellar skippers who need to check their courses on extremely long runs. This was something else.

Burleigh said, "Hmmm...call the others, Harper."

Harper, prudently with him in the control room, put his head into the passage leading away. He called. But Moran observed with grudging respect that he didn't give him a chance to do anything drastic. These people on the *Nadine* were capable. They'd managed to recapture the *Nadine* from him, but they were matter-of-fact about it. They didn't seem to resent what he'd tried to do, or that he'd brought them an indefinite distance in an indefinite direction from their last landing-point, and they had still to relocate themselves.

THEY'D been on Coryus Three and they'd gotten departure clearance from its spaceport. With clearance-papers in order, they could land unquestioned at any other spaceport and take off again—provided the other space-port was one they had clearance for. Without rigid control of space travel, any criminal anywhere could escape the consequences of any crime simply by buying a ticket to another world. Moran couldn't have bought a ticket, but he'd tried to get off the planet Coryus on the *Nadine*. The trouble was that the *Nadine* had clearance papers covering five persons aboard—four men and a girl Carol. Moran made six. Wherever the yacht landed, such a disparity between its documents and its crew would spark an investigation. A lengthy, incredibly minute investigation. Moran, at least, would be picked out as a fugitive from Coryus Three. The others were fugitives too, from some unnamed world Moran did not know. They might be sent back where they came from. In effect, with six people on board instead of five, the *Nadine* could not land anywhere for supplies. With five on board, as her papers declared, she could. And Moran was the extra man whose presence would rouse spaceport officials' suspicion of the rest. So he had to be dumped.

He couldn't blame them. He'd made another difficulty, too. Blaster in hand, he'd made the *Nadine* take off from Coryus III with a trip-tape picked at random for guidance. But the trip-tape had been computed for another starting-point, and when the yacht came out of overdrive it was because the drive had been dismantled in the engine room. So the ship's location was in doubt. It could have traveled at almost any speed in practically any direction for a length of time that was at least indefinite. A liner could re-locate itself without trouble. It had elaborate observational equipment and tri-di star-charts. But smaller craft had to depend on the Galactic Directory. The process would be to find a planet and check its climate and relationship to other planets, and its flora and fauna against descriptions in the Directory. That was the way to find out where one was, when one's position became doubtful. The *Nadine* needed to make a planet-fall for this.

The rest of the ship's company came into the control room. Burleigh waved his hand at the speaker.

"Listen!"

THEY heard it. All of them. It was a trilling, whining sound among the innumerable random noises to be heard in supposedly empty space.

"That's a marker," Carol announced. "I saw a costume-story tape once that had that sound in it. It marked a first-landing spot on some planet or other, so the people could find that spot again. It was supposed to be a long time ago, though."

"It's weak," observed Burleigh. "We'll try answering it."

Moran stirred, and he knew that every one of the others was conscious of the movement. But they didn't watch him suspiciously. They were alert by long habit. Burleigh said they'd been Underground people, fighting the government of their native world, and they'd gotten away to make it seem the revolt had collapsed. They'd go back later when they weren't expected, and start it up again. Moran considered the story probable. Only people accustomed to desperate actions would have remained so calm when Moran had used desperate measures against

10

them.

Burleigh picked up the transmitter-microphone.

"Calling ground," he said briskly. "Calling ground. We pick up your signal. Please reply."

He repeated the call, over and over and over. There was no answer. Cracklings and hissings came out of the speaker as before, and the thin and reedy wabbling whine continued. The *Nadine* went on toward the enlarging cloudy mass ahead.

Burleigh said, "Well?"

"I think," said Carol, "that we should land. People have been here. If they left a beacon, they may have left an identification of the planet. Then we'd know where we are and how to get to Loris."

Burleigh nodded. The *Nadine* had cleared for Loris. That was where it should make its next landing. The little yacht went on. All five of its proper company watched as the planet's surface enlarged. The icecap went out of sight around the bulge of the globe, but no markings appeared. There were cloudbanks everywhere, probably low down in the atmosphere. The darker vague areas previously seen might have been highlands.

"I think," said Carol, to Moran, "that if it's too tropical where this signal's coming from, we'll take you somewhere near enough to the icecap to have an endurable climate. I've been figuring on food, too. That will depend on where we are from Loris because we have to keep enough for ourselves. But we can spare some. We'll give you the emergency kit, anyhow."

THE emergency kit contained antiseptics, seeds, and a weapon or two, with elaborate advice to castaways. If somebody were wrecked on an even possibly habitable plane, the especially developed seed-strains would provide food in a minimum of time. It was not an encouraging thought, though, and Moran grimaced.

She hadn't said anything about being sorry that he had to be marooned. Maybe she was, but rebels learn to be practical or they don't live long. Moran wondered, momentarily, what sort of world they came from and why they had revolted, and what sort of setback to the revolt had sent the five off in what they considered a strategic retreat but their government would think defeat. Moran's own situation was perfectly clear.

He'd killed a man on Coryus III. His victim would not be mourned by anybody, and somebody formerly in very great danger would now be safe, which was the reason for what Moran had done. But the dead man had been very important, and the fact that Moran had forced him to fight, and killed him in fair combat made no difference. Moran had needed to get off-planet, and fast. But space travel regulations are especially designed to prevent such escapes.

He'd made a pretty good try, at that. One of the controls on space traffic required a ship on landing to deposit its fuel-block in the spaceport's vaults. The fuel-block was not returned until clearance for departure had been granted. But Moran had waylaid the messenger carrying the *Nadine's* fuel-block back to that space yacht. He'd knocked the messenger cold and presented himself at the yacht with the fuel. He was admitted. He put the block in the engine's gate. He duly took the plastic receipt-token the engine only then released, and he drew a blaster. He'd locked two of the *Nadine's* crew in the engine room, rushed to the control room without encountering the others; dogged the door shut, and threaded in the first trip-tape to come to hand. He punched the take-off button and only seconds later the overdrive. Then the yacht—and Moran—was away. But his present companions got the drive dismantled two days later and once the yacht was out of overdrive they efficiently gave him his choice of surrendering or else. He surrendered, stipulating that he wouldn't be landed back on Coryus; he still clung to hope of avoiding return—which was almost certain anyhow. Because nobody would want to go back to a planet from which they'd carried away a criminal, even though they'd done it unwillingly. Investigation of such a matter might last for months.

Now the space yacht moved toward a vast mass of fleecy whiteness without any visible features. Harper stayed with the direction finder. From time to time he gave readings requiring minute changes of course. The wabbling, whining signal was louder now. It became louder than all the rest of the space noises together.

THE yacht touched atmosphere and Burleigh said, "Watch our height, Carol."

She stood by the echometer. Sixty miles. Fifty. Thirty. A correction of course. Fifteen miles to surface below. Ten. Five. At twenty-five thousand feet there were clouds, which would be particles of ice so small that they floated even so high. Then clear air, then lower clouds, and lower ones still. It was not until six thousand feet above the surface that the planet-wide cloud-level seemed to begin. From there on down it was pure opacity. Anything could exist in that dense, almost palpable grayness. There could be jagged peaks.

The *Nadine* went down and down. At fifteen hundred feet above the unseen surface, the clouds ended. Below, there was only haze. One could see the ground, at least, but there was no horizon. There was only an end to visibility. The yacht descended as if in the center of a sphere in which one could see clearly nearby, less clearly at a little distance, and not at all beyond a quarter mile or so.

There was a shaded, shadow-less twilight under the cloudbank. The ground looked like no ground ever seen before by anyone. Off to the right a rivulet ran between improbable-seeming banks. There were a few very small hills of most unlikely appearance. It was the ground, the matter on which one would walk, which was strangest. It had color, but the color was not green. Much of it was a pallid, dirty-yellowish white. But there were patches of blue and curious veinings of black, and here and there were other colors, all of them unlike the normal color of vegetation on a planet with a sol-type sun.

Harper spoke from the direction finder, "The signal's coming from that mound, yonder."

There was a hillock of elongated shape directly in line with the *Nadine's* course in descent. Except for the patches of color, it was the only considerable landmark within the half-mile circle in which anything could be seen at all.

The *Nadine* checked her downward motion. Interplanetary drive is rugged and sure, but it does not respond to fine adjustment. Burleigh used rockets, issuing great bellowings of flame, to make actual contact. The yacht hovered, and as the rocket flames diminished slowly she sat down with practically no impact at all. But around her there was a monstrous tumult of smoke and steam. When the rockets went off, she lay in a burned-out hollow some three or four feet deep with a bottom of solid stone. The walls of the hollow were black and scorched. It seemed that at some places they quivered persistently.

There was silence in the control room save for the

14

whining noise, which now was almost deafening. Harper snapped off the switch. Then there was true silence. The space yacht had come to rest possibly a hundred yards from the mound that was the source of the space signal. That mound shared the peculiarity of the ground as far as they could see through the haze. It was not vegetation in any ordinary sense. Certainly it was no mineral surface. The landing pockets had burned away three or four feet of it, and the edge of the burned area smoked noisesomely, and somehow it looked as if it would reek. And there were places where it stirred.

Burleigh blinked and stared. Then he reached up and flicked on the outside microphones. Instantly there was bedlam. If the landscape was strange, here, the sounds that came from it were unbelievable.

THERE were grunting noises. There were clickings, uncountable clickings that made a background for all the rest. There were discordant howls and honkings. From time to time some thing unknown made a cry that sounded very much like a small boy trailing a stick against a picket fence, only much louder. Something hooted, maintaining the noise for an Impossibly long time. And persistently, sounding as if they came from far away, there were booming noises, unspeakably deep-bass, made by something alive. And something shrieked in lunatic fashion and something else still moaned from time to time with the volume of a steam whistle...

"This sounds and looks like a nice place to live," said Moran with fine irony.

Burleigh did not answer. He turned down the outside sound.

"What's that stuff there, the ground!" he demanded.

"We burned it away in landing. I've seen something like it somewhere, but never taking the place of grass!"

"That," said Moran as if brightly, "that's what I'm to make a garden in. Of evenings I'll stroll among my thrifty plantings and listen to the delightful sounds of nature."

Burleigh scowled. Harper flicked off the direction finder.

"The signal still comes from that hillock yonder," he said with finality.

"That ain't no hillock, that's my home!" Moran said bitingly.

Then, instantly he'd said it, he recognized that it could be true. The mound was not a fold in the ground. It was not an up-cropping of the ash-covered stone on which the *Nadine* rested. The enigmatic, dirty-yellow-dirty-red-dirty-blue-and-dirty-black groundcover hid something. It blurred the shape it covered, very much as enormous cobwebs made solid and opaque would have done. But when one looked carefully at the mound, there was a landing-fin sticking up toward the leaden skies. It was attached to a large cylindrical object of which the fore part was crushed in. The other landing-fins could be traced.

"It's a ship," said Moran curtly. "It crash landed and its crew set up a signal to call for help. None came, or they'd have turned the beacon off. Maybe they got the lifeboats to work and got away. Maybe they lived as I'm expected to live until they died as I'm expected to die."

"You'd do what we are doing if you were in our shoes!" Burleigh said angrily.

"Sure," agreed Moran, "but a man can gripe, can't he?"

"You won't have to live here," said Burleigh. "We'll take you somewhere up by the icecap. As Carol said, we'll give you everything we can spare. And meanwhile we'll take a look at that wreck yonder. There might be an indication in it of what solar system this is. There could be something in it of use to you, too. You'd better come along when we explore."

"Aye, aye, sir," said Moran with irony. "Very kind of you, sir. You'll go armed, sir?"

"Naturally!" Burleigh growled.

"Then since I can't be trusted with a weapon," said Moran, "I suggest that I take a torch. We may have to burn through that loathsome stuff to get in the ship."

"Right," growled Burleigh again. "Brawn and Carol, you'll keep ship. The rest of us wear suits. We don't know what that stuff is outside."

MORAN silently went to the spacesuit rack and began to get into a suit. Modem spacesuits weren't like the ancient crudities with bulging metal casings and enormous globular helmets. Non-stretch fabrics took the place of metal, and constant volume joints were really practical nowadays. A man could move about in a late model spacesuit almost as easily as in ship clothing. The others of the landing party donned their special garments with the brisk absence of fumbling that these people displayed in every action.

"If there's a lifeboat left," said Carol suddenly, "Moran might be able to de something with it."

"Ah, yes!" said Moran. "It's very likely that the ship hit hard enough to kill everybody aboard, but not smash the boats!"

"Somebody survived the crash," said Burleigh, "because they set up a beacon. I wouldn't count on a boat, Moran."

"I don't!" snapped Moran.

He flipped the fastener of his suit. He felt all the

17

openings catch. He saw the others complete their equipment. They took arms. So far they had seen no moving thing outside, but arms were simple sanity on an unknown world. Moran, though, would not be permitted a weapon. He picked up a torch. They filed into the airlock. The inner door closed. The outer door opened. It was not necessary to check the air specifically. The suits would take care of that. Anyhow the icecap said there were no water-soluble gases in the atmosphere, and a gas can't be an active poison if it can't dissolve.

They filed out of the airlock. They stood on ash-covered stone, only slightly eroded by the processes that made life possible on this planet. They looked dubiously at the scorched, indefinite substance that had been ground before the *Nadine* landed. Moran moved scornfully forward. He kicked at the burnt stuff. His foot went through the char. The hole exposed a cheesy mass of soft matter that seemed riddled with small holes.

Something black came squirming frantically out of one of the openings. It was eight or ten inches long. It had a head, a thorax, and an abdomen. It had wing cases. It had six legs. It toppled down to the stone on which the *Nadine* rested. Agitatedly, it spread its wing-covers and flew away, droning loudly. The four men heard the sound above even the monstrous cacophony of cries and boomings and grunts and squeaks that seemed to fill the air.

"What the devil—"

Moran kicked again. More holes. More openings. More small tunnels in the cheese-like, curd-like stuff. More black things squirming to view in obvious panic. They popped out everywhere. It was suddenly apparent that the top of the soil, here, was a thick and blanket-like sheet ever the whitish stuff. The black creatures lived and thrived in tunnels under it.

CAROL'S voice came over the helmet-phones:

"They're—bugs!" she said Incredulously. *"They're beetles! They're twenty times the size of the beetles we humans have been carrying around the galaxy, but that's what they are!"*

Moran grunted. Distastefully, he saw his predicament made worse. He knew what had happened here. He could begin to guess at other things to be discovered. It had not been practical for men to move onto new planets and subsist upon the flora and fauna they found there. On some new planets life had never gotten started. On such worlds a highly complex operation was necessary before humanity could move in. A complete ecological complex had to be built up; microbes to break down the rock for soil, bacteria to fix nitrogen to make the soil fertile; plants to grow in the new-made dirt and insects to fertilize the plants so they would multiply, and animals and birds to carry the seeds planet-wide. On most planets, to be sure, there were local, aboriginal plants and animals. But still terrestrial creatures had to be introduced if a colony was to feed itself. Alien plants did not supply satisfactory food. So an elaborate adaptation job had to be done on every planet before native and terrestrial living things settled down together. It wasn't impossible that the scuttling things were truly beetles, grown large and monstrous under the conditions of a new planet. And the ground…

"This ground stuff," said Moran distastefully, "is yeast or some sort of toadstool growth. This is a seedling world. It didn't have any life on it, so somebody dumped germs and spores and bugs to make it ready for plants and animals eventually. But nobody's come back to finish up the job."

Burleigh grunted a somehow surprised assent. But it wasn't surprising, not wholly so. Once one mentioned yeasts and toadstools and fungi generally, the weird landscape became less than incredible. But it remained actively unpleasant to think of being marooned on it.

"Suppose we go look at the ship?" said Moran unpleasantly. "Maybe you can find out where you are, and I can find out what's ahead of me."

He climbed up on the unscorched surface. It was elastic. The parchment—like top skin yielded. It was like walking on a mass of springs.

"We'd better spread out," added Moran, "or else we'll break through that skin and be floundering in this mess."

"I'm giving the orders, Moran!" said Burleigh shortly. "But what you say does make sense."

HE and the others joined Moran on the yielding surface. Their footing was uncertain, as on a trampoline. They staggered. They moved toward the hillock, which was a covered-over wrecked ship.

The ground was not as level as it appeared from the *Nadine's* control room. There were undulations. But they could not see more than a quarter-mile in any direction. Beyond that was mist. But Burleigh, at one end of the uneven line of advancing men, suddenly halted and stood staring down at something he had not seen before. The others halted.

Something moved. It came out from behind a very minor spire of whitish stuff that looked like a dirty sheet stretched over a tall stone. The thing that appeared was very peculiar indeed. It was a—worm. But it was a foot thick and ten feet long, and it had a group of stumpy legs at its fore end—where there were eyes hidden behind bristling hair-like growths—and another set of feet at its tail end. It progressed sedately by reaching forward with its fore-part, securing a foothold, and then arching its middle portion like a cat arching its back, to bring its hind part forward. Then it reached forward again. It was of a dark olive color from one end to the other. Its manner of walking was insane but somehow sedate.

Moran heard muffled noises in his helmet-phone as the others tried to speak. Carol's voice came anxiously:

"What's the matter? What do you see?"

Moran said with savage precision, "We're looking at an inchworm, grown up like the beetles only more so. It's not an inchworm any longer. It's a yard worm." Then he said harshly to the men with him, "It's not a hunting creature on worlds where it's smaller. It's not likely to have turned deadly here. Come on!"

He went forward over the singularly bouncy ground. The others followed. It was to be noted that Hallet, the engineer, avoided the huge harmless creature more widely than most.

THEY reached the mound that was the ship. Moran unlimbered his torch. He said sardonically, "This ship won't do anybody any good. It's old-style. That thick belt around its middle was dropped a hundred years ago, and more." There was an abrupt thickening of the cylindrical hull at the middle. There was an equally abrupt thinning, again, toward the landing-fins. The sharpness of the change was blurred over by the revolting ground-stuff growing everywhere. "We're going to find that this wreck has been here a century at least!"

Without orders, he turned on the torch. A four-foot flame of pure blue-white leaped out. He touched its tip to the fungoid soil. Steam leaped up. He used the flame like a gigantic scalpel, cutting a square a yard deep in the whitish stuff, and then cutting it across and across to destroy it. Thick fumes arose, and quiverings and shakings began. Black creatures in their labyrinths of tunnels began to panic. Off to the right the blanket-like surface ripped and they poured out. They scuttled crazily here and there. Some took to wing. By instinct the other men—the armed ones—moved back from the smoke. They wore space helmets but they felt that there should be an intolerable smell.

Moran slashed and slashed angrily with the big flame, cutting a way to the metal hull that had fallen here before his grandfather was born. Sometimes the flame cut across things that writhed, and he was sickened. But above all he raged because he was to be marooned here. He could not altogether blame the others. They couldn't land at any colonized world with him on board without his being detected as an extra member of the crew. His fate would then be sealed. But they also would be investigated. Official queries would go across this whole sector of the galaxy, naming five persons of such-and-such description and such-and-such fingerprints, voyaging in a space yacht of such-and-such size and registration. The world they came from would claim them as fugitives. They would be returned to it. They'd be executed.

Then Carol's voice came in his helmet-phone. She cried out:

"Look out! It's coming! Kill it! Kill it—"

He heard blast-rifles firing. He heard Burleigh pant commands. He was on his way out of the hollow he'd carved when he heard Harper cry out horribly.

He got clear of the newly burned away stuff. There was still much smoke and stream. But he saw Harper. More, he saw the thing that had Harper.

It occurred to him instantly that if Harper died, there would not be too many people on the *Nadine*. They need not maroon him. In fact, they wouldn't dare. A ship that came in to port with two few on board would be investigated as thoroughly as one that had too many. Perhaps more thoroughly. So if Harper were killed, Moran would be needed to take his place. He'd go on from here in the *Nadine*, necessarily accepted as a member of her crew.

Then he rushed, the flame-torch making a roaring sound.

CHAPTER TWO

THEY went back to the *Nadine* for weapons more adequate for encountering the local fauna when it was over. Blast-rifles were not effective against such creatures as these. Torches were contact weapons but they killed. Blast-rifles did not. And Harper needed to pull himself together again, too. Also, neither Moran nor any of the others wanted to go back to the still un-entered wreck while the skinny, somehow disgusting legs of the thing still kicked spasmodically—quite separate—on the whitish ground-stuff. Moran had disliked such creatures in miniature form on other worlds, let alone enlarged like this.

It seemed insane that such creatures, even in miniature, should painstakingly be brought across light-years of space to the new worlds men settled on. But it had been found to be necessary. The ecological system in which human beings belonged had turned out to be infinitely complicated. It had turned out, in fact, to be the ecological system of Earth, and unless all parts of the complex were present, the total was subtly or glaringly wrong. So mankind distastefully ferried pests as well as useful creatures to its new worlds as they were made ready for settlement. Mosquitoes throve on the inhabited globes of the Rim Stars. Roaches twitched nervous antennae on the settled planets of the Coalsack. Dogs on Antares had fleas, and scratched their bites, and humanity spread through the galaxy with an attendant train of insects and annoyances. If they left their pests behind, the total system of checks and balances that make life practical would get lopsided. It would not maintain itself. The vagaries that could result were admirably illustrated in and on the landscape outside the *Nadine*. Something had been left out of the seeding of this planet. The element—which might be a bacterium or a virus or almost anything at all—that kept creatures at the size called "normal" was either missing or inoperable here. The results were not desirable.

HARPER drank thirstily. Carol had watched from the control room. She was still pale. She looked strangely at Moran.

"You're sure it didn't get through your suit?" Burleigh asked insistently of Harper.

Moran said sourly, "The creatures have changed size. There's no proof they've changed anything else. Beetles live in tunnels they make in fungus growths. The beetles and the tunnels are larger, but that's all. Inchworms travel as they always did. They move yards instead of inches, but that's all. Centipedes—"

"It was—" said Carol unsteadily. "It was thirty feet long!"

"Centipedes," repeated Moran, "catch prey with their legs. They always did. Some of them trail poison from their feet. We can play a blowtorch over Harper's suit and any poison will be burned away. You can't burn a spacesuit."

"We certainly can't leave Moran here," said Burleigh uneasily.

"He kept Harper from being killed," said Carol. "Your blast-rifles weren't any good. The—creatures are hard to kill."

"Very hard to kill," agreed Moran. "But I'm not supposed to kill them. I'm supposed to live with them! I wonder how we can make them understand they're not supposed to kill me either!"

"I'll admit," said Burleigh, "that if you'd let Harper get killed, we'd have been forced to let you take his identity and not be marooned, to avoid questions at the spaceport on Loris. Not many men would have done what you did."

"Oh, I'm a hero," said Moran. "Noble Moran, that's me. What the hell would you want me to do? I didn't think. I won't do it again. I promise!"

The last statement was almost true. Moran felt a squeamish horror at the memory of what he'd been through over by the wrecked ship. He'd come running out of the excavation he'd made. He had for a weapon a four-foot blue-white flame, and there was a monstrous creature running directly toward him, with Harper lifted off the ground and clutched in two gigantic, spidery legs. It was no less than thirty feet long, but it was a centipede. It traveled swiftly on grisly, skinny, pipe-thin legs. It loomed over Moran as he reached the surface and he automatically thrust the flame at it. The result was shocking. But the nervous systems of insects are primitive. It is questionable that they feel pain. It is certain that separated parts of them act as if they had independent life. Legs—horrible things—sheared off in the flame of the torch, but the grisly furry thing rushed on until Moran slashed across its body with the blue-white fire. Then it collapsed. But Harper was still held firmly and half the monster struggled mindlessly to run on while another part was dead. Moran fought it almost hysterically, slicing off legs and wanting to be sick when their stumps continued to move as if purposefully, and the legs themselves kicked and writhed rhythmically. But he bored in and cut at the body and ultimately dragged Harper clear.

Afterward, sickened, he completed cutting it to bits with the torch. But each part continued nauseatingly to move. He went back with the others to the *Nadine*. The blast-rifles had been almost completely without effect upon the creature because of its insensitive nervous system.

I THINK," said Burleigh, "that it is only fair for us to lift from here and find a better part of this world to land Moran in."

"Why not another planet?" asked Carol.

"It could take weeks," said Burleigh harassedly. "We left Coryus three days ago. We ought to land on Loris before too long. There'd be questions asked if we turned up weeks late. We can't afford that! The spaceport police would suspect us of all sorts of things. They might decide to check back on us where we came from. We can't take the time to hunt another planet!"

"Then your best bet," said Moran caustically, "is to find out where we are. You may be so far from Loris that you can't make port without raising questions anyhow. But you might be almost on course. I don't know. But let's see if that wreck can tell us. I'll go by myself if you like."

He went into the airlock, where his suit and the others

had been sprayed with a corrosive solution while the outside air was pumped out and new air from inside the yacht admitted. He got into the suit. Harper joined him.

"I'm going with you," he said shortly. "Two will be safer than one—both with torches."

"Too, too true!" said Moran sardonically.

He bundled the other suits out of the airlock and into the ship. He checked his torch. He closed the inner lock door and started the pump.

Harper said, "I'm not going to try to thank you—"

"Because," Moran snapped, "you wouldn't have been on this planet to be in danger if I hadn't tried to capture the yacht. I know it."

"That wasn't what I meant to say," protested Harper.

Moran snarled at him. The lock-pump stopped and the ready-for-exit light glowed. They pushed open the outer door and emerged. Again there was the discordant, almost intolerable din. It made no sense. The cries and calls and stridulations they now knew to be those of insects had no significance. The unseen huge creatures made them without purpose. Insects do not challenge each other like birds or make mating calls like animals. They make noises because it is their nature. The noises have no meaning. The two men started toward the wreck to which Moran had partly burned a passageway. There were clickings from underfoot all around them.

Moran said abruptly, "Those clicks come from the beetles in their tunnels underfoot. They're practically a foot long. How big do you suppose bugs grow here—and why?"

HARPER did not answer. He carried a flame-torch like the one Moran had used before. They went unsteadily over the elastic, yielding stuff underfoot. Harper halted, to look behind. Carol's voice came in the helmet-phones.

"We're watching out for you. We'll try to warn you if—anything shows up."

"Better watch me!" snapped Moran. "If I should kill Harper after all, you might have to pass me for him presently!"

He heard a small, inarticulate sound, as if Carol protested. Then he heard an angry shrill whine. He'd turned aside from the direct line to the wreck. Something black, the size of a fair-sized dog, faced him belligerently. Multiple-lensed eyes, five inches across, seemed to regard him in a peculiarly daunting fashion. The creature had a narrow, unearthly, triangular face, with mandibles that worked from side to side instead of up and down like an animal's jaws. The head was utterly unlike any animal that might breed and raise their young and fight for them. There was a small thorax, from which six spiny; glistening legs sprang. There was a bulbous abdomen.

"This," said Moran coldly, "is an ant. I've stepped on them for no reason, and killed them. I've probably killed many times as many without knowing it. But this could kill me."

The almost yard-long enormity standing two and a half feet high, was in the act of carrying away a section of one of the legs of the giant centipede Moran had killed earlier. It still moved. The leg was many times the size of the ant. Moran moved toward it. It made a louder buzzing sound, threatening him.

Moran cut it apart with a slashing sweep of the flame that a finger-touch sent leaping from his torch. The thing presumably died, but it continued to writhe senselessly.

"I killed this one," said Moran savagely, "because I

remembered something from my childhood. When one ant finds something to eat and can't carry it all away, it brings back its friends to get the rest. The big thing I killed would be such an item. How'd you like to have a horde of these things about us? Come on!

Through his helmet-phone he heard Harper breathing harshly. He led the way once more toward the wreck.

BLACK beetles swarmed about when he entered the cut in the mould-yeast soil. They popped out of tunnels as if in astonishment that what had been subterranean passages suddenly opened to the air. Harper stepped on one, and it did not crush. It struggled frantically and he almost fell. He gasped. Two of the creatures crawled swiftly up the legs of Moran's suit, and he knocked them savagely away. He found himself grinding his teeth in invincible revulsion.

They reached the end of the cut he'd made in the fungus stuff. Metal showed past burned-away soil. Moran growled:

"You keep watch. I'll finish the cut."

The flame leaped out. Dense clouds of smoke and steam poured out and up. With the intolerably bright light of the torch overwhelming the perpetual grayness under the clouds and playing upon curling vapors, the two space-suited men looked like figures in some sort of inferno.

Carol's voice came anxiously into Moran's helmet-phone:

"Are you all right?"

"So far, both of us," said Moran sourly. "I've just uncovered the crack of an airlock door."

He swept the flame around again. A mass of undercut fungus toppled toward him. He burned it and went on. He swept the flame more widely. There was carbonized matter from the previously burned stuff on the metal, but he cleared all the metal. Carol's voice again:

"There's something flying...it's huge! It's a wasp! It's— monstrous!"

Moran growled, "Harper, we're in a sort of trench. If it hovers, you'll burn it as it comes down. Cut through its waist. It won't crawl toward us along the trench. It'd have to back toward us to use its sting."

He burned and burned, white light glaring upon a mass of steam and smoke which curled upward and looked as if lightning flashes played within it.

Carol's voice:

"It—went on past...it was as big as a cow!"

MORAN wrenched at the port door. It partly revolved. He pulled. It fell outward. The wreck was not standing upright on its fins. It lay on its side. The lock inside the toppled-out port was choked with a horrible mass of thread-like fungi. Moran swept the flame in. The fungus shriveled and was gone. He opened the inner lock-door. There was pure blackness within. He held the torch for light.

For an instant everything was confusion, because the wreck was lying on its side instead of standing in a normal position. Then he saw a sheet of metal, propped up to be seen instantly by anyone entering the wrecked space vessel.

Letters burned into the metal gave a date a century and a half old. Straggly torch writing said baldly:

"This ship the Malabar crashed here on Tethys II a week ago. We cannot repair. We are going on to Candida III in the boats. We are carrying what bessendium we can with us. We resign salvage rights in this ship to its finders, but we have more bessendium with us. We will give that to our rescuers.

Jos. White, Captain."

Moran made a peculiar, sardonic sound like a bark.

"Calling the *Nadine!*" he said in mirthless amusement. "This planet is Tethys Two. Do you read me? Tethys II. Look it up!"

A pause. Then Carol's voice, relieved:

"Tethys is in the Directory! That's good!" There was the sound of murmurings in the control room behind her. *"Yes...Oh—wonderful! It's not far off the course we should have followed! We won't be suspiciously late at Loris! Wonderful!"*

"I share your joy," said Moran sarcastically. "More information. The ship's name was the *Malabar*. She carried bessendium among her cargo. Her crew went on to Candida III a hundred and fifty years ago, leaving a promise to pay more bessendium to whoever should rescue them. More bessendium! That suggests that some bessendium was left behind."

Silence. The bald memorandum left behind the vanished crew was, of course, pure tragedy. A ship's lifeboat could travel four light-years, or possibly even six. But there were limits. A castaway crew had left this world on a desperate journey to another in the hope that life there would be tolerable. If they arrived, they waited for some other ship to cross the illimitable emptiness and discover either the beacon here or one they'd set up on the other world. The likelihood was small, at best. It had worked out zero. If the lifeboats made Candida III, their crews stayed there because they could go no farther. They'd died there, because if they'd been found this ship would have been visited and its cargo salvaged.

MORAN went inside. He climbed through the compartments of the toppled craft, using his torch for light. He found where the cargo-hold had been opened from the living part of the ship. He saw the cargo. There were small, obviously heavy boxes in one part of the hold. Some had been broken open. He found scraps of purple bessendium ore dropped while being carried to the lifeboats. A century and a half ago it had not seemed worth while to pick them up, though bessendium was the most precious material in the galaxy. It couldn't be synthesized. It had to be made by some natural process not yet understood, but involving long-continued pressures of megatons to the square inch with temperatures in the millions of degrees. It was purple. It was crystalline. Fractions of it in blocks of other metals made the fuel-blocks that carried liners winging through the void. But here were pounds of it dropped carelessly...

Moran gathered a double handful. He slipped it in a pocket of his spacesuit. He went clambering back to the lock.

He heard the roaring of a flame-torch. He found Harper playing it squeamishly on the wriggling fragments of another yard-long ant. It had explored the trench burned out of the fungus soil and down to the rock, Harper had killed it as it neared him.

"That's three of them I've killed," said Harper in a dogged voice. "There seem to be more."

"Did you hear my news?" asked Moran sardonically.

"Yes," said Harper. "How will we get back to the *Nadine?*"

"Oh, we'll fight our way through," said Moran, as sardonically as before. "We'll practice splendid heroism, giving battle to ants who think we're other ants trying to rob them of some fragments of an oversized dead centipede. A splendid cause to fight for, Harper."

He felt an almost overpowering sense of irony. The quantity of bessendium he'd seen was worth riches incalculable. The mere pocketful of crystals in his pocket would make any man wealthy if he could get to a settled planet and sell them. And there was much, much more back in the cargo-hold of the wreck. He'd seen it.

But his own situation was unchanged. Bessendium could be hidden somehow—perhaps between the inner and outer hulls of the *Nadine*. But it was not possible to land the *Nadine* at any spaceport with an extra man aboard her. In a sense, Moran might be one of the richest men in the galaxy in his salvagers' right to the treasure in the wrecked *Malabar's* hold. But he could not use that treasure to buy his way to a landing on a colonized world.

Carol's voice, she was frightened:

"Something's coming! It's—terribly big! It's coming out of the mist!"

MORAN pushed past Harper in the trench that ended at the wreck's lock-door. He moved on until he could see over the edge of that trench as it shallowed. Now there were not less than forty of the giant ants about the remnants of the monstrous centipede Moran had killed. They moved about in great agitation. There was squabbling. Angry, whining stridulations filled the air beneath the louder and more gruesome sounds from far-ther-away places. It appeared that scouts and foragers from two different ant-cities had come upon the treasure of dead—if twitching—meat of Moran's providing. They differed about where the noisome booty should be taken. Some ants pulled angrily against each other, whining shrilly. He saw individual ants running frantically away in two different directions. They would be couriers, carrying news of what amounted to a frontier incident in the city-state civilization of the ants.

Then Moran saw the giant thing of which Carol spoke. It was truly huge, and it had a gross, rounded body, and a ridiculously small thorax, and its head was tiny and utterly mild in expression. It walked with an enormous, dainty deliberation, placing small spiked feet at the end of fifteen-foot legs very delicately in place as it moved. Its eyes were multiple and huge, and its forelegs though used so deftly for walking had a horrifying set of murderous, needle-sharp saw-teeth along their edges.

It looked at the squabbling ants with its gigantic eyes that somehow appeared like dark glasses worn by a monstrosity. It moved primly, precisely toward them. Two small black creatures tugged at a hairy section of a giant centipede's leg. The great pale-green creature—a mantis; a praying mantis twenty feet tall in its giraffe-like walking position—the great creature loomed over them, looking down as through sunglasses. A foreleg moved like lightning. An ant weighing nearly as much as a man stridulated shrilly, terribly, as it was borne aloft. The mantis closed its arm-like forelegs upon it, holding it as if piously and benignly contemplating it. Then it ate it, very much as a man might eat an apple, without regard to the convulsive writhings of its victim.

IT moved on toward the denser fracas among the ants. Suddenly it raised its ghastly saw-toothed forelegs in an extraordinary gesture. It was the mantis' spectral attitude, which seemed a pose of holding out its arms in benediction. But its eyes remained blind—seeming and enigmatic—again like dark glasses.

Then it struck. Daintily, it dined upon an ant. Upon another. Upon another and another and another.

From one direction parties of agitated and hurrying black objects appeared at the edge of the mist. They were ants of a special caste—warrior-ants with huge mandibles designed for fighting in defense of their city and its social system and its claim to fragments of dead centipedes. From another direction other parties of no less truculent warriors moved with the swiftness and celerity of a striking taskforce. All the air was filled with the deep-bass notes of something huge, booming beyond visibility, and the noises as of sticks trailed against picket fences, and hootings which were produced by the rubbing of serrated leg-joints against chitinous diaphragms. But now a new tumult arose.

From forty disputatious *formicidae*, whining angrily at each other over the stinking remains of the monster Moran had killed, the number of ants involved in the quarrel became hundreds. But more and more arrived. The special caste of warriors bred for warfare was not numerous enough to take care of the provocative behavior of foreign foragers. There was a general mobilization in both unseen ant-city states. They became nations in arms. Their populations rushed to the scene of conflict. The burrows and dormitories and eating chambers of the underground nations were swept clean of occupants. Only the nurseries retained a skeleton staff of nurses—the nurseries and the excavated palace occupied by the ant queen and her staff of servants and administrators. All the resources of two populous ant-nations were flung into the fray.

FROM a space of a hundred yards or less, containing

mere dozens of belligerent squabblers, the dirty-white ground of the fungus-plain became occupied by hundreds of snapping, biting combatants. They covered—they fought over—the half of an acre. There were contending battalions fighting as masses in the center, while wings of fighting creatures to right and left were less solidly arranged. But reinforcements poured out of the mist from two directions, and soon the situation changed. Presently the battle covered an acre. Groups of fresh fighters arriving from the city to the right uttered shrill stridulations and charged upon the flank of their enemies. Simultaneously, reinforcements from the city to the left flung themselves into the fighting-line near the center.

Formations broke up. The battle disintegrated into an indefinite number of lesser combats; troops or regiments fighting together often moved ahead with an appearance of invincibility, but suddenly they broke and broke again until there was only a complete confusion of unorganized single combats in which the fighters rolled over and over, struggling ferociously with mandible and claw to destroy each other. Presently the battle raged over five acres. Ten. Thousands upon thousands of black, glistening, stinking creatures tore at each other in murderous ferocity. Whining, squealing battle cries arose and almost drowned out the deeper notes of larger but invisible creatures off in the mist.

Moran and Harper got back to the *Nadine* by a wide detour past warriors preoccupied with each other just before the battle reached its most savage stage. In that stage, the space yacht was included in the battleground. Fights went on about its landing-fins. Horrifying duels could be followed by scrapings and bumpings against its hull. From the yacht's ports the fighting ants looked like infuriated machines, engaged in each other's destruction. One might see a warrior of unidentified allegiance with its own abdomen ripped open, furiously rending an enemy without regard to its own mortal wound. There were those who had literally been torn in half, so that only head and thorax remained, but they fought on no less valiantly than the rest.

AT the edges of the fighting such cripples were more numerous. Ants with antenna shorn off or broken, with legs missing, utterly doomed—they sometimes wandered forlornly beyond the fighting, the battle seemingly forgotten. But even such dazed and incapacitated casualties came upon each other. If they smelled alike, they ignored each other. Every ant-city has its particular smell that its inhabitants share. Possession of the national odor is at once a certificate of citizenship in peacetime and a uniform in war. When such victims of the battle came upon enemy walking wounded, they fought.

And the giant praying mantis remained placidly and invulnerably still. It plucked single fighters from the battle and dined upon them while they struggled, and plucked other fighters, and consumed them. It ignored the battle and the high purpose and self-sacrificing patriotism of the ants. Immune to them and disregarded by them, it fed on them while the battle raged.

Presently the gray light overhead turned faintly pink, and became a deeper tint and then crimson. In time there was darkness. The noise of battle ended. The sounds of the day diminished and ceased, and other monstrous outcries took their place.

There were bellowings in the blackness without the *Nadine*. There were chirpings become baritone, and senseless uproars that might be unbelievable modifications of once-shrill and once-tranquil night sounds of other worlds. And there came a peculiar, steady, unrhythmic pattering sound. It seemed like something falling upon the blanket-like upper surface of the soil.

Moran opened the airlock door and thrust out a torch to see. Its intolerably bright glare showed the battlefield abandoned. Most of the dead and wounded had been carried away. Which, of course, was not solicitude for the wounded or reverence for the dead heroes. Dead ants, like dead centipedes, were booty of the only kind the creatures of this world could know. The dead were meat. The wounded were dead before they were carried away.

Moran peered out, with Carol looking affrightedly over his shoulder. The air seemed to shine slightly in the glare of the torch. The pattering sound was abruptly explained. Large, slow, widely separated raindrops fell heavily and steadily from the cloudbanks overhead. Moran could see them strike. Each spot of wetness glistened briefly. Then the raindrop was absorbed by the ground.

But there were other noises than the ceaseless tumult on the ground. There were sounds in the air, the beating of enormous wings. Moran looked up, squinting against the light. There were things moving about the black sky. Gigantic things.

Something moved, too, across the diminishingly lighted surface about the yacht. There were glitterings. Shining armor. Multifaceted eyes. A gigantic, horny, spiked object crawled toward the torch-glare, fascinated by it. Something else dived insanely. It splashed upon the flexible white surface twenty yards away, and struggled upward and took crazily off again. It careened blindly.

IT hit the yacht, a quarter-ton of night-flying beetle. The air seemed filled with flying things. There were moths with twenty-foot wings and eyes that glowed like rubies in the torch's light. There were beetles of all sizes, from tiny six-inch things to monsters in whom Moran did not believe even when he saw them. All were drawn by the light that should not exist under the cloudbank. They droned and fluttered and performed lunatic evolutions, coming always closer to the flame.

Moran cut off the torch and closed the lock-door from the inside.

"We don't load bessendium tonight," he said with some grimness. "To have no light, with what crawls about in the darkness, would be suicide. But to use lights would be worse. If you people are going to salvage the stuff in that wreck, you'll have to wait for daylight. At least then you can see what's coming after you."

They went into the yacht proper. There was no longer any question about the planet's air. If insects that were descendents of terrestrial forms could breathe it, so could men. When the first insect-eggs were brought here, the air had to be fit for them if they were to survive. It would not have changed.

Burleigh sat in the control room with a double handful of purple crystals before him.

"This," he said when Moran and Carol reentered, "this is bessendium past question. I've been thinking what it means."

"Money," said Moran dryly. "You'll all be rich. You'll probably retire from politics."

"That wasn't exactly what I had in mind," said Burleigh distastefully. "You've gotten us into the devil of a mess, Moran!"

"For which," said Moran with ironic politeness, "there is a perfect solution. You kill me, either directly or by leaving me marooned here."

Burleigh scowled. "We have to land at spaceports for supplies. We can't hope to hide you, it's required that landed ships be sterilized against infections from off-planet. We can't pass you as a normal passenger. You're not on the ship's papers and they're alteration-proof. Nobody's ever been able to change a ship's papers and not be caught. We could land and tell the truth, that you hijacked the ship and we finally overpowered you. But there are reasons against that."

"Naturally," agreed Moran. "I'd be killed anyhow and you'd be subject to intensive investigation. And you're fugitives as much as I am."

"Just so," admitted Burleigh.

Moran shrugged. "Which leaves just one answer. You maroon me and go on your way."

BURLEIGH said painfully, "There's this bessendium. If there's more—especially if there's more—we can leave you here with part of it. When we get far enough away, we charter a ship to come and get you. It'll be arranged. Somebody will be listed as of that ship's company, but he'll slip away from the spaceport and not be on board at all. Then you're picked up and landed using his name."

"If," said Moran ironically, "I am alive when the ship gets here. If I'm not, the crew of the chartered ship will be in trouble, short one man on return to port. You'll have trouble getting anybody to run that risk."

"We're trying to work out a way to save you!" insisted Burleigh angrily. "Harper would have been killed but for you. And—this bessendium will finance the underground

41

work that will presently make a success of our revolution. We're grateful! We're trying to help you!"

"So you maroon me," said Moran. Then he said, "But you've skipped the real problem! If anything goes wrong, Carol's in it! There's no way to do anything without risk for her. That's the problem! I could kill all you characters, land somewhere on a colonized planet exactly as you landed here, and be gone from the yacht on foot before anybody could find me. But I have a slight aversion to getting a girl killed or killing her just for my own convenience. It's settled. I stay here. You can try to arrange the other business if you like. But it's a bad gamble."

Carol was very pale. Burleigh stood up.

"You said that, I didn't. But I don't think we should leave you here. Up near the icecap should be infinitely better for you. We'll load the rest of the bessendium tomorrow, find you a place, leave you a beacon, and go."

He went out. Carol turned a white face to Moran.

"Is that—is that the real trouble? Do you really—"

Moran looked at her stonily.

"I like to make heroic gestures," he told her. "Actually, Burleigh's a very noble sort of character himself. He proposes to leave me with treasure that he could take. Even more remarkably, he proposes to divide up what you take, instead of applying it all to further his political ideals. Most men like him would take it all for the revolution!

"But—but—"

Carol's expression was pure misery. Moran walked deliberately across the control room. He glanced out of a port. A face looked in. It filled the transparent opening. It was unthinkable. It was furry. There were glistening chitinous areas. There was a proboscis like an elephant's

42

trunk, curled horribly. The eyes were multiple and mad.

It looked in, drawn and hypnotized by the light shining out on this nightmare world from the control room ports. Moran touched the button that closed the shutters.

CHAPTER THREE

WHEN morning came, its arrival was the exact reversal of the coming of night. In the beginning there was darkness, and in the darkness there was horror.

The creatures of the night untiringly filled the air with sound, and the sounds were discordant and gruesome and revolting. The creatures of this planet were gigantic. They should have adopted new customs appropriate to the dignity of their increased size. But they hadn't. The manners and customs of insects are immutable. They feed upon specific prey—spiders are an exception, but they are not insects at all—and they lay their eggs in specific fashion in specific places, and they behave according to instincts that are so detailed as to leave them no choice at all in their actions. They move blindly about, reacting like automata of infinite complexity that are capable of nothing not built into them from the beginning. Centuries and millennia do not change them. Travel across star clusters leaves them with exactly the capacities for reaction that their remotest ancestors had, before men lifted off ancient Earth's green surface.

The first sign of dawn was deep, deep, deepest red in the cloudbank no more than fifteen hundred feet overhead. The red became brighter, and presently was as brilliant as dried blood. Again presently it was crimson over the entire half-mile circle that human eyes could penetrate. Later still—but briefly—it was pink. Then the sky became gray.

From that color it did not change again.

Moran joined Burleigh in a survey of the landscape from the control room. The battlefield was empty now. Of the thousands upon thousands of stinking combatants who'd rent and torn each other the evening before, there remained hardly a trace. Here and there, to be sure, a severed saw-toothed leg remained. There were perhaps as many as four relatively intact corpses not yet salvaged. But something was being done about them.

There were tiny, brightly-banded beetles hardly a foot long which labored industriously over such frayed objects. They worked agitatedly in the yeasty stuff, which on this world took the place of soil. They excavated, beneath the bodies of the dead ants, hollows into which those carcasses could descend. They pushed the yeasty, curdy stuff up and around the sides of those to-be-desired objects. The dead warriors sank little by little toward oblivion as the process went on. The up-thrust, dug-out material collapsed upon them as they descended. In a very little while they would be buried where no larger carrion-eater would discover them, and then the brightly-colored sexton beetles would begin a banquet to last until only fragments of chitinous armor remained.

BUT Moran and Burleigh, in the *Nadine's* control room, could hardly note such details.

"You saw the cargo," said Burleigh, frowning. "How's it packed? The bessendium, I mean."

"It's in small boxes too heavy to be handled easily," said Moran. "Anyhow the *Malabar's* crew broke some of them open to load the stuff on their lifeboats."

"The lifeboats are all gone?"

"Naturally," said Moran. "At a guess they'd have used

all of them even if they didn't need them for the crew. They could carry extra food and weapons and such."

"How much bessendium is left?"

"Probably twenty boxes unopened," said Moran. "I can't guess at the weight, but it's a lot. They opened six boxes," he paused. "I have a suggestion."

"What?"

"When you've supplied yourselves," said Moran, "leave some spaceport somewhere with papers saying you're going to hunt for minerals on some plausible planet. You can get such a clearance. Then you can return with bessendium coming out of the *Nadine's* waste pipes and people will be surprised but not suspicious. You'll file for mineral rights, and cash your cargo. Everybody will get busy trying to grab off the mineral rights for themselves. You can clear out and let them try to find the bessendium lode. You'll be allowed to go, all right, and you can settle down somewhere rich and highly respected."

"Hmmm," said Burleigh. Then he said uncomfortably, "One wonders about the original owners of the stuff."

"After a hundred and fifty years," said Moran, "who'd you divide with? The insurance company that paid for the lost ship? The heirs of the crew? How'd you find them?" Then he added amusedly, "Only revolutionists and enemies of governments would be honest enough to worry about that '"

Brawn came into the control room. He said broodingly that breakfast was ready. Moran had never heard him speak in a normally cheerful voice. When he went out, Moran said, "I don't suppose he'll be so gloomy when he's rich!"

"His family was wiped out," said Burleigh curtly, "by the government we were fighting. The girl he was going to marry, too."

"Then I take back what I said," said Moran ruefully.

THEY went down to breakfast. Carol served it. She did not look well. Her eyes seemed to show that she'd been crying. But she treated Moran exactly like anyone else. Harper was very quiet, too. He took very seriously the fact that Moran had saved his life at the risk of his on the day before. Brawn breakfasted in a subdued, moody fashion. Only Hallet seemed to have reacted to the discovery of a salvageable shipment of bessendium that should make everybody rich—everybody but Moran, who was ultimately responsible for the find.

"Burleigh," said Hallet expansively, "says the stuff you brought back from the wreck is worth fifty thousand credits, at least. What's the whole shipment worth?"

"I've no idea," said Moran. "It would certainly pay for a fleet of space liners, and I'd give all of it for a ticket on one of them."

"But how much is there in bulk?" insisted Hallet.

"I saw that half a dozen boxes had been broken open and emptied for the lifeboat voyagers," Moran told him. "I didn't count the balance, but there were several times as many untouched. If they're all full of the same stuff, you can guess almost any sum you please."

"Millions, eh?" said Hallet. His eyes glistened. "Billions? Plenty for everybody."

"There's never plenty for more than one," said Moran mildly. "That's the way we seem to be made."

Burleigh said suddenly, "I'm worried about getting the stuff aboard. We can't afford to lose anybody, and if we have to fight the creatures here…well every time we kill one its carcass draws others."

Moran took a piece of bread. He said, "I've been thinking about survival tactics for myself as a castaway. I think a torch is the answer. In any emergency on the yeast surface, I can burn a hole and drop down in it. The monsters are stupid. In most cases they'll go away because they stop seeing me. In the others, they'll come to the hole and I'll burn them. It won't be pleasant, but it may be practical."

Burleigh considered it.

"It may be," he admitted. "It may be."

"I want to see that work before I trust the idea," said Hallet.

"Somebody has to try it," agreed Moran. "Anyhow my life's going to depend on it."

Carol left the room. Moran looked after her as the door closed.

"She doesn't like the idea of our leaving you behind," said Burleigh. "None of us do."

"I'm touched."

"We'll try to get a ship to come for you, quickly," said Burleigh.

"I'm sure you will," said Moran politely.

BUT he was not confident. The laws governing space travel were very strict indeed, and enforced with all rigor possible. On their enforcement, indeed, depended the law and order of the planets. Criminals had to know that they could not escape to space whenever matters got too hot for them aground. For a spaceman to trifle with interstellar traffic laws meant at the least that they were grounded for life. But the probabilities were much worse than that. It was most likely that Burleigh or any of the others would be reported to spaceport police instantly if they attempted to charter a ship for any kind of illegal activity. Moran made a mental note to warn Burleigh about it.

By now, though, he was aware of a very deep irritation at the idea of being killed, whether by monsters on this planet or men sent to pick him up for due process of law. When he made the grand gesture of seizing the *Nadine*, he'd known nothing about the people on board, and he hadn't really expected to succeed. His real hope was to be killed without preliminary scientific questioning. Modern techniques of interrogation were not torture, but they stripped away all concealments of motive and to a great degree revealed anybody who'd helped one. Moran had killed a man in a fair fight that the other man had not wanted to engage in. If he were caught on Coryus or returned to it, his motivation could be read from his mind. And if that was done, the killing—and the sacrifice of his own future and life—would have been useless. But he'd been prepared to be killed. Even now he'd prefer to die here on Tethys than in the strictly painless manner of executions on Coryus. But he was now deeply resistant to the idea of dying at all. There was Carol…

He thrust such thoughts aside.

MORNING was well begun when they prepared to transfer the wreck's treasure to the *Nadine*. Moran went first. At fifteen-foot intervals he burned holes in the curd-like, elastic groundcover. Some of the holes went down only four feet to the stone beneath it. Some went down six. But a man who jumped down one of them would be safe against attack except from directly overhead, which was an unlikely direction for attack by an insect. Carol had seen a wasp fly past the day before. She said it was as big as a cow. A sting from such a monster would instantly be fatal. But no wasp would have the intelligence to use its sting on something it had not seized. A man should be safe in such a foxhole. If a creature did try to investigate the opening, a torch could come into play. It was the most practical possible way for a man to defend himself on this world.

Moran made more than a dozen such holes of refuge in the line between the *Nadine* and the wreck. Carol watched with passionate solicitude from a control room port as he progressed. He entered the wreck through the lock-doors he'd uncovered. Harper followed doggedly, not less than two foxholes behind. Carol's voice reassured them, the while, that within the half-mile circle of visibility no monster walked or flew.

Inside the wreck, Moran placed emergency lanterns to light the dark interior. He placed them along the particularly inconvenient passageways of a ship lying on its side instead of standing upright. He was at work breaking open a box of bessendium when Harper joined him.

"I've brought a bag," Harper said heavily, "it was a pillow. Carol took the foam out."

"We'll fill it," offered Moran. "Not too full. The stuff's heavy."

Harper watched while Moran poured purple crystals into it from his cupped hands.

"There you are," said Moran. "Take it away."

"Look!" said Harper. "I owe you plenty—"

"Then pay me," said Moran, exasperatedly, "by shutting up! By making Burleigh damned careful about who he tries to hire to come after me! And by getting this cargo-shifting business in operation! The *Nadine*'s almost due on Loris. You don't want to have the spaceport police get suspicions. Get moving!"

HARPER clambered over the side of doorways. He disappeared. Moran was alone in the ship. He explored. He found that the crew that had abandoned the *Malabar* had been guilty of a singular oversight for a crew abandoning ship. But, of course, they'd been distracted not only by their predicament but by the decision to carry part of the ship's precious cargo with them, so they could make it a profitable enterprise to rescue them. They hadn't taken the trouble to follow all the rules laid down for a crew taking to the boats.

Moran made good their omission. He was back in the cargo hold when Brawn arrived. Burleigh came next. Then Harper again. Hallet came last of the four men of the yacht. They did not make a continuous chain of men moving back and forth between the two ships. Three men came, and loaded up, and went back. Then three men came again, one by one. There could never be a moment when a single refuge-hole in the soil could be needed by two men at the same time.

Within the first hour of work at transferring treasure, the bolt-holes came into use. Carol called anxiously that a gigantic beetle neared the ship and would apparently pass between it and the yacht. At the time, Brawn and Harper were moving from the *Malabar* toward the *Nadine*, and Hallet was about to leave the wreck's lock.

He watched with wide eyes. The beetle was truly a monster, the size of a hippopotamus as pictured in the culture books about early human history. Its jaws, pronged like antlers, projected two yards before its huge, faceted eyes. It seemed to drag itself effortfully over the elastic surface of the ground. It passed a place where red, foleated fungus grew in a fantastic absence of pattern on the surface of the ground. It went through a streak of dusty-blue mould, which it stirred into a cloud of spores as it passed. It crawled on and on. Harper popped down into the nearest bolt-hole, his torch held ready. Brawn stood beside another refuge, sixty feet away.

Carol's voice came to their helmet-phones, anxious and exact. Hallet, in the lock-door, heard her tell Harper that the beetle would pass very close to him and to stay still. It moved on and on. It would be very close indeed. Carol gasped in horror.

The monster passed partly over the hole in which Harper crouched. One of its clawed feet slipped down into the opening. But the beetle went on, unaware of Harper. It crawled toward the encircling mist upon some errand of its own. It was mindless. It was like a complex and highly decorated piece of machinery, which did what it was wound up to do, and nothing else.

Harper came out of the bolt-hole when Carol, her voice shaky with relief, told him it was safe. He went doggedly on to the *Nadine*, carrying his bag of purple crystals. Brawn followed, moodily.

HALLET, with a singularly exultant look upon his face, ventured out of the airlock and moved across the fungoid world. He carried a king's ransom to be added to the riches already transferred to the yacht.

Moving the bessendium was a tedious task. One plastic box in the cargo-hold held a quantity of crystals that three men took two trips each to carry. In mid-morning the bag in Hallet's hand seemed to slip just when Moran completed filling it. It toppled and spilled half its contents on the cargo-hold floor, which had been a sidewall. He began painstakingly to gather up the precious stuff and get it back in the bag. The others went on to the *Nadine*. Hallet turned off his helmet-phone and gestured to Moran to remove his helmet. Moran, his eyebrows raised, obeyed the suggestion.

"How anxious," asked Hallet abruptly, gathering up the dropped crystals, "how anxious are you to be left behind here?"

"I'm not anxious at all," said Moran.

"Would you like to make a deal to go along when the *Nadine* lifts? —*If* there's a way to get past the spaceport police?"

"Probably," said Moran. "Certainly! But there's no way to do it."

"There is," said Hallet. "I know it. Is it a deal?"

"What is the deal?"

"You do as I say," said Hallet significantly. "Just as I say! Then…"

The lock-door opened, some distance away.

Hallet stood up and said in a commanding tone, "Keep your mouth shut. I'll tell you what to do and when."

He put on his helmet and turned on the phone once more. He went toward the lock-door. Moran heard him exchange words with Harper and Brawn, back with empty bags to fill with crystals worth many times the price of diamonds. But diamonds were made in half-ton lots, now-adays.

Moran followed their bags. He was frowning. As Harper was about to follow Brawn, Moran almost duplicated Hallet's gestures to have him remove his helmet.

"I want Burleigh to come next trip," he told Harper, "and make some excuse to stay behind a moment and talk to me without the helmet-phones picking up everything I say to him. Understand?"

Harper nodded. But Burleigh did not come on the next trip. It was not until near midday that he came to carry a load of treasure to the yacht.

When he did come, though, he took off his helmet and turned off the phone without the need of a suggestion.

"I've been arranging storage for this stuff," he said. "I've opened plates between the hulls to dump it in. I've told Carol, too, that we've got to do a perfect job of cleaning up. There must be no stray crystals on the floor."

"Better search the bunks, too," said Moran dryly, "so nobody will put aside a particularly pretty crystal to gloat over. Listen!"

He told Burleigh exactly what Hallet had said and what he'd answered. Burleigh looked acutely unhappy.

"Hallet isn't dedicated like the rest of us were," he said distressfully. "We brought him along partly out of fear that if he were captured he'd break down and reveal what he knows of the Underground we led, and much of which we had to leave behind. But I'll be able to finance a real revolt, now!"

MORAN regarded him with irony. Burleigh was a capable man and a conscientious one. It would be very easy to trust him, and it is all-important to an Underground that its leaders be trusted. But it is also important that they be capable of flint-like hardness on occasion. To Moran, it seemed that Burleigh had not quite the adamantine resolution required for leadership in a conspiracy that was to become a successful revolt. He was—and to Moran it seemed regrettable—capable of the virtue of charity.

"I've told you," he said evenly. "Maybe you'll think it's a scheme on my part to get Hallet dumped and myself elected to take his identity. But what happens from now on is your business. Beginning this moment, I'm taking care of my own skin. I've gotten reconciled to the idea of dying, but I'd hate for it not to do anybody any good."

"Carol," said Burleigh unhappily, "is much distressed."

"That's very kind," said Moran sarcastically. "Now take your bag of stuff and get going."

Burleigh obeyed. Moran went back to the business of breaking open the strong plastic boxes of bessendium so their contents could be carried in forty-pound lots to the *Nadine.*

Thinking of Carol, he did not like the way things seemed to be going. Since the discovery of the bessendium, Hallet had been developing ideas. They did not look as if they meant good fortune for Moran without corresponding bad fortune for the others. Obviously, Moran couldn't be hidden on the *Nadine* during the spaceport sterilization of the ship, which prevented plagues from being carried from world to world. Hallet could have no reason to promise such a thing. Before landing here, he'd urged that Moran simply be dumped out the airlock. This proposal to save his life...

Moran considered the situation grimly while the business of ferrying treasure to the yacht went on almost monotonously. It had stopped once during the forenoon while a giant beetle went by. Later, it stopped again because a gigantic flying thing hovered overhead. Carol did not know what it was, but its bulging abdomen ended in an organ which appeared to be a sting. It was plainly hunting. There was no point in fighting it. Presently it went away, and just before it disappeared in the circular wall of mist it dived headlong to the ground. A little later it rose slowly into the air, carrying something almost as large as itself. It went away into the mist.

Again, once a green-and-yellow caterpillar marched past upon some mysterious enterprise. It was covered with incredibly long fur, and it moved with an undulating motion of all its segments, one after another. It seemed well over ten yards in length, and its body appeared impossibly massive. But a large part of the bulk would be the two-foot-long or longer hairs that stuck out stiffly in all directions. It, too, went away.

But continually and constantly there was a bedlam of noises. From underneath the yielding skin of the yeast-ground, there came clickings. Sometimes there were quiverings of the surface as if it were alive, but they would be the activities of ten and twelve-inch beetles who lived in subterranean tunnels in it. There were those preposterous noises like someone rattling a stick along a picket fence— only deafening—and there were baritone chirpings and deep bass booming from somewhere far away. Moran guessed that the last might be frogs, but if so they were vastly larger than men.

SHORTLY after what was probably midday, Moran brushed off his hands. The bessendium part of the cargo of the wrecked *Malabar* had been salvaged. It was hidden between the twin hulls of the yacht. Moran had, quite privately, attended to a matter the wreck's long-dead crew should have done when they left it. Now, in theory, the *Nadine* should lift off and take Moran to some hastily scouted spot not too far from the icecap. It should leave him there with what food could be spared, and the kit of seeds that might feed him after it was gone, and weapons that might but probably wouldn't enable him to defend himself, and with a radio-beacon to try to have hope in. Then—that would be that.

"Calling," said Moran sardonically into his helmet-phone. "Everything's cleaned up here. What next?"

"You can come along," said Hallet's voice from the ship. It was shivery. It was gleeful. *"Just in time for lunch!"*

Moran went along the disoriented passages of the *Malabar* to the lock. He turned off the beacon that had tried uselessly during six human generations to call for help for men now long dead. He went out the lock and closed it behind him. It was not likely that this planet would ever become a home for men. If there were some strangeness in its constitution that made the descendents of insects placed upon it grow to be giants, humans would not want to settle on it. And there were plenty of much more suitable worlds. So the wrecked spaceship would lie here, under deeper and ever deeper accumulations of the noisome stuff that passed for soil. Perhaps millennia from now, the sturdy, resistant metal of the hull would finally rust through, and then—nothing. No man in all time to come would ever see the *Malabar* again.

Shrugging, he went toward the *Nadine*. He walked through bedlam. He could see a quarter-mile in one direction, and a quarter-mile in another. He could not see more than a little distance upward. The *Nadine* had landed upon a world with tens of millions of square miles of surface, and nobody had moved more than a hundred yards from its landing place, and now it would leave and all wonders and all horrors outside this one quarter of a square mile would remain unknown...

He went to the airlock and shed his suit. He opened the inner door. Hallet waited for him.

"Everybody's at lunch," he said. "We'll join them."

Moran eyed him sharply. Hallet grinned widely.

"We're going to take off to find a place for you as soon

as we've eaten," he said.

There was mockery in the tone. It occurred abruptly to Moran that Hallet was the kind of person who might, to be sure, plan complete disloyalty to his companions for his own benefit. But he might also enjoy betrayal for its own sake. He might, for example, find it amusing to make a man under sentence of death or marooning believe that he would escape, so Hallet could have the purely malicious pleasure of disappointing him. He might look for Moran to break when he learned that he was to die here after all.

Moran clamped his lips tightly. Carol would be better off if that was the answer. He went toward the yacht's mess-room. Hallet followed close behind. Moran pushed the door aside and entered. Burleigh and Harper and Brawn looked at him. Carol raised her eyes. They glistened with tears.

"Here goes!" Hallet said gleefully.

Standing behind Moran, he thrust a hand-blaster past Moran's body and pulled the trigger. He held the trigger down for continuous fire as he traversed the weapon to wipe out everybody but Moran and himself.

CHAPTER FOUR

MORAN responded instantly. His hands flew to Hallet's throat, blind fury making him unaware of any thought but a frantic lust to kill. It was very strange that Moran somehow noticed Hallet's hand insanely pulling the trigger of the blast-pistol over and over and over without result. He remembered it later. Perhaps he shared Hallet's blank disbelief that one could pull the trigger of a blaster and have nothing at all happen in consequence. But nothing did happen, and suddenly he dropped the weapon and clawed desperately at Moran's fingers about his throat. But that was too late.

There was singularly little disturbance at the luncheon table. The whole event was climax and anticlimax together. Hallet's intention was so appallingly murderous and his action so shockingly futile that the four who were to have been his victims tended to stare blankly while Moran throttled him.

Burleigh seemed to recover first. He tried to pull Moran's hands loose from Hallet's throat. Lacking success he called to the others. "Harper! Brawn! Help me!"

It took all three of them to release Hallet. Then Moran stood panting, shaking, his eyes like flames.

"He—he—" panted Moran. "He was going to kill Carol!"

"I know," said Burleigh, distressfully. "He was going to kill all of us. You gave me an inkling, so while he was packing bessendium between the hulls, and had his spacesuit hanging in the airlock, I doctored the blaster in the spacesuit pocket," he looked down at Hallet. "Is he still alive?"

Brawn bent over Hallet. He nodded.

"Put him in the airlock for the time being," said Burleigh. "And lock it. When he comes to, we'll decide what to do."

HARPER and Brawn took Hallet by the arms and hauled him along the passageway. The inner door of the lock clanged shut on him.

"We'll give him a hearing, of course," said Burleigh conscientiously. "But we should survey the situation first."

To Moran the situation required no survey, but he viewed it from a violently personal viewpoint that would neither require or allow discussion. He knew what he meant to do about Hallet. He said harshly,

"Go ahead. When you're through I'll tell you what will be done."

HE went away. To the control room. There he paced up and down, trying to beat back the fury that rose afresh at intervals of less than minutes. He did not think of his own situation, just then. There are more important things than survival.

He struggled for coolness, with the action before him known. He didn't glance out the ports at the half-mile circle in which vision was possible. Beyond the mist there might be anything: an ocean, swarming metropoli of giant insects, a mountain range. Nobody on the *Nadine* had explored. But Moran did not think of such matters now. Hallet had tried to murder Carol, and Moran meant to take action, and there were matters that might result from it. The matter the crew of the *Malabar* had forgotten to attend to—

He searched for paper and a pen. He found both in a drawer for the yacht's hand-written log. He wrote. He placed a small object in the drawer. He had barely closed it when Carol was at the control room door.

"They want to talk to you," she said in a small voice.

He held up the paper.

"Read this later. Not now," he said curtly. He opened and closed the drawer again, this time putting the paper in it. "I want you to read this after the Hallet business is settled. I'm afraid that I'm not going to look well in your eyes."

She swallowed and did not speak. He went to where the others sat in official council.

"We've come to a decision," Burleigh said heavily. "We shall call Hallet and hear what he has to say, but we had to consider various courses of action and decide which were possible and which were not."

Moran nodded grimly. He had made his own decision. It was not too much unlike the one that, carried out, had made him seize the *Nadine* for escape from Coryus. But he'd listen. Harper looked doggedly resolved. Brawn seemed moody as usual.

"I'm listening," said Moran.

"Hallet," said Burleigh regretfully, "intended to murder all of us and with your help take the *Nadine* to some place where he could hope to land without spaceport inspection."

"He didn't discuss that part of his plans," Moran observed. "He only asked if I'd make a deal to escape being marooned."

"Yes," said Burleigh, nodding. "I'm sure—"

"My own idea," said Moran, "when I tried to seize the *Nadine*, was to try to reach one of several newly-settled planets where things aren't too well organized. I'd memos of some such planets. I hoped to get to ground somewhere in a wilderness on one of them and work my way on foot to a new settlement. There I'd explain that I'd been hunting or prospecting or something of the sort. On a settled planet that would be impossible. On a brand-new one people are less fussy and I might have been accepted quite casually."

"Hallet may have had some such idea in his mind," agreed Burleigh. "With a few bessendium crystals to show, he would seem a successful prospector. He'd be envied but not suspected. To be sure."

"But," said Moran dryly, "he'd be best off alone. So if

he had that sort of idea, he intended to murder me too."

BURLEIGH nodded. "Undoubtedly. But to come to our decision. We can keep him on board under watch—as we did you—and leave you here. This has disadvantages. We owe you much. There would be risk of his taking someone unawares and fighting for his life. Even if all went as we wished, and we landed and dispersed, he could inform the spaceport officials anonymously of what had happened, leading to investigation and the ruin of any plans for the future revival of our underground. Also, it would destroy any hope for your rescue."

Moran smiled wryly. He hadn't much hope of that, if he were marooned.

"We could leave him here," said Burleigh unhappily, "with you taking his identity for purposes of landing. But I do not think it would be wise to send a ship after him. He would be resentful. If rescued, he would do everything possible to spoil all our future lives, and we are fugitives."

"Ah, yes!" said Moran, still more wryly amused.

"I am afraid," said Burleigh reluctantly, "that we can only offer him his choice of being marooned or going out the airlock. I cannot think of any other alternative."

"I can," said Moran. "I'm going to kill him."

Burleigh blinked. Harper looked up sharply.

"We fight," said Moran grimly. "Armed exactly alike. He can try to kill me. I'll give him the same chance I have. But I'll kill him. They used to call it a duel, and they came to consider it a very immoral business. But that's beside the point. I won't agree to marooning him here. That's murder. I won't agree to throwing him out the airlock. That's murder, too. But I have the right to kill him if it's in a fair fight. That's justice! You can bring him in and let him decide if he wants to be marooned or fight me. I think he's just raging enough to want to do all the damage he can, now that his plans have gone sour."

Burleigh fidgeted. He looked at Harper. Harper nodded grudgingly. He looked at Brawn. Brawn nodded moodily.

Burleigh said fretfully, "Very well...Harper, you and Brawn bring him here. We'll see what he says. Be careful!"

Harper and Brawn went down the passageway. Moran saw them take out the blasters they'd worn since he took over the ship. They were ready. They unlocked and opened the inner airlock door.

There was silence. Harper looked shocked. He went in the airlock while Brawn stared, for once startled out of moodiness.

Harper came out.

"He's gone," he said in a flat voice. "Out the airlock."

ALL the rest went instantly to look. The airlock was empty. By the most natural and inevitable of oversights, when Hallet was put in it for a temporary cell, no one had thought of locking the outer door. There was no point in it. It only led out to the nightmare world. And out there Hallet would be in monstrous danger; he'd have no food. At most his only weapon would be the torch Moran had carried to the *Malabar* and brought back again. He could have no hope of any kind. He could feel only despair unthinkable and horror undiluted.

There was a buzzing sound in the airlock. A spacesuit hung there. The helmet-phone was turned on. Hallet's voice came out, flat and metallic and desperate and filled with hate:

"What're you going to do now? You'd better think of a bargain to

offer me! You can't lift off! I took the fuel-block so Moran couldn't afford to kill me after the rest of you were dead. You can't lift off the ground! Now give me a guarantee I can believe in or you stay here with me!"

Harper bolted for the engine room. He came back, his face ashen. "He's right. It's gone. He took it."

Moran stirred. Burleigh wrung his hands. Moran reached down the spacesuit from whose helmet the voice came tinnily. He began to put it on. Carol opened her lips to speak, and he covered the microphone with his palm.

"I'm going to go out and kill him," said Moran very quietly. "Somebody else had better come along just in case. But you can't make a bargain with him. You can't believe in any promise he might make, because he wouldn't keep any."

Harper went away again. He came back, struggling into a spacesuit. Brawn moved quickly. Burleigh suddenly stirred and went for a suit.

"We want torches," said Moran evenly, "for our own safety, and blasters because they'll drop Hallet. Carol, you monitor what goes on. When we need to come back, you can use the direction finder and talk us back to the yacht."

"But—but—"

"What are you going to do?" rasped the voice shrilly. *"You've got to make a bargain! I've got the fuel-block! You can't lift off without the fuel-block! You've got to make a deal."*

THE other men came back. With the microphone still muffled by his hand, Moran said sharply, "He has to keep talking until we answer, but he won't know we're on his trail until we do. We keep quiet when we get the helmets on. Understand?" Then he said evenly to Carol. "Look at that paper I showed you if—if anything happens. Don't forget! Ready?"

Carol's hands were clenched. She was terribly pale. She tried to speak, and could not. Moran, with the microphone still covered by the palm of his hand, repeated urgently:

"Remember, no talking! He'll pick up anything we say. Use gestures. Let's go!"

He swung out of the airlock. The others followed. The one certain thing about the direction Hallet would have taken was that it must be away from the wreck. And he'd have been in a panic to get out of sight from the yacht.

Moran saw his starting point at once. Landing, the *Nadine* had used rockets for easing to ground because it is not possible to make delicate adjustments of interplanetary drive. A take-off, yes. But to land even at a spaceport one uses rockets to cushion what otherwise might be, a sharp impact. The *Nadine's* rockets had burned away the yeasty soil when she came to ground. There was a burnt-away depression down to bedrock in the stuff all around her. But Hallet had broken the scorched, crusty edge of the hollow as he climbed up to the blanket-like surface-skin.

Moran led the way after him. He moved with confidence. The springy, sickeningly uncertain stuff underfoot was basically white-that-had-been-soiled. Between the *Nadine's* landing spot and the now-gutted wreck, it happened that only that one color showed. But, scattered at random in other places, there were patches of red mould and blue mould and black dusty rust and greenish surface fungi. Twenty yards from the depression in which the *Nadine* lay, Hallet's footprints were clearly marked in a patch of orange-yellow groundcover, which gave off impalpable yellow spores when touched. Moran gestured for attention and pointed out the trail. He gestured again for the others to spread out.

Hallet's voice came again. He'd left the *Nadine's* lock because he could make no bargain for his life while in the hands of his companions. He could only bargain for his life if they could not find him or the precious fuel-block without which the *Nadine* must remain here forever. But from the beginning he knew such terror that he could not contrive, himself, a bargain that could possibly be made.

He chattered agitatedly, not yet sure that his escape had been discovered. At times he seemed almost hysterical. Moran and the others could hear him pant, sometimes, as a fancied movement aroused his panic. Once they heard the noise of his torch as he burned a safety-hole in the ground. But he did not use it. He hastened on. He talked desperately. Sometimes he boasted, and sometimes he tried cunningly to be reasonable. But he hadn't been prepared for the absolute failure of what should have been the simplest and surest form of multiple murder. Now in a last ditch stand, he hysterically abused them for taking so long to realize that they had to make a deal.

HIS four pursuers went grimly over the elastic surface of this world upon his trail. The *Nadine* faded into the mist. Off to the right a clump of toadstools grew. They were taller than any of the men, and their pulpy stalks were more than a foot thick. Hallet's trail in the colored surface-moulds went on. The giant toadstools were left behind. The trail led straight toward an enormous object the height of a three-story house. When first glimpsed through the mist, it looked artificial. But as they drew near they saw that it was a cabbage; gigantic, with leaves impossibly huge and thick. There was a spike in its middle on which grew cruciform faded flowers four feet across.

Then Hallet screamed. They heard it in their helmet-phones. He screamed again. Then for a space he was silent, gasping, and then he uttered shrieks of pure horror. But they were cries of horror, not of pain.

Moran found himself running, which was probably ridiculous. The others hastened after him. And suddenly the mistiness ahead took on a new appearance. The ground fell away. It became evident that the *Nadine* had landed upon a plateau with levels below it and very possibly mountains rising above. But here the slightly rolling plateau fell sheer away. There was a place where the yeasty soil—but here it was tinted with a purplish overcast of foleate fungus—where the soil had given way. Something had fallen, here.

It would have been Hallet. He'd gone too close to a precipice, moving agitatedly in search of a hiding place in which to conceal himself until the people of the *Nadine* made a deal he could no longer believe in.

His cries still came over the helmet-phones. Moran went grimly to look. He found himself gazing down into a cross-valley perhaps two hundred feet deep. At the bottom there were incredible, green growing things. But they were not trees. They were some flabby weeds with thick reddish stalks and enormous pinnate leaves. It grew here to the height of oaks. But Hallet had not dropped so far.

From anchorages on bare rock, great glistening cables reached downward to other anchorages on the valley floor. The cables crossed each other with highly artificial precision at a central point. They formed the foundation for a web of geometrically accurate design and unthinkable size. Cross cables of sticky stuff went round and round the center of the enormous snare, following a logarithmic spiral with absolute exactitude. It was a spider's web whose cables stretched hundreds of feet; whose birdlimed ropes would trap and hold even the monster insects of this world. And Hallet was caught in it.

HE'D tumbled from the cliff-edge as fungoid soil gave way under him. He'd bounced against a sloping, fungus-covered rocky wall and with fragments of curdy stuff about him had been flung out and into the snare. He was caught as firmly as any of the other creatures on which the snare's owner fed.

His shrieks of horror began when he realized his situation. He struggled, setting up insane vibrations in the fabric of the web. He shrieked again, trying to break the bonds of cordage that clung the more horribly as he struggled to break free. And the struggling was most unwise.

"We want to cut the cables with torches," said Moran sharply. "If we can make the web drop we'll be all right. Web spiders don't hunt on the ground. Go ahead! Make it fast!"

Burleigh and the others hastened to what looked like a nearly practicable place by which to descend. Moran moved swiftly to where one cable of the web was made fast at the top. It was simple sanity to break down the web—by degrees, of course—to get at Hallet. But Hallet did not cooperate. He writhed and struggled and shrieked.

His outcry, of course, counted for nothing in the satanic cacophony that filled the air. All the monsters of the planet seemed to make discordant noises. Hallet could add nothing. But his struggles in the web had meaning to the owner of the trap.

They sent tiny tremblings down the web-cables. And this was the fine mathematical creation of what was quaintly called a "garden spider" on other worlds. *Epeira fasciata.* She was not in it. She sat sluggishly in a sheltered place, remote from her snare. But a line, a cord, a signal-cable went from the center of the web to the spider's retreat. She waited with implacable patience, one foreleg—sheathed in ragged and somehow revolting fur—resting delicately upon the line. Hallet's frantic struggles shook the web. Faintly, to be sure, but distinctively. The vibrations were wholly unlike the violent, thrashing struggles of a heavy beetle or a giant cricket. They were equally unlike those flirtatious, seductive pluckings of a web-cable, which would mean that an amorous male of her own species sought the grisly creature's affection.

Hallet made the web quiver as small prey would shake it. The spider would have responded instantly to bigger game, if only to secure it before the vast snare was damaged by frenzied plungings. Still, though there was no haste, the giant rose and in leisurely fashion traversed the long cable to the web's center. Moran saw it.

"Hallet!" he barked into his helmet-phone, "Hallet! Hold still! Don't move!"

He raced desperately along the edge of the cliff, risking a fall more immediately fatal than Hallet's. It was idiotic to make such an attempt at rescue. It was sheer folly. But there are instincts one has to obey against all reason. Moran did not think of the fuel-block. Typically, Hallet did.

"I've got the fuel-block," he gasped between screams. *"If you don't help me—"*

But then the main cable nearest him moved in a manner not the result of his own struggles. It was the enormous weight of the owner of the web, moving leisurely on her own snare, which made the web shake now. And Hallet lost even the coherence of hysteria and simply shrieked.

MORAN came to a place where a main anchor-cable reached bedrock. It ran under yeasty groundcover to an anchorage. He thrust his torch deep, feeling for the cable. It seared through. The web jerked wildly as one of its principal supports parted. The giant spider turned aside to investigate the event. Such a thing should happen only when one of the most enormous of possible victims became entangled.

Moran went racing for another cable-anchorage. But when he found where the strong line fastened, it was simply and starkly impossible to climb down to it. He swore and looked desperately for Burleigh and Brawn and Harper. They were far away, hurrying to descend but not yet where they could bring the web toppling down by cutting other cables.

The yellow-banded monster came to the cut end of the line. It swung down. It climbed up again. Hallet shrieked and kicked.

The spider moved toward him. Of all nightmarish creatures on this nightmare of a planet, a giant spider with a body eight feet long and legs to span as many yards was most revolting. Its abdomen was obscenely swollen. As it moved, its spinnerets paid out newly formed cord behind it. Its eyes were monstrous and murderously intent. The ghastly, needle-sharp mandibles beside its mouth seemed to move lustfully with a life of their own. And it was somehow ten times more horrible because of its beastly fur. Tufts of black hairiness, half-yards in length, streamed out as its legs moved.

There was another cable still. Moran made for it. He reached it where it stretched down like a slanting tightrope.

He jerked out his torch to sever it—and saw that to cut it would be to drop the spider almost upon Hallet. It would seize him then because of his writhings. But not to cut it—

He tried his blaster. He fired again and again. The blaster-bolts hurt. The spider reacted with fury. The blaster would have killed a man at this distance, though it would have been ignored by a chitin-armored beetle. But against the spider the bolts were like bites. They made small wounds, but not serious ones. The spider made a bubbling sound that was more daunting than any cry would have been. It flung its legs about, fumbling for the thing that it believed attacked it. It continued the bubbling sounds. Its mandibles clashed and gnashed against each other. They were small noises in the din, which was the norm on this mad world, but they were more horrible than any other sounds Moran had ever heard.

THE spider suddenly began to move purposefully toward the spot where Hallet jerked insanely and shrieked in heart-rending horror.

Moran found himself attempting the impossible. He knew it was impossible. The blast-pistol hurt but did not injure the giant because the range was too long. So—it was totally unjustifiable—he found himself slung below the downward-slanting cable and sliding down its slope. He was going to where the range would be short enough for his blast-pistol to be effective. He slid to a cross-cable, and avoided it and went on.

Burleigh and Brawn and Harper were tiny figures, very far away. Moran hung by one hand and used his free hand to fire the blaster once more. It hurt more seriously, now. The spider made bubbling noises of infinite ferocity. And it moved with incredible agility toward the one object it could imagine as meaning attack.

It reached Hallet. It seized him.

Moran's blast-pistol could not kill it. It had to be killed. Now! He drew out his torch and pressed the continuous-flame stud. Raging, he threw it at the spider.

It spun in the air, a strange blue-white pinwheel in the gray light of this planet's day. It cut through a cable that might have deflected it. It reached the spider, now reared high and pulling Hallet from the sticky stuff that had captured him.

The spinning torch hit. The flame burned deep. The torch actually sank into the spider's body.

And there was a titanic flame and an incredible blast and Moran knew nothing.

A LONG time later he knew that he ached. He became aware that he hurt. Still later he realized that Burleigh and Brawn and Harper stood around him. He'd splashed in some enormous thickness of the yeasty soil, grown and fallen from the cliff-edge, and it was not solid enough to break his bones. Harper, doubtless, had been most resolute in digging down to him and pulling him out.

He sat up, and growled at innumerable unpleasant sensations.

"That," he said painfully, "was a very bad business."

"It's all bad business," said Burleigh in a flat and somehow exhausted tone. "The fuel-block burned. There's nothing left of it or Hallet or the spider."

Moran moved an arm. A leg. The other arm and leg. He got unsteadily to his feet.

"It was bessendium and uranium," added Burleigh hopelessly. "And the uranium burned. It wasn't an atomic explosion, it just burned like sodium or potassium would do. But it burned fast! The torch-flame must have reached it," he added absurdly. "Hallet died instantly, of course. Which is better fortune than we are likely to have."

"Oh, that…" said Moran. "We're all right. I said I was going to kill him. I wasn't trying to at the moment, but I did. By accident," he paused, and said dizzily, "I think he should feel obliged to me. I was distinctly charitable to him."

Harper said grimly:

"But we can't lift off. We're all marooned here now."

Moran took an experimental step. He hurt, but he was sound.

"Nonsense," he said. "The crew of the *Malabar* went off without taking the fuel-block from the wreck's engines. It's in a drawer in the *Nadine's* control room with a note to Carol that I asked her to read should something happen to me. We may have to machine it a little to make it fit the *Nadine's* engines. But we're all right."

Carol's voice came in his helmet-phone. It was shaky and desperately glad.

"You're—all right? Quite all right? Please hurry back?"

"We're on the way," said Moran.

HE was pleased with Carol's reaction. He also realized that now there would be the right number of people on the *Nadine*; they would take off from this world and arrive reasonably near due time at Loris without arousing the curiosity of spaceport officials.

He looked about him. The way the others had come down was a perfectly good way to climb up again. On the surface, above, their trail would be clear on the multi-colored surface rusts. There were four men together, all with blast-pistols and three with torches. They should be safe.

Moran talked cheerfully, climbing to the plateau on which the *Nadine* had landed, trudging with the others across a world on which it was impossible to see more than a quarter-mile in any direction. But the way was plain. Beyond the mist Carol waited.

THE END

If you've enjoyed this book, you will not want to miss these terrific titles...

ARMCHAIR SCI-FI & HORROR DOUBLE NOVELS, $12.95 each

D-1   **THE GALAXY RAIDERS** by William P. McGivern
SPACE STATION #1 by Frank Belknap Long

D-2   **THE PROGRAMMED PEOPLE** by Jack Sharkey
SLAVES OF THE CRYSTAL BRAIN by William Carter Sawtelle

D-3   **YOU'RE ALL ALONE** by Fritz Leiber
THE LIQUID MAN by Bernard C. Gilford

D-4   **CITADEL OF THE STAR LORDS** by Edmond Hamilton
VOYAGE TO ETERNITY by Milton Lesser

D-5   **IRON MEN OF VENUS** by Don Wilcox
THE MAN WITH ABSOLUTE MOTION by Noel Loomis

D-6   **WHO SOWS THE WIND...** by Rog Phillips
THE PUZZLE PLANET by Robert A. W. Lowndes

D-7   **PLANET OF DREAD** by Murray Leinster
TWICE UPON A TIME by Charles L. Fontenay

D-8   **THE TERROR OUT OF SPACE** by Dwight V. Swain
QUEST OF THE GOLDEN APE by Ivar Jorgensen and Adam Chase

D-9   **SECRET OF MARRACOTT DEEP** by Henry Slesar
PAWN OF THE BLACK FLEET by Mark Clifton.

D-10   **BEYOND THE RINGS OF SATURN** by Robert Moore Williams
A MAN OBSESSED by Alan E. Nourse

ARMCHAIR SCIENCE FICTION CLASSICS, $12.95 each

C-1   **THE GREEN MAN**
by Harold M. Sherman

C-2   **A TRACE OF MEMORY**
By Keith Laumer

C-3   **INTO PLUTONIAN DEPTHS**
by Stanton A. Coblentz

ARMCHAIR MASTERS OF SCIENCE FICTION SERIES, $16.95 each

M-1   **MASTERS OF SCIENCE FICTION, Vol. One**
Bryce Walton—"Dark of the Moon" and other tales

M-2   **MASTERS OF SCIENCE FICTION, Vol. Two**
Jerome Bixby—"One Way Street" and other tales

ETERNAL GUARDIAN OF THE STAR CIRCUIT

Because of the long years it took to travel between the worlds of the galaxy, interplanetary peace could only be maintained by a small band of men known as The Deathless Legion. And of these cosmic policemen, Chaan Fritag of Earth was the first to cross the path of the man who wanted to be Napoleon of the stars.

From the first it seemed an unequal fight. On the one side, the ruler of a planet with a million armed followers to do his bidding. On the other side, one man in galactic blue.

But Chaan Fritag had two secrets none could surmise—one buried in the childhood of his past, the other lying in wait for him somewhere in his future. And those two secrets would be worth an army if he could but understand them!

CAST OF CHARACTERS

CHAAN FRITAG
Something most unusual had happened to him as a boy. Now, as an adult, the stars were child's play to him.

ILLITA
Even though her husband had ceased to exist, she would never really be a widow.

JAHR
As a spy, it was his duty to be Chaan's best friend—and Chaan made the most of it.

MARL
This smiling young man saw himself as the mastermind of an entire star system.

HILDI
Was there more behind this pretty blonde's beauty than an evening's amusement?

RAMITZ
Officially he was the Chief Psychologist, but unofficially he was the Chief Torturer.

TWICE UPON
A TIME

By
CHARLES L. FONTENAY

ARMCHAIR FICTION
PO Box 4369, Medford, Oregon 97501-0168

*For more information about Armchair Books and products, visit our
website at...*

www.armchairfiction.com

Or email us at...

armchairfiction@yahoo.com

CHAPTER ONE

WHEN CHAAN FRITAG was a very small boy, a being gave him a dodecahedron.

He was given the dodecahedron long before he found the hole into the upper attic. There was really no connection between them.

Chaan did not remember the being very well, for he could not have been more than five years old when it visited them. He retained the impression of a very tall, ghost-like creature with long white fur and a square mouth that did not close. Stretched across the being's square mouth were chords which vibrated like the strings of a harp when it talked musically with Father. Father, who worked for the Space Service and was very wise, used a little stringed instrument to talk back to it.

The being was strange and awesome, but when it placed the dodecahedron in Chaan's small hand its eyes were big and dark and soft. Looking into them was like looking into the deep sky on a moonless night.

The dodecahedron was very small, about two inches in diameter, and it was transparent. Looking into it, one could see not only its twelve facets, but apparently many, many more. It was a fascinating thing. It sparkled in the light, and in the dark Chaan sometimes fancied it glowed with a light of its own.

When he was a few years older, he asked Father about the dodecahedron. By then, he had forgotten how he came by it.

"A wise and kind being from a world that is far away gave it to you, Chaan," said his father, a reminiscent light coming into his eyes. "He was a friend of mine, and he came from an old, old race of creatures."

"Why did he give it to me, Father?" asked Chaan.

"He said it was because he saw something in your face that made him want you to have it. I think...Kreel's language is very hard to understand...but I think he said you would use it one day. His people sometimes know the future."

This sort of thing was beyond Chaan's comprehension. His interest was more immediate.

"What is it?" he asked for the first time in the many months he had owned it.

"It's a dodecahedron," answered Father. "You'll learn some day that a dodecahedron is a figure that has twelve equal pentagrams as its facets. What else this is that Kreel gave you, I don't know."

As he had done before, Chaan played with the dodecahedron for a while and then tossed it aside for other toys. Father found it in a corner and used it as a paperweight on his desk, until they left the spaceport in Alabama and moved to the three centuries-old house in the flat country near Memfis. Chan saw it no more for a while.

The house had three attics, as Chaan discovered early. One of them was big enough to stand in, and there all the discarded furniture was kept. In the second, where one had to crouch to get around, were boxes of his grandfather's old books, for the house had belonged to Father's father.

The third was just a space between the ceilings over the rest of the big house, and its roof. It wasn't considered an attic, really, and nobody ever went into it—until Chaan found the hole.

It was just a place where a wide plank had fallen loose, up under the eaves of the second attic. Chaan stood on a pile of three boxes of his grandfather's books the day he found it, and peered through it into musty blackness.

There was a little, dimly-lit space into which he could crawl, and a corner that promised other vistas beyond. With some difficulty, Chaan pulled himself through the hole and crawled forward along the tie beams. The upper attic was so shallow that he had to lie flat and pull himself along with his elbows, and his head bumped the rafters and struts above.

The corner was more than a corner, he found. It was a meeting place of rafters and shingles of several gables, and the way through the mélange twisted into some curious angles. There was nothing beyond it but more low-roofed space; but it was an ideal hideout for a boy.

So for a time Chaan used the third attic as a retreat and an extra special hiding place for valuables. He kept such things there as a sheep skull (to frighten away intruders), his bow and arrows, and his pony's bridle when he was convinced someone was taking the pony out and riding it around the countryside while he was asleep.

Chaan was nine years old when he found the dodecahedron again. He was pawing through the bottom drawer of an ancient dresser, and it winked up at him in the afternoon sunlight.

He cupped it in his two hands and peered into it. The planes and angles of its many sides swam and dissolved in its depths.

That was Chaan's spaceman period. He had determined that when he grew up he would be the captain of a spaceship and go out to the stars.

He cogitated over the possible value of such an object to a spaceman, and decided it would be an ideal celestial globe in which to chart the course of his racing spaceship.

He took it up to the attic, for that was where he was currently piloting his spaceship. The close-fitting black suit and plastic helmet were hot and sweaty in the dusty attic, but the two shiny ray-guns were a comforting weight in the dimness.

The plastic helmet had a light on it—for space was dark, wasn't it—and he switched it on as soon as he crawled into the third attic. The battery was weak from much use, but he didn't really need the light. It was one of the formalities of the game.

The dodecahedron made a fine celestial globe. Chaan had rounded far Centaurus and was considering a routine return flight to the Solar System, when a space pirate thumbed his nose at him and blasted off at a tangent. That was a challenge no captain of the Centaurus Patrol could ignore; so of course Chaan gave chase.

The fleeing pirate was making for distant regions. Chaan was quite sure he was making for Arcturus, and Arcturus was around the comer made by the gables. There were immense vistas beyond that corner in which a pirate could hide, and Chaan could not afford to lose sight of his quarry.

He crawled determinedly across the rafters, holding the dodecahedron in front of him in one hand to steer by.

The odd comer was a hard pull for Chaan, especially as he peered steadfastly into the dodecahedron while negotiating it, in order not to get off course.

The little object did seem to have a light of its own. In it were reflected the gables and rafters and shingles, mingled with its own planes and angles—and something else.

Chaan made it around the corner.

He wasn't in another part of the attic at all. He emerged between the roots of a very large tree into a grassy glade lit by a red sun.

Now, if Chaan had been more than nine years old, he would have been frightened. But stories of fairies and magic were still very real to him. It was obvious that the upper attic was an enchanted land that, somehow, he never had discovered before. All he felt was a queer thrill, which was as much a thrill of discovery as anything else.

Standing up, he made a feeble effort to rid himself of some of the dust of the attic. Then, marking the tree well in his mind—he was experienced enough as an adventurous spaceman to keep his bearings at all times—he stuck the dodecahedron resolutely in his pocket and set forth on a tour of exploration.

As an enchanted land, it was very satisfying. The grass and foliage of the trees were bluish-purple, the sky was a very dark blue and the sun was tremendous and crimson. It was a little chilly, too, which didn't strike Chaan so well, because he was dressed for a Southern summer under his spacesuit.

Through a break in the trees he saw the distant turrets of a city, and he started toward it. The thought entered his mind that he might not make it there and back before suppertime, but he felt duty-bound to find out something about it.

As he neared the edge of the glade, the animal stepped forth from the bushes. Such an old spaceman as Chaan knew at once it wasn't an intelligent inhabitant of another world; though it was a weird creature, he had never seen it pictured in The Children's Encyclopedia of Space.

For an instant Chaan and the animal observed each other with scientific detachment. At the same moment the animal decided that Chaan was edible. Chaan decided the animal was ferocious.

The animal crouched for a rush, the tips of its tentacles waving ominously. Chaan pulled his trusty ray-guns from their holsters and at the same time realized, with a sinking heart, that the spectacular sparks they emitted would have no effect on the animal.

This animal was real, and the ray-guns were only toys.

But he valiantly pointed the ray-guns at the animal, and pulled the triggers as the animal leaped toward him with an ear-splitting roar. Sparks flashed colorfully and futilely from the ray-guns.

The animal burst into smoking flame in mid-air and fell writhing in its death agony at his feet.

Chaan holstered the ray-guns in mingled triumph and puzzlement. Then a hand fell on his shoulder. He turned.

A real spaceman, a grown-up one in a blue-and-silver uniform but without a helmet, stood at his side. A real ray-gun dangled from the big spaceman's hand, and Chaan recognized it from the pictures he had seen as a regulation heat-gun.

"That was a narrow escape," said the big spaceman.

"Yes, sir," agreed Chaan. "I'm afraid my guns weren't strong enough for such an animal. It's lucky you came along."

The big spaceman looked down at him, and amazed recognition spread across his face.

"You're Chaan, aren't you?" he asked in a voice that trembled a little.

"Yes, sir. Captain Chaan of the Centaurus Patrol. I'm here trying to run down a space pirate, but I've got to get back in time for supper."

The big spaceman smiled.

"Do you think I'll have time to take a look at the city?" asked Chaan. "The pirate may be hiding out there."

"The city's pretty far away," said the big spaceman gravely. "I think we'd better just go to the top of the hill and look down on the city from there."

Together they walked to the top of the slope that overlooked the city. The big spaceman told Chaan what world this was, but Chaan didn't recognize the name.

"I hope I can come here again some day," said Chaan, looking down on the beautiful city with eager eyes. "On a spaceship I mean, not through the attic. I want to be a spaceman when I grow up. A spaceman like you."

"Why, Chaan?" asked the big spaceman.

"I study history in school. People are always fighting in the history books because some people want things one way and some people want them another way. They don't have to do that any more."

"And what does that have to do with being a spaceman?" asked his companion.

"Why, there's plenty of room out there for everybody. If people don't like the way things are on one world, they can move on to another one. There are lots of worlds—that's what they teach us in school, you know—and there won't be any reason for fighting when people who think one thing can have a world all to themselves."

"You're right," said the big spaceman softly. "There won't be any fighting. Now, I think we'd better go back if you're going to make it to supper on time."

The huge red sun was still high as the big spaceman accompanied Chaan back to the glade, past the scorched body of the animal and right to the tree Chaan remembered. The big spaceman looked longingly at the little hole between the roots, just big enough for a little spaceman like Chaan.

"I wish I could go back with you," he said.

"I wish you could, too," said Chaan. "I'm sure my mother and father would be glad to meet you."

"Perhaps," said the big spaceman. "But, then, it might not work for me now."

Chaan started to climb down in the hole, then hesitated. He put his hand in his pocket and pulled out the dodecahedron.

"You should have something for saving my life," he said gravely to the big spaceman. "I don't carry any medals on my spaceship, but maybe this will do."

He laid the dodecahedron in the hand of the big spaceman and slipped through the hole among the roots.

He was somewhat disconcerted to find himself in a little cave, facing a bare wall of dirt. Almost, he turned around and crawled back out into the red world. But the big spaceman had said he ought to get home for supper.

Chaan shut his eyes and remembered what he had seen in the dodecahedron. It was not as clear as actually looking into it had been, but he could still imagine the shifting of the planes and the angles: and in them, instead of the reflections of the red world, he imagined a picture of the shingles and rafters of the dim attic.

When he opened his eyes, he was in the attic again.

Chaan got back in time for supper, but Mother and Father were not happy at his being so dirty. Chaan tried to explain to them, but they acted like grown-ups usually do.

"Too many comic tapes and three-Ds," said Mother severely.

"I'll be glad when school starts," said Father. "When he gets into advanced school they'll teach him what space is really like."

Chaan went into the upper attic again many times, but he never did come out in the red world again. It occurred to him more than once that maybe that was because he had given away his dodecahedron, and he half-regretted his generosity.

CHAPTER TWO

THE YEARS PASS swiftly on the worlds that turn around the stars, and even more swiftly in the lonely depths of space. And so there came a time when Chaan Fritag stood in a house far removed in time and space from his grandfather's house near Memfis, and tried to console a weeping woman.

The woman's name was Illita, and she was Chaan's wife. He felt very sorry for her, but not sorry enough to do what she asked. He had lived through this same leave-taking four times before with four other women, three times on other worlds and once here on Greyhound, the sixth planet of Sirius A.

"When we were married, you said you loved me," she sobbed, clinging to his shoulder. Her tear-bright eyes were black, and black was the hair that tumbled over her shoulders.

"I did," said Chaan. "I do."

"I'm going to give birth to your son in four months, and you don't even want to see him," she accused.

"I'll see him when he's a grown man," said Chaan, smiling faintly over her head at the luminescent wall.

She pulled away from him, angrily, and flung herself face down on the sofa. She clenched her small fists over her head and wailed.

"That's no way for the wife of a spaceman to act," he chided gently.

She rolled over swiftly, turning a tear-stained face up to him.

"I know wives of other spacemen," she said. "Their husbands come back to them."

"They aren't of the Deathless Legion," said Chaan proudly. "That's your honor, Illita, and the sorrow you must bear. Those men travel slow rocketships among the planets of Sirius, and time for them runs as swiftly as it does for their wives.

"But, my dear, the last time I was in the Sirius System you weren't even born, and yet that was less than five years ago for me. You're only two years younger than I, yet you're more than a quarter of a century younger. I have seen my son, born just after I left Greyhound before, and he is older than you. He's older than I am.

"And when I come back after this tour, you'll be old enough to be my mother."

"I know that, Chaan," she said, quietly now. "That's why I'm asking you not to go. Why won't you stay?"

He looked away from her and a light kindled in his eyes, a light she had seen before at times when he grew restless.

"I suppose space is in my blood, Illita," he said. "I've always wanted adventure, even as a little boy, and I've found it in the Deathless Legion. I don't suppose I could explain to you how I feel, but I've never found a life on any world that could compare with these jumps between the stars."

"Not even a wife and child?" she asked.

"Not yet. One of these days, I suppose. Don't forget, Illita, I've had four wives before, and two of them bore me children."

"So I'm nothing but another in the procession," she said bitterly.

"Don't look at it that way. I do love you, Illita. But the scouts of the Deathless Legion have it drilled into them, again and again, that any associations they have on the worlds they visit must be temporary as long as they're in the service. You understood when we were married that the time would be short, and I could never come back to you."

He smiled, tenderly.

"I'll say this," he added: "I'm sure that if and when I find a woman who will make me want to leave the service and settle down, she'll have black eyes and black hair."

This brought a faint, gratified smile from Illita. She took one of his hands in both of hers.

"I've never asked you about those other wives of yours," she said. "Did all of them act like this when you had to leave them?"

"At first they did," he replied. "It's normal, after all. But all but one of them were resigned at last and tried to make the last night a memorable one for both of us."

"Then I shall, too," she whispered softly, and turned her lips up to his.

Much later, Chaan walked alone along the streets of Stellopolis, capital city of Greyhound and of the Sirius System. He would have preferred to stay with his wife until morning, but there were certain things that had to be done before the morrow's briefing and blastoff.

Trim in the blue-and-silver uniform of the Deathless Legion, the Solar Council's far-flung patrol of Space Scouts, he walked along a viaduct that was flung from skyscraper to towering skyscraper high above the ground. Below and above it crisscrossed other aerial roads, some carrying vehicles and others pedestrians over the gardens of the city. Three of the planet's five moons hung in the sky, dimmed by the pervading radiance of the city lights.

As he walked, Chaan cogitated on the paradox that had converted time from a steady, dependable thing, equal for all men, to a fluid, relative matter that made him years older than that old man walking there, though Chaan was in his twenties and the old man was nearing the end of his existence. Speed had done this, the speed of man streaking between the stars: and of all the tremendous speed that man had reached in his technological progress, the speed of the Deathless Legion was supreme.

It made Chaan feel aloof and apart from all these millions of people on Greyhound, the millions on other worlds. It made him feel something like a god. It was this feeling that Illita and other planet-bound people could not understand, but which prevented him from giving up space for her or for his previous wives.

The Solar Space Command recognized the power of this feeling in its key intelligence personnel, and counted on it as much as on loyalty to the System itself to keep them in space. The Command recognized, too, that these men needed more solid emotional relationships during their stays on the various worlds than were offered by casual bachelor associations.

For that reason, the Deathless Legion had special dispensation on every world, no matter what its customs. Where there was marriage, as on most planets, they could marry for the year or two they would remain. In such cases, the wife understood that the marriage was ended—was as though it never had been—once the husband took flight again to the stars. She was assured support for her and for a child, if there was one, for the remainder of her life, and she could marry again at will.

Often such a wife would see her star-husband once more during her lifetime, when he returned to that world on his ageless round. She would be an old woman then, perhaps a grandmother, and he would be as young as she remembered him in her heart.

Chaan's private rooms, a second lodging made necessary by his job, were in a building only a quarter of a mile from the home in which he had lived with Illita for the past year. He had walked the distance through choice, rather than take a cab.

Now he entered the building at the fiftieth level and took an elevator ten floors down. He walked down the corridor, unlocked his door and entered his suite.

The lights went on automatically. But they were not steady. The illumination pulsed faintly, so faintly that he would not have noticed it except for his rigid training as a Space Scout. The pulsation was slow and throbbing.

At the same time there was a low, insistent humming sound, at the very edge of audibility.

Chaan's razor-keen senses shrieked a warning.

HYPNO-TRAP!

He whirled and switched off the lights. The humming sound died with them.

It wasn't probable, but there was a possibility that an enemy was in the room, shielded against the trap he had set. Chaan shook his cuff and a tiny, vicious needler slid into the palm of his right hand.

Silently and surely, Chaan moved through the pitch darkness, across the room. At the window, he touched a button and leaped aside as the blinds flung open, letting the city lights flood in. There was no one in the room.

He repeated this procedure in every room, then searched every closet and corner with a hand-light. He was alone in his suite.

Chaan returned the needler to his cuff and strapped on his heat-gun. If there was going to be trouble, he preferred the larger, cleaner weapon.

His pale, blue eyes hard and alert, Chaan sat down by the communicator in his parlor, and dialed the call letters of Space Command headquarters in the dark.

"Get me Aken at home," he instructed the duty officer who answered. The man obeyed, and in a moment the sleepy voice of the Quadrilateral commander came in on the line. Chaan told Aken what had happened.

"I don't know what it's all about, sir," he said. "Perhaps you can tell me."

"Possibly," said Aken. "But not until tomorrow. You don't have to know the background to find out all you can tonight."

"No, sir. I'm going to try to get to the heart of the hypno-trap, and find out what instructions are in it."

"Do you need any help?"

"Not just now," said Chaan, scratching his yellow head thoughtfully. "I'm on the fortieth level, halfway between two skyways. The blinds were shut when I came in, and there's no way whoever set the hypno-trap can tell I turned it off. If they're still around, I don't want to scare them off."

"All right," said Aken, "But be careful. There'll be a unit alerted, but it'll take them half an hour to get there after you call for them."

Chaan disconnected, and went to work with a hand-light.

He found the light projector in the light fixture of his parlor fifteen minutes later. He disconnected it and switched the lights on. Now they burned steadily, and there was no accompanying pulsation of sound.

In the brighter light, he began tracing the almost invisible wires that stretched across the ceiling. Someone had done a thorough job while he was absent from the apartment.

He was standing in the center of the parlor, head thrown back, studying the ceiling intently, when a slight noise behind him alerted him.

Chaan moved to one side silently, turning and drawing his heat-gun. The door to the apartment was inching open, slowly, cautiously.

A man stepped in carefully as the door opened, holding a paralyzer in his hand. On seeing Chaan standing by the sofa, he started a convulsive upward swing of the gun, but froze as Chaan wiggled the nose of the heat-gun warningly.

"Drop it," said Chaan in a low, cold voice.

The paralyzer fell to the floor, a snub-nosed weapon with a pistol grip.

The man was a mild-looking, average sort of fellow, dressed in the shorter Sirian garb that permitted more freedom of action than the toga. He gazed at Chaan's ominous figure with distressed brown eyes.

"Your hypno-trap?" asked Chaan.

"I...I helped," the man managed, gulping.

"How many of you?"

"Th-three."

"Where are the others?"

"Well..." The man hesitated, and suddenly Chaan saw at least part of the answer. A hand bearing a paralyzer was poking cautiously around the edge of the door behind the intruder.

Chaan pressed the stud of the heat-gun, and a narrow beam took the paralyzer square. There was an agonized yelp from the corridor. Red-hot, the paralyzer fell to the floor, and flames sprang up around it on the plastic surface.

The man in the door leaped desperately backward, and vanished futilely into the air of the corridor. Running for the door, Chaan heard hasty footsteps beating a retreat down the hall.

He leaped through the door to see the backs of two men crowding each other into the elevator. He raised his heatgun, then lowered it. It was too late. The elevator door slid shut.

There were seventy-five levels in this building. If he took another elevator, he could not possibly predict their course.

He turned back, and stamped out the fire that was crawling in a circle from the still-smoking paralyzer. Then he called headquarters on the communicator.

"We'll ring the area right away," said the duty officer.

"I'll send a squad of men up to your place, too."

The only source of information left was the hypno-trap. Carefully, Chaan traced the tiny wires, and found the loudspeaker behind a painting in the short corridor connecting the parlor and the bedroom. Other wires led from it to the sound projector, attached to the springs of his bed.

Almost a full roll of tape was still wound on the sound projector. Only a few inches of it had run before Chaan had turned it off with the lights.

Chaan turned the volume down on the loudspeaker, went back into the bedroom and switched on the sound projector. There was a blinding flare of light, an explosion muffled by the mattress of the bed. Chaan staggered back, throwing his arm over his face.

For a moment he could see nothing but red-starred blackness. His vision cleared gradually, and he leaped to the task of extinguishing the flames that licked from beneath his bed.

A fire extinguisher from the corridor did the trick in a few minutes. But the hypno-trap's sound projector was charred and twisted, and its roll of tape had gone up in smoke. The air conditioners slowly cleared the swirling fumes from the room.

The hypno-trap had been booby-trapped. He never would know what instructions had been on the tape.

Chaan stared at the ruins of his bed, puzzled. He was accustomed to intrigue, for the efforts of dissident elements often gravitated naturally to the work of the Space Scouts, key men in the Solar Council's intelligence system. But he had had no reason to expect anything like this on Greyhound itself.

There was something afoot, something he had not even suspected before.

CHAPTER THREE

CHAAN, AFTER A completely sleepless night, sat in the office of Lex Aken, Sirius Quadrilateral Commander for the Solar Space Command. The big, cubical Space Command headquarters building was near the edge of Stellopolis, about five miles from the spaceport. Through the glass wall of Aken's office, Chaan could see the towering buildings of the city and the flying network of its multi-level thoroughfares, spun like a great spider web above its neat gardens.

Chaan liked the city. He liked the whole planet and its people. They were more civilized than any he had seen any where. He wondered what changes would be brought in the thirty years, their time, which would elapse before he returned. Probably not many major ones. Their civilization was too stable. It was the mainspring of all the worlds of the Sirius Quadrilateral.

Aken relaxed in a comfortable chair, clad in the toga-like garment that was the Sirian fashion of the day. That was another thing Chaan would miss. Greyhound, revolving around the main component of Sirius, was more than five times as far from Sirius A as Earth was from Sol, yet the planet was more Earthlike than any he would encounter on his tour.

"Your experience fits another piece into the jigsaw puzzle we've been trying to put together," said Aken gruffly. He was a clean-shaven, heavy-jowled man. "We suspected they might have agents on Greyhound by now, but we weren't sure."

"Who is 'they'?" asked Chaan. "I didn't know anything out of the way was going on."

Aken smiled thinly.

"You'd have been told today," he replied, "because that will be an important part of your job on this tour. All available evidence points to the secret build-up of a revolt against the Solar Council somewhere in the Sirius Quadrilateral."

"Then I failed in my last tour," said Chaan.

"Not necessarily. Our sociologists tell us the build-up of anything big enough to challenge the Council would have to move so slowly it could proceed for ten years without being detectable, even by a trained Scout. It has been six years, planetary time, since you were in the Procyon System. Of course, if the trouble should be in one of the other two systems, it has been much longer since you were there."

"But you think it's at Procyon," ventured Chaan.

Aken smiled again.

"It's logical," he said. "The fleet is at Lalande. Wolf is small and has only one inhabitable planet. Procyon is the only system that compares to that of Sol, and thus of Sirius. Just plain local pride would lead a good many of the Procyonites to feel that Procyon should be the central system of the Quadrilateral, or at least independent."

"I don't see why the fleet hasn't been ordered to Procyon, then," said Chaan.

"There are a couple of reasons; the lesser of which is that Lalande is still in a state of disorganization and we might lose the colony completely if the fleet doesn't remain there until some order is achieved.

"The more important reason, though, is that a space fleet isn't a scout ship. It requires acceleration and deceleration time. It would take the fleet twenty years to cover the two and a half parsecs from Lalande to Procyon, and if it turned out that Wolf was the offender, it would take twenty more years to reach Wolf from Procyon. A build-up takes a long time, but in forty years after getting this much of a start, a rebellious world might amass the strength to wipe out the fleet.

"On the other hand, a Scout can be at Procyon in five years, at Wolf in nine. Since the Quadrilateral evens itself out, a Scout detecting trouble can be at Lalande within fourteen years of leaving Sirius. We save six years that way, and I shouldn't have to tell you how important six years can be in a situation like this."

"Sol is only two and a half parsecs from Wolf," Chaan pointed out. "The fleet could go to Procyon from Lalande and you could call on the Solar Council to send an emergency fleet to Wolf, just in case."

"It takes nine years to get a message to Earth," replied Aken, "and twenty more for another fleet to reach the Quadrilateral from there. Admittedly, that would be faster than a Scout, but the economy of the Council can't support sending fleets hither and yon at random: that could create more danger than we're trying to cure. So you see the job that lies before you."

"Yes, I do," said Chaan, smiling and rising. "You want me to reverse my route this time, and go to Procyon first, instead of Wolf, don't you?"

"No. I want you to go to Wolf, as planned."

Chaan was astounded.

"That's senseless, if the trouble's probably at Procyon!" he exclaimed. "Don't you realize it will take me twenty-four years to reach Procyon, making the regular round by way of Wolf and Lalande?"

"Certainly, but don't forget that Wolf has to be checked too. We're sending another agent on an extraordinary tour by the reverse route, checking Procyon first. You two should reach Lalande about the same time."

"But I'm the regular Scout on this schedule," protested the dismayed Chaan.

"That's exactly why you're going to follow the regular routine, and there will be no further discussion about it," said Aken firmly. "Now, as to the hypno-trap. What's your theory about it?"

Chaan sat down again and scratched his close-cropped head. Aken hitched up closer to his huge desk, picked up a pencil and held it posed for notes.

"If they wanted to stop me from blasting off, the simplest thing would have been to plant a bomb instead of the hypno-trap," Chaan said. "Obviously, that would be useless, because another Scout would just be sent in my place."

"Correct," said Aken. "They aren't after you personally. They're after the Scout, whoever he may be, who will make this tour."

"The same thing could be said of an effort to prevent my going into stardrive in the ship," said Chaan. "You'd know that here, and again another Scout would be sent."

"Correct again. Now, theoretically, nothing could touch you while in star drive. What's your opinion on that, from experience?"

Chaan shook his head.

"Impossible," he said. "Even if they had the secret of the stardrive, the speed is so near that of light that no driveoff could be scheduled accurately enough for interception."

"Then what!"

"Trouble at the other end."

"Interception at Wolf, you mean?"

"Or Procyon," said Chaan. "I'm sure you don't underestimate our opponents, Commander, and I wouldn't want to. They must know that suspicion would be directed logically at Procyon, and probably guessed that the Scout tour would be reversed this time."

"Possibly. But such interception would do them no good. If our reverse-tour Scout doesn't reach Lalande on schedule, the fleet will blast off for Procyon at once. And if you don't get there on schedule, it blasts off for Wolf. As you know, that's standard procedure."

"Our opponents may not know that. At any rate, trouble at the other end is the only thing that makes sense out of the hypno-trap. It means trouble before landing, too, in my opinion. If it didn't, it would be easier for them to set a hypno-trap at the other end."

Aken tapped his pencil on the desk and frowned.

"There's only one thing wrong with your theory of trouble at the other end," he said. "The maximum effectiveness of a hypno-trap is two years. Its effect on you would be dissipated long before you reach either Wolf or Procyon."

"Again, maybe they don't know that," said Chaan. "Don't forget, our opponents don't have the stardrive. Or do they?" he asked, on sudden suspicion.

"No," said Aken, smiling. "Not as far as we know. It certainly isn't likely."

"Well, then, we know that mental and emotional effects during the stardrive proceed just as they would if the person aboard the ship were experiencing planetary time, so hypnotic effects from a hypno-trap would expire a fourth of the way to Wolf or halfway to Procyon. But they may think that the effects are based on the traveler's subjective time; if they were, the hypnosis would last long after reaching either system."

"All that would be a very satisfactory explanation if I had your confidence that our enemies, whoever they are, are ignorant on so many points," said Aken.

"I don't know of any other explanation that fits the facts."

"Nor do I. But, leaving explanations aside for the time, I hope you're convinced of the necessity of being exceptionally alert, even though you are going to Wolf instead of Procyon."

"I am, sir."

CHAPTER FOUR

WHEN CHAAN LEFT Aken, he took the elevator down to the residential floor of the headquarters building and slept for three hours. Normally he would have returned to his apartment for the nap, but Aken had decided it best not to, since the hypno-trap incident.

Chaan had argued that he should be in the apartment in case the enemy agents returned in force to attempt any other action against him. Aken vetoed that. Precautions would be taken to capture the spies if that happened, he said, and he did not want to risk anything happening to one of his Scouts.

Neither of them thought the spies would return. After learning the hypno-trap was ineffective, and the Command alerted, they could be expected to give the place a wide berth.

At noon he awoke and took a cab to the Amphitheater, half a mile away. It was a tremendous round arena, without walls, covered by a domed metal roof.

As he got out and paid the cab driver, another cab pulled up behind it. Two men emerged. They did not look toward him, but Chaan knew what they were. They were Space Command agents, tailing him to protect him—or perhaps to catch a spy.

Chaan paid his admission at the entrance to the Amphitheater. The ticket-seller recognized him. He had been there often before.

"Good afternoon, Captain Fritag," said the man. "Mrs. Fritag isn't with you today?"

"No," said Chaan. "She isn't feeling well today."

"They get that way sometimes," said the man with a smile, winking at him as he handed over the ticket. The ticket agent knew of the expected child; but he had no way of knowing that this was blastoff day for Chaan, that Chaan would see Illita no more for thirty years.

Chaan looked at his stub. It was the usual seat: Row G, Seat 30. They usually saved that seat for him—and Seat 31 for Illita.

As he moved under the edge of the big dome, he saw the two men following him out of the corner of his eye. They stopped at the window and talked seriously for a minute to the ticket agent.

One of them flashed a badge, surreptitiously. Chaan grinned, and walked on.

The outer area of the Amphitheater, under the edge of the dome, was a huge circular restaurant for its patrons. There was no better food in Stellopolis. Chaan took a table near the low outside wall, where he could look out over the gardens, and ordered lunch by number, without paying any attention to his selection.

He could have had Illita meet him here, or he could have gone back to the home they had shared for a year. But it would have been only prolonging the agony of farewell. It was best that she should remember him by last night.

She thought her love for him would not let her be happy, ever again, when he was gone. He smiled, wryly. It would be difficult for her, but she would recover. She'd find another man and marry again, wisely or foolishly, in a few years.

He hoped it would be wisely, for her sake, but it was out of his hands. For her, he was dead now. For him, she was dead. He might see her again, much later—five years for him, thirty years for her—but they would be nothing but memories to each other then.

It was a hard price to pay, for her. It was a little hard for him, too, for he did love her. But with that price they purchased the safety of the Solar Council, the peace that must be guarded among the far-flung worlds of man's interstellar quests. It was not too heavy a price for the Deathless Legion and those who loved them.

If he had loved her more...Strange, Chaan thought, how one can love one person genuinely, but another time can love someone else just as genuinely. Not too strange, perhaps. When he had been on Greyhound before, long ago, a sentimental song had been popular: *"For every man there is a woman, somewhere out among the stars..."* For every man there were many possible women, really. No man or woman was unique.

Still, if he had loved her more, perhaps he would not have left her. He could conceive of himself loving someone so much that he would leave the service and stay with her. The Space Command expected it, periodically. They released their Scouts, when their Scouts requested it, and they did so freely.

Even if he had loved her so, he didn't think he would ask release now, after the hypno-trap, after what he had learned from

Aken. The Space Command needed its most experienced Scouts in this emergency. They needed the experience he had gained in one previous tour of the Sirius Quadrilateral, even though he was starting at Wolf, instead of Procyon where the trouble probably was. He was glad he had not learned of this before he had taken leave of Illita, that he made the choice to leave of his own free will. It was easier for him this way.

He ate his lunch almost mechanically, thinking furiously. At a nearby table sat the two Space Command agents, eating too, keeping an eye on him.

It was nearly time for the concert to begin when he arose and went in to his seat. It was far down, near the front. A moment after he had taken it, the two agents took seats directly behind him.

He turned to look casually at them, and saw Illita coming in.

His heart almost stopped. Of course, she had known the blastoff time. She had figured it out. She had guessed that if he had any time left before blastoff, he'd spend it here.

She was coming down the aisle. Quickly Chaan pulled from his pocket an emergency kit. Padding went into his cheeks, a mustache on his upper lip, spray changed the color of his eyes and another spray tinted his hair. He breathed a brief thanksgiving that he wasn't in uniform.

He turned to the men behind him.

"I know who you are," he said urgently. "One of you must change seats with me."

No questions were asked. It was done in a moment. He climbed over the back of the seat, keeping low, and one of the agents took his place. Chaan fell back into the seat beside the other agent.

Illita came down between the rows of seats and sank into Seat 31. Her eyes searched the face of the agent, and he returned the look of a stranger, although he undoubtedly knew who she was. The look of disappointment on her face tore at Chaan's heart.

She looked all around. Chaan kept his head low. If he had been in his regular seat, she might have penetrated the disguise, but she did not recognize him sitting behind her.

The musicians came on stage. There was a moment of utter silence in the great Amphitheater, then the conductor's hand came down and the soft opening strains of *"Beyond the Stars"* floated across its vast circle.

Chaan sat back with eyes closed, and let the music capture him. It was a fitting farewell for him. The violins cried the loneliness of space, the horns inserted the insistent urge of man to conquer the stars. Then the drums rolled, louder and louder, their triumphant theme and Chaan let his heart revel with their thunder in its powerful narrative of the human spirit's achievement.

This was the real call that drew him to the Deathless Legion. This was the real power space had over him. This was the real reason that he could forsake love and comfort and human companionship. It was not just loyalty to the Solar Council, not even the safety of all the worlds of the inhabited systems that lay upon his shoulders, but the exciting lure of adventure, of riding free on the crest of space and time, far above the creeping affairs of planetary humanity.

He opened his eyes and saw Illita's black head just in front of him. It was bent, and he realized she was sobbing. At once he felt ashamed, and very sorry for her. He rose and left the Amphitheater, in the middle of the symphony's first movement.

On the way back to the headquarters building, Chaan stripped off the mustache and took out the cheek pads. When he arrived at his temporary quarters there, he washed away the tints of his eyes and hair. Once more he had his normal blue eyes and sandy hair. He slipped into space coveralls, checked his kit, took an elevator down and rode the under-ground belt to the spaceport.

He emerged from the control building onto the flat landing area of the spaceport. It stretched, a huge oval a mile across on its narrowest diameter, under the violet-white sky of Greyhound. It was mid-afternoon of the planet's twenty-six-hour day, and the double sun of Sirius shone in the western heavens, a tremendously brilliant orb one-seventeenth the size of Sol at Earth, with a bright star riding near the horizon. Back to the east, the towers of Stellopolis speared the sky.

There were half a hundred ships lined around the edge of the oval, ranging from the stubby, winged G-boats that ferried from the surface to the more conventional ships to the newer, spherical anti-gravity ships that traveled directly from planet to planet.

Different from all of them was Chaan's scout ship, readied in the center of the spaceport. It was a hundred-foot needle, standing on its tail, its sharp nose pointed at the invisible stars.

Chaan took a car across the field to the ship. They were waiting for him there, the five-man maintenance crew in their soiled coveralls and the Space Command inspector in his toga. Chaan greeted them and took the check-sheet from the inspector.

He went over each item carefully, and at the end of each section, he called the name of each crewman and showed him the signature on the sheet.

"This represents your work on this section, and this is your signature?" he asked in each case.

Each crewman answered affirmatively. Chaan searched the face of each one. Each one returned an open, honest look. He recognized each one. He had known all five for the year he had lived on Greyhound.

Then he checked the entire sheet with the inspector. The inspector he did not know, but his Space Command credentials were in order.

Chaan shook hands with each of the six and walked up the short ramp into the ship. Lined up outside, they waved goodbye as he entered. He saluted and pulled the lever that pulled the ramp into the ship and sealed the airlock.

He climbed the short ladder into the lower control room and watched the six men climb into the two cars and roll back across the field toward the control building. He pressed the "ready" button. A green light on the control panel began to blink slowly off and on, and in a moment the loudspeaker announced: *"X minus five minutes..."*

Chaan climbed to the nose. As he reached it, the ship's loudspeakers blared: *"X minus four minutes..."*

He came back down through the ship slowly, checking everything about it as thoroughly as could be done on the surface, drawing on long familiarity with its every lever and corner. There was the upper control room—the stardrive room—the cramped living quarters—the storage deck—the sealed stardrive deck to which even he had no access—the anti-gravity engine deck.

Everything was in order. He returned to the lower control deck as the green light changed to amber and the loudspeaker said: *"X minus one minute..."*

He dropped into the control chair. A three-minute inspection wasn't much to go on, but it would take him an entire day to inspect the ship thoroughly. That was the job of the Space Command inspector who had just left.

"X minus fifty seconds..."

There was some reason for the hypno-trap. What was the enemy's objective with him? Completely alerted, he had detected nothing out of the ordinary, either about the only men who had access to the ship or about the ship itself.

"X minus forty seconds..."

Aken had given him no instructions, no help. He had just told him to remain alert. Surely the Space Command was doing more than this to solve the puzzle. Scouts were expendable, but they were not expended unnecessarily.

"X minus thirty seconds..."

At least he was safe at blastoff, and at driveoff. They weren't after him personally.

"X minus twenty seconds..."

Their plan must be at the other end. But what could it be? Even assuming that they didn't know the effects of the hypno-trap would wear off within two light-years, there was no way of their predicting where or when he would emerge from stardrive. It could only be something they had planned between his emergence from stardrive and his landing on a planet of Wolf...or Procyon.

"X minus ten seconds..." The light changed to red.

Chaan shrugged. He had not been ordered to delay blastoff. If he could find anything between blastoff and driveoff, he would act.

"X minus five seconds...four...three...two...one..."

"FIRE!"

Chaan pressed the anti-gravity drive lever down and the needle-ship leaped smoothly upward. It raced like an arrow into the sky. He felt no pressure of acceleration, for the anti-gravity field affected everything in the ship alike.

A buzzer sounded and a light shone on the control board. Chaan pressed a button and the radio receiver automatically spun to the channel calling.

"Fritag, this is Aken," said the gruff voice on the sealed beam. "When you've cleared the atmosphere, take her to the other side of Greyhound and drop down at Caniport. That's all."

"Yes, sir."

An hour later, the needle backed down onto the oval at Caniport, a duplicate of that at Stellopolis. There were not so many ships here. This was not plains country like that at Stellopolis. High mountains ringed the spaceport. Four moons lit the night sky.

Aken and two other men were waiting for him on the field when he set the starship down. The two men, with a perfunctory salute, brushed past him and entered the ship as Chaan walked down the ramp. Aken shook hands with him.

"That's the best pair of Space Command inspectors in the Quadrilateral," Aken said dryly. "They'll go over your ship with a fine comb."

"Why didn't you just have them inspect it at Stellopolis?" asked Chaan.

"We don't want the enemy to know their plan has failed," answered Aken. "You see, we still have some spies to catch around here. One of your mechanics or the inspectors, or both, may be either enemy agents or victims of a hypno-trap."

Twenty hours later it was found, in a portion of the ship where Chaan could not have looked and would not have recognized anything out of order if he had the sealed stardrive section.

The senior inspector, Filen, held up the tiny gadget, a bit of metal and wire that weighed perhaps three pounds. It ticked.

"Very clever," he said. "It was timed to put the stardrive out of commission about two light-years out. The only thing Captain Fritag could have done would be to limp in on anti-gravity, which would have taken him quite a few years longer."

"That means they know the secret of the stardrive, then," said Aken unhappily.

"No, sir. Not necessarily. They wouldn't have to know it for this to operate. It would just explode in the stardrive chamber, putting it out of commission without damaging the ship."

"At least, sir," suggested Chaan, "it indicates they don't know that if I fail to appear at Lalande on schedule the fleet will move to Wolf."

"Not necessarily," said Aken slowly. "If the trouble is at Procyon, they might want the fleet to move to Wolf on a false alarm. Or if the trouble is at Wolf, they may have thought you were going to Procyon and this would draw the fleet there.

"Or they may know that you would be able to get an emergency message back to Sirius in two years after the accident. The course was actually would take...and they may have guessed it...would be to send out another Scout to Wolf immediately, and a message to Lalande saying the tour had been delayed by four years.

"They're guessing at our actions, and we're guessing at their guesses. We don't know any more than we did before."

CHAPTER FIVE

THE NEEDLE-NOSED scout ship moved out from Caniport on anti-gravity to a point in space about 200 million miles beyond Greyhound, halfway to the orbit of Deerhound, the seventh planet of Sirius. There Chaan aimed it at Wolf 359 and threw it into star drive.

The stardrive of the scout ships was a mechanism that utilized the energy that filled space to create a space warp and throw the ship instantaneously into a speed near that of light. Like anti-gravity, the sudden acceleration had no effect on the ship or its passengers, because in the space warp every atom of the ship and passengers was accelerated at once. The stardrive could not be used near a planet, for the energy it generated was enough to incinerate the surface of any world within several million miles.

So it was that Aken, watching from the night side of Greyhound, saw a nova bloom, expand to moon-size and gradually fade away. And Chaan, in the starship, saw the disc of Sirius A and the stars that jeweled the sky dissolve momentarily into a uniform gray.

A fraction of an instant later, the forward and rear screens cleared. The side screens were, still gray, but in the rear screen Sirius and the stars around it were bright and clear, while in the forward screen Wolf 359 and the stars near its position were pinpoints of light. Near the edges of these screens the stars were streaks of light, that accelerated and vanished on the forward screen and gradually slowed into points on the rearward screen: for the ship was not only moving at near light-speed, but Chaan was living more than a hundred times more slowly than planet bound humans.

That was the secret of the longevity of the Space Scouts...the Deathless Legion. As the ship approached the speed of light, it became more and more elongated in space, more and more tenuous in its substance. Chaan's subjective time moved more and more slowly in relation to the "objective time" of the creeping planets.

For him, no more than a few days would elapse before the stardrive automatically reversed itself and he dropped instantly to normal interplanetary speed in the vicinity of Wolf 359. But objectively nothing could travel faster than light, and Wolf 359 was 8.64 light-years from Sirius. So to those who lived on the worlds of the two systems, it would be nine years between the time a temporary star blossomed in the Sirius System and the moment a similar star heralded Chaan's arrival at Wolf 359.

That was why Illita would be thirty years older when Chaan returned to Sirius, but Chaan, stopping a year at each of his ports of call, would be only about four years older.

The drive was set, and Chaan pushed himself, floating, along the corridors of the ship to the living quarters. Here at the largest bulge of the ship, the quarters were ten feet in diameter. They were big enough for two, and there were supplies for two aboard.

He had not told Illita of this, nor any of his other wives. It would have just made them unhappy to know there was room for them to accompany him, for it would have done them no good. The extra room and the extra supplies were for emergencies, and no star scout would have been permitted to take a wife with him on his tour of duty.

The supplies aboard were twice enough for one man for one month of stardrive, plus the several weeks involved in maneuvering among the planetary systems on anti-gravity. Had the plan succeeded to put Chaan's stardrive out of commission a quarter of the way to Wolf he would have starved to death long before he reached the system.

The quarters, though not commodious, were comfortable. Chaan put a tape of *"Beyond the Stars"* on the sound projector and relaxed on the curved sofa against one wall. He closed his eyes and lay back, feeling himself drift slowly up against the restraining straps.

Chaan loved the starhops. If ever he could find a planetary civilization that would arouse in him the same emotions and sensations, he believed he would be ready to leave the service and settle down.

There was a strange telescoping effect of the mind and emotions during the starhops. Chaan lived subjectively at a slow rate that made the time pass for him in a few days, and with his eyes open and senses alert the things he did aboard the ship followed that time scale. But his emotional and mental processes had a trick of moving with the swiftly passing objective time: so that when he arrived at Wolf, his memories of Illita and his feelings for her and for all the things they had done together would be those of nine years gone.

The starhop was a tremendously healing experience. He came out of it every time as though born again, with mind and heart fresh for the new world that would greet him. All the griefs and heartaches of the world he had left were in the dim past behind him. In the gray womb of space-time, he was soothed and rejuvenated.

At the same time, it was an exciting experience. It seemed to him that he rode on the swiftly-flying crest of human history, while great events revolved slowly below him. Occasionally, when he reached a planetary system, he would descend into these events and influence them one way or another for a time.

The last thundering strains of *"Beyond the Stars"* died in the room. Chaan aroused himself and switched off the machine with a sigh. Even during the starhop, there was work to be done.

Chaan glanced at the chronometer. It showed days, months and years, rather than hour and minutes, for it was geared to planetary time. The days spun by on the dial almost as fast as miles on a speeding car. Already two weeks had passed since he entered stardrive, and he had been in stardrive less than an hour.

From the files he took the dossiers of the planetary systems of the Sirius Quadrilateral and reviewed them. Most of the information was based on his own reports, when he had returned to Greyhound a year ago, but it was supplemented by information received since then over light-beam transmission.

He started with the Procyon System, most likely site of the trouble. Procyon was a star bigger and brighter than Sol, with a tiny, faint companion revolving around it. It had three inhabitable planets, of which the fifth, Proteus, was Earth-type in size and temperature as well as atmosphere. It was the capital planet of the system. The other two were not colonies, for the Solar Council theory of interstellar government did not permit colonies after a world was established well enough for political independence. But they were dependent on Proteus economically and culturally.

The culture that he remembered on Proteus, and which was outlined in the reports, was aggressively mercantile. Big business, politics and the planet's formal religion went hand in hand. Everything was geared to commercialism. A rigid class system was based on wealth. Family relationships and family honor were emphasized, music was heavily romantic and art standards were baroque. Clothing was stiff, formal and heavily ornamented.

Chaan would have called it a Victorian planet, a Carthaginian world. But his sociological knowledge gave the lie to the popular concept that a commercial culture is by nature a peaceful one. He knew that there is no pride like the pride of wealth, and no incentive to war like the fancied opportunity for commercial gain.

The Proteans were insular and conservative, farthest from the Mother Earth of any inhabitants of the Sirius Quadrilateral. If they were plotting rebellion against the Solar Council, jealousy of the preeminent position of the Sirian System in the Quadrilateral might have something to do with it. But the principal incentive would more likely be a desire to tie the other two worlds of the Procyon System more dependently to Proteus as outright economic colonies, and to gain a more favorable position for commercial exploitation in the Quadrilateral.

At the opposite corner of the Quadrilateral from Sirius lay Lalande 21185. It was a red star two-fifths as large as Sol, much fainter but surprisingly warm. Most of its radiation was in the heat range, and its two inner planets were inhabitable by man, although men had to live under domes because of the hostile atmosphere.

The Solar Council's fleet had been at Lalande for years. Its colonists had broken up into warring groups. There was no homogeneous culture on either of the two planets, and the dome cities were constantly at each other's throats, over boundaries, mineral deposits, fancied slights, any pretext. The presence of the fleet enforced an uneasy peace and kept the peoples of Lalande from exterminating each other while Solar Council sociologists worked to manipulate the culture into stable society.

It was hardly likely that the Lalande peoples could brew a rebellion under the nose of the fleet, even if they could achieve the cooperation among themselves to make such a thing possible. Lalande could be marked off as the trouble spot, with even more certainly than the highly civilized Sirian System itself.

It had been something over twenty years, planetary time, since Chaan had left Volksweld, the single planet that hovered around Wolf 359 like a lone chick to its mother hen. Wolf itself was a planet-sized star, no bigger than Uranus, and Volksweld swung so close to it—only a few thousand miles out—that its crimson orb filled half the planet's daytime sky. Even so, Volksweld was a chill, snowy world, with brief summers and hard winters.

Despite these inhospitable conditions, the hardy colonists had thriven and multiplied, for the atmosphere here was similar to that of Earth and no domes were necessary. Chaan remembered that culture with a pleasant nostalgia and was looking forward to spending time on Volksweld again.

The Volksweldvolken, as they called themselves, were an independent, informal people. They had to be, to settle such a world. They had brought no traditions with them that they were not willing to break if occasion demanded it, so their culture had grown in a free, haphazard way, like Topsy.

If Proteus was a Victorian world, Chaan would call the Volksweld he remembered a Polynesian world, despite its near-Arctic climate. Government was so democratic that it was founded on no formal constitution and its very form was changed when the citizens became dissatisfied. Religion, art, and dress were individual things and convention was almost non-existent. There was no legal marriage, although there were some permanent unions through choice: almost everyone loved children and they were always cared for, regardless of parentage.

No, there could be no danger of peace-breaking from that relaxed, happy-go-lucky society. It must be Procyon. Chaan knew he should wish he had been sent to Procyon first, and he was slightly peeved that Aken hadn't given him that important assignment. But he could not suppress a feeling of pleasure that he was returning to Volksweld.

The Sirius Quadrilateral was, as its name indicated, a quadrilateral whose corners were the four star systems Chaan visited on his tour. It was one of several similar sectors into which the Solar Council had divided the inhabited star systems that surrounded the Solar System within a distance of a dozen light-years. There was no "Centaurus Patrol" in the sense Chaan had imagined it as a boy, for the Alpha Centauri System and Innes Star were part of the Solar Triangle.

The theory of the Sirius Quadrilateral, as in other sectors, was based on the fact that Sirius was 8.64 light-years from Wolf 359, Wolf was 4.03 light-years from Lalande 21185, Lalande was 8.3 light-years from Procyon and Procyon was 4.64 light-years from Sirius. The Quadrilateral was not in a single plane, so the diagonal distances were little longer than those on its sides.

Chaan's tour as Solar Council Scout, with a year's stopover in each system, took him around the Quadrilateral about every thirty years, planetary time. The sociological theory was that no culture could develop a challenge to the power of the Solar Council fleet in less than sixty to seventy-five years, and trends in that direction could be detected early by a trained Scout. The maximum period required for Chaan to reach the fleet and warn of a trouble spot, and for the fleet to reach it, was something over twenty years, representing what was considered to be an adequate margin.

Chaan wondered if he had failed in his last visit to Procyon. He had left that system only six years ago, planetary time, and if a revolt move was far enough advanced for the Council to worry about it, he should have detected it. Perhaps that was why Aken did not trust him enough to send him back to Procyon on the reverse swing.

The days passed swiftly. Chaan studied his reports, drew theories from them and ran them through the ship's small calculator without decisive results. He relaxed and let the happy languor of the starhop capture his soul, and he slept, wrapped in pleasant and significant dreams.

Then came the day when there was a flare of blinding light on the screens, the stars reappeared and the baleful crimson orb of Wolf 359 hung ahead of him. Biting into it, a black disc a third of its diameter, was Volksweld.

Chaan moved the ship in close to the planet and set it in an orbit that crisscrossed above Volksweld's surface. Then he settled down to make his preliminary inspection.

Volksweld was a planet somewhat larger than Earth. Due to the eccentricity of its orbit, much of the northern hemisphere was glaciated. About half of the southern hemisphere was land area.

No effort had been made to hide what he saw. There was no other planet in the system to spy on Volksweld; and it could not have been hidden from the scout ship's instruments.

There were three tremendous spaceports, thrice again the size of those on Greyhound. On them were scores of big starships, already completed or being built. Thirty years ago the planet had fielded fewer than half a dozen ships.

Volksweld had not had nuclear power thirty years before. Despite its advantages, it was a power source that required a big and well-integrated society to develop and support it. Now the evidence was startling, overwhelming. The danger spot was not Procyon, *it was Wolf!*

During his survey, two dark, bulky ships passed near him, looking him over. They were well armed, but no challenge was issued. No effort was made to contact him by radio.

Chaan put in a call to the Space Command station on Volksweld. There was no answer on the Space Command's private channel.

He called the spaceport on an open beam, and received a reply at once.

"This is Chaan Fritag, Solar Council Scout from Sirius," he said. "Please notify Space Command I am attempting to reach them by radio."

"Sorry, sir," said a polite but firm voice on the other end. "Space Command radio is temporarily out. May we relay a message?"

Chaan hesitated. That sounded ominous.

He could kick the ship into stardrive and head for Lalande at once. The fleet would be en route to Wolf within hours of his arrival there.

But what if he was wrong, despite the evidence? Nuclear power was not banned among the stellar worlds, and neither was heavy spaceship construction. Procyon had both.

It was the culture, the sociological development of a planet, that made it either a peaceful member of the family of worlds or a potential threat to the safety of others. Chaan remembered Volksweld as it had been. There was no hint in that recollection of a dangerous trend, or even a possibility of danger.

If he called the fleet to Wolf and the trouble actually was at Procyon, the fleet could be delayed a dangerously long time in getting back to Procyon. The way the Quadrilateral's distances coincided, he and the other Scout were scheduled to get to Lalande at the same time, but that schedule contemplated each of them remaining a full year in the other system.

His duty was to be sure. If they attempted to hold him against his will on Volksweld, the fleet would move in from Lalande as soon as he did not arrive on schedule. And if his landing on Volksweld meant danger...well, that was part of his job.

"No message," he said to the radio. "Please notify Space Command I'm landing as soon as I'm cleared at the planet's major spaceport."

He checked the chronometer to enter the date of arrival in the log.

It was the twenty-third day of April, 3503, Earth Standard—the time that was used as a common denominator by all the human worlds.

Hours later, Chaan backed the ship down slowly onto the spaceport at Regn, capital city of Volksweld. When he had been here before, the planet had not had a capital. Much more than at Stellopolis, the tiny starship was dwarfed by the vessels that clustered on the field. The ships at Stellopolis were interplanetary craft, designed for travel within the Sirius System; these were starships.

As Chaan stepped out onto the descending ramp of his ship, a double line of armed, uniformed men formed a lane a hundred feet long to a little cluster of brightly clad people waiting for him. They raised their weapons in salute. Behind the lines of the honor guard, several hundred people had gathered on the field to watch the starship land.

Chaan hesitated, then stepped firmly down the ramp. Clutching his thick briefcase under his arm, he strode down the lane formed for him with hardly a sidelong glance, challenging the grim crimson-and-black of their garb with the blue-and-silver of the Solar Council Space Scout.

He reached the group of people waiting for him, and saw Victad, the Space Command agent, among them, recognizing Victad from the light-beam transmission pictures sent to headquarters at Greyhound.

Victad stepped forward with outstretched hand. As Chaan grasped it and opened his mouth for a greeting, there was a commotion behind him.

Both men turned toward the starship. There was a moment of confusion near it, then two figures in the crimson-and-black uniforms raced up the ramp and into the ship's open port.

Someone shouted an order, and heat-beams splashed futilely around the port. Half a dozen soldiers started up the ramp, but staggered and fell to the ground as it was pulled up and the port closed.

Seconds later, with Chaan and scores of Volksweldvolken gaping helplessly from the ground, the scout ship rose slowly and streaked with increasing speed into the dark blue sky.

CHAPTER SIX

CHAAN WHIRLED on the man whose elaborate uniform proclaimed him the head of the Volksweld welcoming delegation. Chaan's blue eyes blazed.

"What's the meaning of this?" he demanded furiously in the Volkswelden tongue. "Do you realize the Solar Council can abolish a government for such an action?"

The man's face was white under the plumed helmet. His mouth hung open and his eyes bulged.

"Sir...sir, it is not our doing," he managed to stammer. "I don't know what to say, sir. Our soldiers should have prevented it."

The Volksweld official was so obviously stunned that Chaan believed him. But he snapped:

"The thieves wore the uniform of your soldiers!"

The man turned helplessly to Victad.

"We had nothing to do with it. Assure him it was not our action," he pleaded.

Victad was a short, fat man, but he drew himself up with such regal dignity that he seemed to tower over the taller Volksweld official.

"I am not at all sure it isn't some scheme of yours, in view of your government's recent attitude, Tregor," he retorted coldly. "Perhaps by the time you've attempted to talk your way out of this one, you'll realize you're dealing now with a Council Scout—not just a local Space Command agent."

Tregor turned back to Chaan, literally with tears in his eyes.

"Sir!" he exclaimed. "Captain Fritag! You must believe the Volksweld government had nothing to do with the theft of your craft! We cannot antagonize...Sir, we shall do everything we can, anything you recommend, to explain this incident and make restitution for it."

"Don't you think you'd better get busy, then?" suggested Chaan dryly. "My only recommendation is that I get my ship back."

"But, Captain, how can we? No ship can match the stardrive."

"I see you're not a spaceman, Tregor. No one but a Scout knows how to operate the stardrive."

Tregor's face cleared. His shoulders straightened and the drooping plumes of his helmet seemed to assume a jauntier air.

"Yes, sir! At once, sir!" he exclaimed. He snapped orders, and two of his subordinates left at a hasty trot.

The honor guard had re-formed now, in quadruple ranks near them. Around the little group were clusters of onlookers, crowding in curiously. Chaan studied them with interest.

There was a change here from thirty years ago. The Volksweldvolken he remembered had been individualistic, with a free-and-easy, live-and-let-live attitude toward customs and morals. But that very attitude, unstrained, had engendered in them a sensible, almost conservative, outlook.

There was the mark of fanaticism on many of these faces. The old Volksweld people had worn loose, warm garments that protected them from the chill air. Despite the cool of the afternoon, these, both men and women, wore only tight trousers reaching from waist to calf, tucked into short boots. Perhaps half of them had a short cape thrown over their shoulders, but even most of these had the cape thrown back to expose arms and chest.

The only people around him wearing more than this skimpy dress were the gaudily uniformed soldiers and officials, and Victad, who wore a fur jacket and trousers.

The surface analysis was simple. This was far from a tropical world, which would have justified light dress and made it a foregone conclusion from the Volksweld people's casual attitude. Somewhere along the line, since his last visit to Volksweld, they had developed a strong strain of exhibitionism and body worship. Most of those around him were fine physical specimens.

He found Tregor at his side, waiting respectfully.

"If it is your pleasure, sir, we shall escort you to your quarters," said Tregor. "We have reserved a suite for you in the city's best residential hotel."

"I think I'd prefer to talk to Victad for a while," said Chaan. "Thank you for your offer, but he'll see that I get to my quarters tonight."

Tregor looked slightly disappointed, but said only: "As you wish, sir."

The honor guard came to attention and saluted as Chaan and Victad walked away together. A car emblazoned with the Space Command's star-and-lightning insignia was waiting for them at the gate. They got in, Victad set the automatic controls and the car moved smoothly away.

The spaceport was about ten miles east of Regn, and they were in the outskirts of the city in a few minutes. This was no metropolis of soaring towers and sky-spanning viaducts like Stellopolis. Its broad streets were all at ground level and were lined with wide outdoor sidewalks. The buildings were square and low, of megalithic stone construction, some of them covering wide areas. They were heavily ornamented with gargoyle-like carving.

There was very little vehicular traffic, but as they moved toward the heart of Regn there were more and more pedestrians crowding the sidewalks. Tight trousers, bare chests and capes predominated, but there were many of the crimson-and-black military uniforms. Frequently the streets along which they traveled were broken by great circles, centered with a heroic human figure of stone, or other statuary.

Regn was a large city, of perhaps a million or two people, but no more than a twentieth the total size of Stellopolis. Yet, because it was all spread at ground level, it encompassed an area almost equal to that of the Greyhound capital.

Space Command headquarters was a small building near the center of the city. Victad's living quarters were a suite in the rear of the building, opening to a wall-enclosed garden. The car took them through a gate in the wall to the door, and when they got out it purred off to its garage.

They stepped through the door of Victad's home into a tiny segment of the graceful Sirian civilization Chaan had just left. Here was no heavy architecture, here were no gloomy statues. The simple, curved walls were adorned with a few calligraphic paintings, the resilient floor gleamed with soft color, and flowers perfumed the air from glass tables.

A gray-haired woman in a Sirian toga greeted them, and Victad introduced her to Chaan as his wife, Leah. He spoke in Sirian, seeming to derive pleasure from use of his native tongue. Chaan bowed formally to her, in the Sirian fashion. Victad waved Chaan to one of the low, comfortable chairs as Leah left to oversee the preparation of supper. He slipped out of his furs and into a toga, and produced two long-stemmed Sirian glass pipes before taking a seat facing Chaan.

"The trouble with the Space Service is that you're an old man before you get started at your post," said Victad, as they ceremoniously lit each other's pipes. "Now you Deathless Legion

TWICE UPON A TIME

boys get here in a couple of months, subjective time, from Sirius, but it took us twelve years aboard a starliner. I don't see how the early settlers ever had the energy left to colonize these worlds after they got here."

"They didn't ban the birth of children in transit then," said Chaan. "The Volksweld settlers seem to have arrived here with plenty of energy."

Victad shook his balding head sadly.

"They are an energetic and aggressive people," he agreed. "They have done wonders on a world that would cause lesser people to despair. But I am very much afraid of the aims of their present government."

"That's why I wanted to talk to you first," said Chaan. "My initial inspection showed a very heavy starship construction program and widespread evidence of the use of nuclear energy. I was sure you had relayed that much to Sirius, or I might have headed for Lalande at once, but since I wasn't able to establish radio contact with you from space, I wonder if you aren't being held incommunicado."

"No, it isn't that bad. The radio actually was out, though there might have been sabotage. They know that any long suspension of contact with me would bring real trouble. But there hasn't been much that I could report except those things."

"You mean Volksweld isn't a threat to the peace of the Quadrilateral, then?" asked Chaan, relieved.

"No, I mean that I don't know whether it is or not. They don't have to censor my reports. They can prevent my seeing what I need to see to know exactly what's going on, and some limitation on the freedom of a Space Command agent isn't likely to get Sirius excited. That's why I'm glad you're here. They can't hide things from a trained Space Scout."

Chaan puffed the fragrant tobacco and cogitated.

"The starship construction could be a program for expanded trade with other systems," he thought aloud. "The nuclear program could be an accompaniment of a corresponding expansion in the domestic economy. The note that strikes me as ominous, when taken in connection with these two together, is the heavy emphasis on the military and the indication of a national egomania in the dress and faces of the civilians."

"I've tried to investigate that military concentration," said Victad. "Their answer to me is that they must guard against revolt from dissatisfied elements. There is supposed to be an organized terrorist revolutionary group, the Wasser."

"Possibly a psychological whipping boy. I've studied the dossier on Volksweld thoroughly, but light-beam reports are necessarily skimpy. Perhaps you'd better fill me in on developments here in the past thirty years."

"Well, I've been agent here for eighteen years," said Victad. "When I arrived, the change was already under way from the pastoral sort of existence which you must remember. A government had been formed, with very strong popular support, to organize the resources of the planet, which, as you can understand, had not been very well developed in their previous rather easygoing society. In itself it was a very sound step…but have you ever heard of Philip of Macedon?"

"Philip? A terrestrial leader, wasn't he?"

"Yes, in very ancient times, even before space travel. He organized the small country of Macedonia and brought order to the warring cities of Greece. His son, Alexander the Great, inherited a unified Greece and led it to the conquest of the world."

"Yes, I remember now. But what does that have to do with Volksweld?"

"The leader of their new government was a tremendously popular figure, and a man with far-reaching ambition. His name was Adarl. When he died seven years ago he had built the government of Volksweld into a powerful organization, he had welded the army into its right arm, and he had inaugurated the starship construction program and the nuclear power program. He handed it—along with his long-range aims, whatever they were—down to his son, Marl, and Marl has been even more aggressive than his father in continuing the plan."

"Hmm. One-man government. That's even worse than I thought. Tell me, do you think they stole my ship?"

"I can't say, with certainty. I'm inclined to doubt it. When the effort was made to sabotage your ship at Greyhound, I was notified by light-beam as a routine matter. I suspected Volksweld agents, and I talked pretty straight to Marl about it. He was appalled to learn, as he did not know before, that the delay could have brought the fleet down on him from Lalande."

"He didn't know that failure of a Space Scout to arrive on schedule would activate the fleet? And he does know now?"

"That's correct. That's why I suspect the Wasser, rather than the Volksweld government, of stealing your ship. You can be assured that the government will do everything in its power to get you off to Lalande on time, with a favorable report."

"Hmm. Well, of course the government could have stolen the ship as part of a psychological offensive to make me think the Wasser is a menace that needs strong control. They have a year to get it back without bringing trouble down on their heads."

Chaan's first meal on Volksweld was a Sirian one, expertly prepared and served under Leah's direction. After the meal, he took his leave from Victad and his wife, and was escorted by one of the servants to his suite at the Regnal Hotel.

On Volksweld, Chaan had seen none of the robot servitors that were so common in the Sirius System. He found his suite attended by three human servants, two men and a woman, clad in the tight pants of the Volksweld civilians. On inquiry, he learned that one of the men, Jahr, was his personal servant, while the other man, Oler, and the woman, Ingra were house servants.

"Tell me, Jahr," said Chaan when he had relieved himself of his boots, "who is this man Tregor?"

"Tregor is our minister of defense, sir," answered Jahr. He was a powerfully-muscled blond man, half a head taller than Chaan, with sky-blue eyes and a ready smile.

"Well, they spread the red carpet more than I realized!" exclaimed Chaan, surprised. "Call him in the morning, Jahr, and tell him I want to be supplied with clothing in every style that is currently worn on Volksweld, in my size, including the uniforms of both ordinary soldiers and officers in the army."

"Yes, sir."

"I want them by noon," said Chaan. He studied Jahr and added: "And Jahr, tell him to supply the same in your size."

"Very little will be necessary, sir," answered Jahr, smiling. "I am an army officer."

CHAPTER SEVEN

CHAAN'S ROOMS were high-ceilinged and luxuriously furnished with heavy, carved furniture. There was a rug—something he hadn't seen since he left Procyon—into which his bare feet sank as though into thick moss. Colorful tapestries draped the bed and windows, and gloomy landscapes in gold-worked frames hung on the walls. The suite had an air of barbaric magnificence such as Chaan never had seen before, and it rather appealed to him.

He liked Jahr, too. The big blond man was open and friendly, with none of that obsequious respect so often accorded a Space Scout. Oler was a different proposition: a thin, dark man who said little and often seemed on the verge of sneering. Ingra was a chubby girl with corn-colored hair and good-natured, stupid blue eyes.

Of the three, Chaan decided, Jahr was most likely to be the Volksweld spy assigned to keep tabs on him—always assuming that all three of them weren't espionage agents. It didn't matter a whit. Chaan was accustomed to being spied upon.

Chaan's work as a Space Scout involved some activities that would appear completely useless to people unfamiliar with his procedure—that is, to almost everyone in the inhabited universe. For the one he contemplated now he needed local companionship, and he chose Jahr as being both well-suited and readily available.

When the clothing Chaan had ordered arrived the next day—shortly after noon, although Chaan knew the government could have complied on time without difficulty—he donned the uniform of a Volksweld soldier. It consisted of a pair of baggy, crimson-striped black trousers, close-fitting at the ankles; short black boots; a loose, black-trimmed crimson jacket; and a simple black helmet of some light material that covered the back of the neck.

Chaan instructed Jahr to dress similarly. Jahr protested slightly: as an officer, he objected to being garbed as a common soldier. But he complied.

"Now," said Chaan, "where would a soldier go to pass away afternoon and evening?"

"He'd spend the afternoon in drill and weapons practice," replied Jahr with a grin. "He'd spend the first part of the evening in wrestling, swimming and physical exercise, but he might be free in time for a game or two of cards in the barracks before lights out."

"I don't mean when he's on duty. Don't the Volksweld soldiers ever get a day's leave?"

"Oh, I didn't understand, sir. Why, if we're off for a bit of fun, there's a section of the city filled with taverns and amusement houses, that caters to the military."

"That's more like it. Let's go there. What unit will we be from?"

"Well, sir," said Jahr, a twinkle in his eye, "from our insignia we're under sergeants from the Third Sector of the Northern Fleet."

"Fleet?" murmured Chaan, wondering how that terminology fitted into an army organization, but he did not press the matter farther.

Under sergeants, he learned from questioning Jahr, certainly would not own a car. They might be able to afford a cab, but it was more likely they would take the moving street across the city. So the moving street they took.

The moving streets radiated out like spokes from the heart of Regn. They were below the level of the crisscrossing stationary streets, which passed over them by means of viaducts. At this point, near the middle of the city, they were only a block from the nearest outward-moving street.

Chaan and Jahr walked to it and descended a short flight of steps to its level. It was an endless belt, about forty feet wide. A narrow belt on either side moved about five miles an hour, while the main central belt moved at twice that speed. The main belt was well populated with passengers moving away from the midst of the city.

The two men stepped onto the five-mile belt and from it to the ten-mile belt, then added the pace of their own walking to the speed of the belt. They reached their destination within twenty minutes and left the belt.

They were in the midst of a section of the city called the

Wehmer. It was crowded with soldiers. Shops, amusement places and small hotels were jammed together, advertised by garishly painted signs. Chaan grinned. Soldiers were much alike, anywhere. Taverns, girlie shows, and gambling dens predominated among the amusement houses, while souvenir stores and pawnshops outnumbered all other shops.

"What do we do first, sir?" asked Jahr.

"Don't call me 'sir' here. We're a couple of under sergeants on leave, remember? Call me Chaan. And what would you like to do?"

"Well, sir...Chaan, there's a spot near here where they serve good ale and a man can usually get into a good game of quadrangle."

"You seem to know the district pretty well, for an officer."

Jahr grinned.

"I was a common soldier for five years before I won my comets," he said.

They crossed the street, shouldered their way through a group of laughing, tipsy soldiers and ducked down into a basement restaurant which bore the sign: The Titian Queen. The interior, dim with tobacco smoke, was not large but contained about a dozen large round tables and several booths along the street-side wall. Against the opposite wall was a bar, behind which stacked bottles partially concealed a relief wood-carving of a reclining nude woman.

Drinkers sat at all the tables and in the booths, but there were empty places. Chaan and Jahr pushed their way to seats at one of several tables on which players were manipulating wire rings on rectangular three-dimensional figures of wire. This, Jahr informed Chaan in an undertone, was the game of quadrangle.

"Next in," said Jahr, and the four players nodded without looking at him or interrupting their game.

A huge squat man with a hairy chest and an apron tied over his tight trousers took their order for ale and presently returned with two tall tankards. Chaan dipped his nose gratefully into the good Volksweld ale. It was as he remembered, sweet and rich.

He looked around the tavern. Not only did he see it with his eyes, but he let its atmosphere sink into him. With his emotions he sought to sense the general feelings and attitudes of these people from their reactions in relaxation. It was a sampling method he used often in his work: the tavern was a microcosm of its planet.

Most of the tavern's customers were soldiers, but there were three civilian men, two in one of the booths and another in a second booth. The single civilian was accompanied by a woman, as were four of the soldiers, all in the comparative privacy of the booths.

Most of these men were like Jahr: blond and athletic. Not one was fat, except the bartender, although a couple were somewhat chubby; and Chaan counted only half a dozen with brown or dark hair. There was one freckle-faced redhead, with a chest like a barrel and muscles like cords. Chaan, with his own sandy hair and blue eyes, fit quite well into the overall picture, although he was slenderer and wirier than most of them.

The four women gave Chaan a uniform initial impression. They were healthy-looking, even rangy, compared to the soft, slight women representing the universal type in the Sirian System. It occurred to Chaan that perhaps the low-cut costume of these women contributed to his impression of them.

The broad, freckled shoulders of one husky red-head with her back to him bespoke the Amazon. Two of the others drew his notice only casually, but the fourth...she was a youngster of eighteen or twenty with a round, open face, round blue eyes and pale hair cut in bangs over her forehead. She sat facing him, in a booth with two soldiers.

For a brief moment, Chaan remembered flaxen-haired Ilse, who had been his wife when he had been on Volksweld before. Where was she now? he wondered. He probably had grandchildren on this planet.

What surprised him about the people in this tavern was the carefree, almost joyous, attitude that could be sensed instantly. From what Victad had told him of the government and Volksweld's recent history, he had anticipated one of two things: either that they would cower, talk in whispers, fearful of the secret police; or that they would be drinking excessively, talking too boisterously, escaping from the frustrations of a rigid existence.

There was none of either. Some of the talk and laughter were loud, but it was the exuberance of natural energy. They drank freely and they talked freely, but they drank and talked as free men and women. They reminded him very much of the courageous, individualistic Volksweldvolken he remembered, except that now there was an undercurrent of vast and confident excitement.

What was the significance of this new facet to the Volksweld mentality? He searched the compartments of his mind, but he could not pinpoint it. He only knew that it appealed to him mightily, as though he stood at the brink of a tremendous current that invited him to plunge in and be swept along to fulfillment of some spiritual destiny he had always sought.

Jahr now had entered the game of quadrangle, replacing one of the players who had dropped out, and the coldly logical habit of observation took command of Chaan's mind. He watched closely as they moved the little rings of metal through the intricacies of the wire cubicle by turns. Presently, the significance of the game dawned upon him.

The quadrangle represented the Sirius Quadrilateral! This game of three-dimensional chess was, in miniature, a space war among the four star systems of the Quadrilateral. Jahr, manipulating the Wolf corner, pitted his skill against the combined wits of his three opponents, though with equal strength of pieces. Should he lose, he, like his predecessor, would suffer a minor disgrace and retire from the game.

As a people's games are played, so run their thoughts, thought Chaan. It was stronger evidence of that which he sought than anything Victad had learned.

The ale flowed freely. Chaan was not sure how many of the cool, rich tankards he had drained, but his head was swimming slightly, when there was a slight commotion in one of the booths.

Voices were raised in argument. The round-faced young girl slid out of her seat, her blue eyes flashing in anger, and shook off the detaining hand of one of the soldiers.

"Argue all you like, but not over me!" she snapped in a husky voice sharpened by wrath. "I haven't said yes to either of you."

She turned and started toward the door. One of the soldiers sat and watched her with a rueful grin, but the other, hotter-tempered, leaped after her. As she passed Chaan's table with long-legged strides, her pursuer grabbed the cape that trailed behind her and pulled her off balance. She fell sidewise, gasping and clutching, into Chaan's lap.

Almost knocked from his chair, Chaan instinctively clasped her about the waist with one arm, clutching the edge of the table with the other hand. The young soldier grasped her wrist and attempted to pull her away, and for an instant there was a minor tug-of-war, with Chaan at a disadvantage. Then a new factor entered the picture.

Getting to his feet, Jahr said quietly:

"Let her alone, soldier. She's said her say."

"You stay out of this!" shouted the soldier, and impulsively swung at Jahr.

His fist bounced off Jahr's chest, and Jahr hurled him across the room with a sweep of his arm.

"Here!" shouted a voice from behind them, as the soldier's companion came to his aid, armed with an ale bottle. Before Jahr could turn, he shattered the bottle over Jahr's head.

Jahr turned around with a contemptuous smile and swung a fist into the surprised soldier's face. The man did a backward arc through the air and skidded across the floor under a table.

By this time, Chaan had disengaged himself from the girl and was on his feet. As the first soldier leaped at Jahr from behind, Chaan's hand flicked out viciously and the attacker sprawled sidewise to the floor, unconscious.

Jahr grinned down at Chaan.

"My mistake, comrade," he said. "I thought you might need protection."

"It came in handy," replied Chaan, smiling back. "I was tied up." He turned to the girl. "You're free to go now, miss."

"No!" she exclaimed, her round eyes on Jahr. "Your friend...he's hurt."

"Nothing but a few scratches," denied Jahr, rubbing the back of his blond head with his hand. His palm came away bloody.

"It needs disinfecting," said the girl. She turned to the bartender, who was dragging the two unconscious soldiers to the door. "Hann, bring us some disinfectant and cotton."

"And some cold ale," added Jahr, as the three moved together to a booth.

She was Hildi Gretten, daughter of a minor government official, she told them as she swabbed the back of Jahr's head. She and a girl friend had made an engagement to go out with the two soldiers, and when her friend had been unable to go, she had foolishly agreed to go out with both of them. They had drunk too much ale.

"Well, the evening has hardly begun," said Jahr, exploring her medical ministrations gingerly, "but I wouldn't want to get into the same sort of an argument with my friend Chaan. Maybe we'd better find another girl."

"I haven't said I want to go out with either of you," she retorted, but her eyes were merry.

"Oh, sure you do," said Jahr carelessly. "The only problem's to make it a foursome. We'll have to find another girl for Chaan."

"We'll find another girl for you," she answered firmly. "I like your friend, if you don't mind."

"Me?" asked Chaan, surprised. "Jahr disposed of those other two fellows for you."

"I like whom I like," said Hildi. "And I like you. We'll go by and pick up Gretl. The only reason she couldn't come along was that these boys wanted to start out in the middle of the afternoon."

They took the moving street back uptown. The huge crimson sun of Volksweld was setting, and with the evening chill coming on Hildi pulled her sky-blue cape around her. Chaan found himself rather regretting this. He had been admiring her figure. She was slim and virginal, with mobile hips and firm breasts. Her round eyes, tilted nose and full lips gave her an air of appealing Dutch innocence.

Hildi, he learned, lived with her father on the northern outskirts of the city, but Gretl, a government secretary, kept an apartment downtown. They found her at her apartment, just in from work, a rather thin, dark, attractive girl.

They did not return to the Wehmer, but ate supper in a downtown restaurant where Chaan and Jahr were the only ones in uniform among a huge crowd of civilians. From there they moved to one of the city's nightspots, where Chaan discovered that the free swing of Hildi's frame fulfilled its promise: she danced like a breeze, and initiated him without difficulty into the boisterous steps that were the current Volksweld mode.

Hildi's disposition toward him was warm from the start, and for a time he tried to analyze whether the mood arose from her own general nature, was a reflection of the Volksweld social attitude or was brought about—as he rather hoped—by her liking for him. After a while he stopped worrying about it and accepted it without question.

This fact, combined with the frankly hedonistic air that pervaded the place and the exciting intimacy of Hildi in his arms, soon captured him from the task he had appointed himself. He no longer observed, he experienced. It was one of those rare evenings which dissolve into something that is memorable and yet not remembered in detail.

Very late, the four of them were in Gretl's apartment, enjoying drinks and talking animatedly of such subjects as the true meaning of the universe and the real nature of man's mission.

And then, without any appreciable interval that he could recollect at once, Chaan was coming dizzily awake to a vigorous and cheerful voice:

"Wake up, comrade! Breakfast is almost ready."

Chaan sat up with a start. He was on one side of one of the gigantic Volksweld beds. Over a nearby chair was tossed the crimson-and-black uniform, tangled with a mass of familiar sky-blue cloth.

Jahr stood in the doorway, grinning, leaning against the jamb with one hand. He was fully dressed, but his uniform was rumpled.

And on the other side of the big bed, sleeping peacefully on her stomach, lay Hildi.

CHAPTER EIGHT

"WHERE ARE WE?" asked Chaan, his mind still fuzzy. "In Gretl's apartment?"

Jahr roared with laughter.

"You must have enjoyed the evening!" he replied. "Don't you

recognize your own bedroom, sir? We're in your suite."

"Well, it's just my second night in the place," said Chaan defensively. He put a hand to his blond head, which throbbed slightly. "I remember now. We came over here when Gretl's supply of drinks ran out."

"And Gretl's been wondering all morning how two common soldiers can afford a suite in the Regnal Hotel, with two servants," said Jahr.

Chaan looked over at Hildi. Surprisingly, in view of the natural volume of Jahr's voice, their conversation hadn't awakened her.

She was stretched out at full length, clean-limbed and lovely. The blonde hair was tousled at the back of her neck, and her cherubic face was cradled on one forearm, lips slightly parted. Her shoulders moved with her breathing.

Looking down at her, memory returning to him, Chaan shivered with a twinge of indefinable emotion.

Jahr either was unaware of Chaan's sentimental reflections, or he had no patience with them. Striding into the room, he brought Hildi to startled and resentful wakefulness with a resounding thwack of his palm. With a yelp, she rolled over on her back and propped herself on her elbows. Then, tilting her head sidewise, she smiled and fixed sleepy blue eyes on Chaan's face.

"Hello," she said softly. "I love you."

Impulsively, Chaan leaned over and kissed her soft lips.

"Get dressed," commanded Jahr as he went out the door. "Breakfast is almost ready."

As they bathed and dressed, with few words spoken between them, Chaan sought to analyze the experience he had just been through.

It was something that could have happened, with variations, on any world in the Quadrilateral, except perhaps Lalande, where relations between the sexes were rigidly formalized in almost all the splinter societies. Yet here there was a different flavor, and a more significant one, from the same sort of thing on one of the planets of Sirius or Procyon.

Chaan remembered last night's conversations. These people, Hildi, Jahr and Gretl, were not boisterous feather-heads; they had talked seriously and intelligently. The community of views and affection that had built up between him and Hildi at no time had struck any jarring note of cheapness.

Hildi squeezed his arm and smiled demurely up into his face as they left the room together. Chaan sighed. He liked these people.

Breakfast, consisting largely of some sort of fried little Volksweld animals on toasted cakes, was served to them in the big dining room by Oler, who gazed sourly upon the spectacle of Jahr seated at the table with their master. Occasionally Ingra peeked in, wide-eyed, from the kitchen.

Chaan saw no point in delaying the inevitable reckoning.

"Well, what's the convention here now?" he asked.

"What do you mean, Chaan?" asked Hildi. "What sort of convention?"

Realizing all at once how undiplomatic he was being, Chaan wished fervently he had waited to take Jahr aside and question him, but there was no way out of it now.

"Am I expected to marry you now?" he asked, trying to alleviate the brutality of it with a smile. "Or was last night...well, just a night to remember?"

Hildi averted her face suddenly.

"Whatever you wish," she said in a hurt tone.

"Wait, Hildi, you don't understand," interposed Jahr. "You don't realize it, but Chaan has no way of knowing what's expected of him. If you're ready for the girls to learn the truth, Chaan, perhaps you'd better tell us what the significance of our little social event of last night would have been on other...in other places you've been."

"I don't find it necessary to conceal my identity often," answered Chaan with a wry smile. "As a matter of fact, this sort of thing probably couldn't happen with a girl like Hildi on any world except Volksweld as it was when I was here before. Then it could mean anything Hildi and I wanted it to mean: that we live together permanently or that we never see each other again. Essentially; it would mean we liked each other very much last night."

"What do you mean, when you were on Volksweld before?" interrupted Gretl. "Where else have you been at your age?"

"A great many places," said Chaan slowly. "I'm not Volksweldvolken. I'm the Solar Council's Space Scout."

The two women stared at him with wide, awed eyes.

"I told Jahr soldiers don't have apartments like this!" exclaimed Gretl triumphantly.

"Now I know why you asked what you did," said Hildi softly, and her voice caught in a sob.

"Why, what's the matter, Hildi?" asked Chaan, instantly solicitous.

"Space Scouts never stay on one world more than a year," she murmured tearfully.

Jahr frowned at her impatiently.

"You can relax, Chaan," he said, "Volksweld hasn't changed as much as it may appear to you. If a man and woman love each other they live together or meet each other, as they prefer, and if they stop loving each other they part."

"Well spoken, my fine philosopher," said Gretl. "And just what are your plans for us?"

"Why," said Jahr carelessly, "I know where you live, my dear. I don't imagine Chaan wants too many dependent females cluttering up his premises, so expect me when you see me."

"I'm curious," said Hildi. "Since Chaan's a Space Scout, where do you fit in, Jahr? Are you really a soldier?"

Very much so, said Jahr. I'm...

"He's a very high-ranking and important officer," interposed Chaan dryly, "who was assigned to pose as one of my servants so he could report my activities to the government."

Jahr exploded into delighted laughter.

"I told them I wasn't cut out for a spy!" he exclaimed joyously. "Instead of being properly discreet and respectful, I start calling the young master by his first name and going out on binges with him!"

"I won't file any official complaints," said Chaan with a grin. "Report all you like, and let's stay good friends. I don't think I've ever met such a likeable spy."

"Done!" retorted Jahr and stuck out a huge hand impulsively. Chaan shook hands with him solemnly across the table.

After breakfast, Jahr took Gretl back to her apartment, with the understanding he probably wouldn't return before mid-afternoon. They left, carrying on an animated discussion about how she was to explain her absence from her office.

Chaan and Hildi retired to the big living room for a second cup of *fehr*, the strong, sweetish Volksweld substitute for Sirian coffee, Oler served it to them, disapprovingly.

"Don't you have a job to explain about?" asked Chaan.

"No," she answered. "I'm completing studies in interstellar sociology at Regn University this year, and I can cut my classes today."

"You said you live with your father. Won't he be worried about your staying out all night?"

"You must have lived on some very strange worlds," she said wonderingly, "I've read about such societies. But no woman has to fear harm, anywhere on Volksweld. I'm sure my father knows exactly why I didn't go home last night."

"In a culture like this, I'm sure fathers grow accustomed to such absences," remarked Chaan dryly.

She looked at him steadily. The gaze of her honest blue eyes was disconcerting.

"I'd like you to understand this, Chaan," she said, "I know that the overwhelming love of a woman for her first man is sometimes just the wonderful discovery of love itself. I've seen women for whom that first love lasted a lifetime, and I've seen them for whom it lasted only a day. No woman who is honest can say how she'll feel tomorrow, but I know that today I love you with all my heart."

"I wouldn't love you if you weren't honest, and I find I do love you very much," said Chaan quietly. "Love is not a single thing that can be pinpointed and defined, Hildi. It can be brief and sweet and memorable, or it can grow deeper and richer throughout a long life together. In my job of star-hopping, I've experienced the brief kind very sincerely several times, and I've always hoped that some day I'll know the other kind."

"I hope so, too," she said.

They sat in silence for a few moments, and Chaan watched her as she sat demurely sipping her *fehr*. He half expected her to suggest that she could offer him the permanent love he sought, but she didn't.

Chaan found the idea not unattractive to him. There was something about the girl that struck a chord deep within him. He was tempted to offer her the Solar Council marriage that was his right on any world, but somehow it seemed too casual a thing to do. Instead, he said:

"If you don't mind taking Jahr's place as my companion today, I'd like for you to show me the city, Hildi. And I want you to spend tonight here with me again. But tomorrow I'm going to take you back to your home for a while."

"Whatever you say," she agreed. "But if you loved me last night and still love me today, why do you think you won't love me tomorrow?"

He laughed.

"It isn't that at all," he said. "I just don't want you to run the risk of any trouble, and I have no way of knowing what the atmosphere around here is going to be after I talk to Marl tomorrow."

"You're going to see Marl?" she asked with wide eyes.

"The Leader?"

"The sooner I see him, the sooner I can bring my investigation of Volksweld to a head. So I'm going to have Jahr make the necessary arrangements when he gets back for an audience with Marl tomorrow."

"But how do you know he'll see you right away?"

"When a Space Scout suggests an audience," commented Chaan with a grim smile, "I don't think the leader of a planet is going to try to put him off. Any planet."

CHAPTER NINE

DESPITE HIS WORDS, Chaan did expect a certain amount of delay. If Marl was playing a game with the Solar Council, it was reasonable to expect him to employ irritating tactics on the Council's Scout.

He was mildly surprised, therefore, when Jahr reported that Marl was willing to see him at Chaan's convenience. Since Chaan had suggested originally that the conference be at the hour of 1400, he did not consider it necessary to notify Marl further that he would arrive at that time.

"You know," he told Hildi after breakfast the next morning, "you'd look charming in a Sirian toga. Or, better, one of those fur outfits people used to wear on Volksweld."

She stretched charmingly, favoring him with a smile that came as near to being seductive as her artless face permitted.

"Don't you like my body?" she asked. "I've always thought I was too long-legged and bony."

"Your body is the most delectable combination of youth and maturity I've ever seen," he affirmed devoutly. "But that cape-and-trousers costume is the only thing I've actually seen about Volksweld that I dislike. It reminds me of the children's Star Ranger programs on the Tri-D screens on Greyhound."

For their tour of the city the previous day, Chaan had worn the black-and-crimson Volksweld uniform, to avoid being conspicuous. Now he donned his blue-and-silver Solar Council garb, and Hildi exclaimed in delight. He didn't blame her. Tailored smoothly to his figure, it contrasted startlingly with the Volksweld uniform.

They took one of the city's few automatic cabs to Hildi's home. Chaan gathered that luxury vehicles were rare in an economy committed heavily to space fleet construction, and only wealthy persons and high officials owned cars or used cabs; most people utilized the moving streets.

The vehicle's quality, however, compared with anything hoe had seen on Greyhound and was superior to most of those in the Procyon System. Hildi punched the address on its controls, and it moved smoothly and swiftly to the outskirts of Regn. It pulled up before a modest house, surrounded by gardens. Chaan punched the wait button and escorted Hildi to the door.

"Father is at his office, but why don't you have lunch here?" suggested Hildi.

"No," said Chaan. "I have some intensive, studying to do before I see Marl. As Jahr told Gretl, expect me when you see me: the difference being that you can be assured you'll see me again."

He kissed her and took the cab back to the hotel. At 1330, he and Jahr went to the Volksheim building, which covered a quarter of a square mile in the very heart of Regn.

The big square building was swarming with people, both

military and civilian. Chaan had assumed it was merely a palatial residence for Marl, but apparently it was the nerve center of the government, too. On a magnified scale, Marl followed the practice—or perhaps he had set the example—of having his living quarters where he worked, a practice that seemed common in Regn.

Chaan was in for another surprise. He assumed that Marl would be seated in regal magnificence in a vast room, surrounded by retainers. But he and Jahr were led to no such throne room:

Instead, he was ushered into a small room from which Jahr was barred by a pair of uniformed guards. It was a small room with a single window that overlooked an inner courtyard of the Volksheim building. Its walls were lined with shelves of microfilm, and there was a reading screen in one corner. Behind a desk bearing a globe of Volksweld and a plastic model of the Sirius Quadrilateral, a dark-haired young man wearing old-fashioned spectacles arose with a smile.

"Captain Fritag," he said. "Welcome."

"Thank you," said Chaan, looking around. The receptionist was holding out his hand across the desk, so Chaan shook it.

"Won't you have a seat?" suggested the young man cordially, gesturing at a comfortable chair before the desk.

Chaan sank into the chair and glanced at his wrist chronometer impatiently. It was now 1400.

"I hope I won't have to wait too long to see Marl," he said, rather sternly.

"Not long at all," said the young man. "I am Marl."

Chaan gulped and lurched to his feet. As a Space Scout, he owed Marl no obeisance, but he was put at a disadvantage by having treated Volksweld's leader as a servant. He felt his ears turning pink.

"I'm very sorry," he said. "I just assumed…"

"Please be seated," said Marl, smiling. "It's not an unusual mistake. I'm afraid I rather encourage it. It gives me a certain psychological advantage."

"I can see how it might," remarked Chaan, regaining his composure and sitting down again.

He took in Marl with a quick, photographic glance. So this was the Volksweld leader! He wasn't impressive at all, as Chaan had expected. He was a slight man, with a squarish face and a wide, firm mouth. His keen black eyes seemed to glitter behind the heavy-rimmed spectacles, and his black hair was neatly combed. He was swarthier than most of the Volksweldvolken, and his black garb, cut along the lines of the Volksweld uniform but unrelieved by any color, seemed to make him a part of the shadows of the dim room.

"I hope you've been enjoying your stay on Volksweld so far," said Marl.

"Yes, thanks to the fine fellow you sent to take care of me."

"Jahr? Yes, Jahr is a good man, if a little impulsive at times. I thought you'd like him. And I see he's already plunged you into the city's night life."

"Oh, he's reported that already, has he?"

Marl laughed gently.

"Jahr forgets such routine matters as regular reports sometimes," he said. "No, I had to depend on other sources this time. But completely reliable ones, as I'm sure you guessed. I understand that Hildi and Gretl are very pleasant companions."

Chaan flushed to his sandy eyebrows.

"Very," he replied. "I didn't get to know Gretl very well, but I consider Jahr and Hildi among the more pleasant aspects of Volksweld life."

"You found unpleasant ones, Captain? You surprise me."

"I doubt that, Marl. I hope I'm not being disrespectful in calling you by your first name—or is it your last name?"

"My only name," said Marl. "My father abandoned the family name entirely. No, my people ordinarily address me as Leader Marl, but you are not of Volksweld. At present you might say we are of equal rank, so I'll address you as 'Chaan' if you have no objection."

"None at all. Now as to Volksweld's more unfortunate aspects. I shouldn't have to enumerate them to you: the starship construction program, nuclear power, one-man government, a heavy military training program.

"Putting aside the military organization for the moment, heavy starship construction is permissible and nuclear power is permissible. They're permissible together, and they usually develop together.

"Neither does the Solar Council interfere with a totalitarian form or government, unless there is evidence that it is indulging in certain excesses.

"But the combination simply isn't allowed. A totalitarian form of government cannot be tolerated on a planet that has achieved a certain level of technological progress. It's too dangerous. On a planet of a high technological level we have grades for them, but that isn't important—one man or a group of men could make a decision that would destroy that world or plunge it into war with other worlds."

"And my military organization just adds to the danger, in the eyes of the Solar Council?" murmured Marl.

"Exactly."

"Then I'm faced with the choice of resigning and plunging Volksweld into political chaos, or trying to revoke the planet's technological progress and throw it back to savagery."

"The choice isn't as stringent, as you make it. I don't know whether you could reorganize Volksweld's form of government on a more representative basis without unfortunate results in any reasonable length of time. I agree it would be impractical to try to reverse and prohibit nuclear power and research. But among the things you can do to prove your peaceful intentions and good faith, are reduction of your military establishment and immediate suspension of your starship construction program."

Marl leaned back and put the tips of his fingers together.

"You have already decided to call the fleet to Wolf," he said positively.

"Yes, I made that decision before I asked to see you, Marl. I can't stay here long enough to assure myself that you would do these things, even if you agreed."

"I'm not going to waste time trying to argue you out of your judgment of Volksweld," said Marl. "I just want to ask you one thing before I present my alternative suggestion: is it true that the fleet will come here automatically if you don't report to Lalande on schedule?"

Chaan grinned. His eyes twinkled with the triumph of the

moment.

"Quite true," he replied. "So you may as well return my ship to me. Any attempt to interfere with a Space Scout's duties can bring some pretty severe punitive measures."

Marl stared at him soberly.

"I'm being honest with you, Chaan," he said. "We don't have your ship."

"Then who does?"

"I don't know. The Wasser, perhaps. At any rate, it doesn't matter. The fleet will come down on us without any effort on your part, because, whoever has it, we can't catch them now. There was a stardrive explosion in space on the other side of Volksweld last night."

Chaan arose from his chair and went to the window. He looked out into the pleasant little courtyard below.

Marl did seem to be telling the truth about this. He had no reason to lie about it. And the apparent burst of the ship into stardrive was something no one on Volksweld except Chaan could be expected to anticipate.

"I should let you go on thinking that," said Chaan, turning back to Marl. "Perhaps then you'd scurry to clean house here. But I want my ship back. Don't you know that no one but a Space Scout can put a ship into stardrive, Marl?"

"That's what I had been led to believe. But there was a stardrive explosion."

"Somebody tried to put it into stardrive," replied Chaan. "When anyone who doesn't know how attempts to put the ship into stardrive you get a spectacular fake explosion. All it does is drain off the excess energy that's built up during the anti-gravity flight, but the ship remains on anti-gravity."

Marl breathed a deep sigh of relief.

"You have no idea how much that changes things," he said. "I have every available ship scouring that section of space, and if your ship is still on anti-gravity it will be brought back to Volksweld eventually.'"

Chaan scratched his head and sat down again.

"Marl, you puzzle me," he said. "I've told you that the fleet's coming to Wolf, whether I get to Lalande or not. You act as though cooperating with me and getting my ship back will make a major difference in the Solar Council's action."

Marl smiled at him. He arose behind his desk and removed his spectacles, revealing deceptively mild, dark eyes.

"With your Space Scout training, you should be able to predict my next move from my attitude, if they hadn't made such a thing inconceivable to you," he said softly. "Don't you think I counted on the arrival of a Space Scout here on schedule? Don't you think I planned to meet this very contingency?

"Oh, the Council has the Scout system well set up, so there's no way of getting around it. If I let you go, you report; if I hold you here, the fleet comes when you don't show up at Lalande. An insoluble situation, my advisors said, but I found the answer.

"Chaan, I want you to desert the Solar Council and join the Volksweld cause! I want you to take your ship to Lalande on schedule and report that there is no danger here and there is no need for the fleet to come to Wolf!"

Chaan's jaw fell, but he caught himself before speaking. His every instinct warned him of the most terrible danger to himself and to all the far-flung worlds of the Solar Council, in Marl's quiet words.

The danger lay in the fact that Marl was no fool...and that Marl knew Chaan was no fool. Here was no egotistical dictator making a wild, blind proposal, nor a clever man attempting to outwit an opponent he considered stupid. Whatever Marl had in mind, he had figured his chances and considered the effort worthwhile.

And what did he have in mind? Was it an honest proposal, which Marl had some hidden reason to believe he could persuade Chaan to accept? Or was it a bold smokescreen for some other plan?

"What makes you think I would accept such a proposal?" he asked cautiously. He knew no other approach.

"You've been on Volksweld before. Don't you think it's improved now?"

"In many respects, yes," Chaan conceded slowly. "It has made a tremendous amount of technological progress. But I rather like the old air of freedom and individualism."

"Wait a minute." Marl leaned forward and his voice took on a new intensity. His eyes were almost hypnotic. "You say that because you've been taught that a totalitarian government always means a loss of individuality and freedom. Be honest, Chaan, as I'm being honest with you. There is a singleness of community purpose on Volksweld now, but other than that can you say you've seen evidence of any abridgement of freedom?"

"No, but I've hardly had time for that yet. I expect all the people I've seen here, except Victad of course, agree with your aims."

"The great majority of Volksweldvolken do. I need no secret police. The Solar Council asks a democratic form of government, and I assure you that Volksweld is democratic. It's just that the people of Volksweld choose, for reasons of efficiency, to have a government headed by one man.

"You must consider this, Chaan: there comes a time in the history of every culture when it must have bold, unified leadership to progress. My father and I provided that leadership for Volksweld and now, as always, selfish dissenters would discard us once the major task is accomplished."

Chaan held up his hand. To his trained ear, Marl protested too much for his opposition to be as minor as he pictured it, but Chaan wanted to direct the conversation away from any pure-propaganda line.

"Let me concede that you and your father have done a good job of lifting Volksweld by its bootstraps, and probably with comparatively little dislocation of basic human freedoms," he said. "But the Solar Council is not interested in your domestic affairs, as such. You haven't proposed that I commend you for what you have done for Volksweld. You've proposed that I close my eyes to your obvious intention to interfere in the affairs of other worlds."

Marl seemed to come out of a semi-daze. With a slight effort, he regained his air of detached composure.

"Please excuse me," he apologized. "I'm afraid I'm too accustomed to dealing with underlings who must have their doubts resolved. Now how long has the Council fleet been at Lalande?"

"An academic question, I'm sure. About sixty years."

"Why?"

"The colonies at Lalande haven't had the benefit of an Adarl or a Marl," answered Chaan with a smile. "They never could achieve unification, and developed into bitterly warring groups. Without the fleet to enforce peace, they might exterminate each other."

"There you are!" said Marl triumphantly. "They need a strong hand to guide them. The Solar Council fleet sits there, merely a restraining force, supported at great expense which is borne by all the other worlds men inhabit. Let me take the task from the shoulders of the Solar Council, and I'll have those Lalande societies organized into a decent, productive culture within a few years."

"And then Procyon," said Chaan sardonically. "And after that, Sirius. A pretty pattern for conquest. What in space ever made you think I'd go along with a plan like that?"

"Look, Chaan," said Marl, leaning forward intently and clasping his hands on his desk. "You like Volksweld. You like the people here. You like our ways and the way we think and face the future with courageous hearts. I know this, because we've had agents out ever since my father took control here, and the psychology and background of every Space Scout in the Quadrilateral has been studied intensively. The only thing that stands in the way of throwing your lot with Volksweld is the loyalty to the Solar Council that was beaten into you with your training.

"You know our situation. We need time. If you give a favorable report at Lalande, we have thirty more years to get ready, and that will be enough. But if the fleet comes here from Lalande in half that time, we can't fight it."

"Unfortunately for your theory, there is another Space Scout on a reverse tour," said Chaan. "He is en route from Procyon to Lalande now, and you certainly couldn't expect to persuade two of us to your plot when he arrives here and sees what's going on."

"We plan to detain him," said Marl. "By the time he makes the round and fails to show up at Sirius, twenty years will have passed, and it will take eight or nine more years for them to get a light-beam message to Lalande. You see, we've considered every contingency, and it all hinges on your decision.

"We don't ask you to do this just because you like Volksweld. But, deep within you, we know it doesn't matter to you whether you're loyal to the Solar Council or Volksweld.

"When you return to Volksweld, the highest place in the government, next to mine, is reserved for you. Or if you prefer the life of a Space Scout, you can be a scout for Volksweld instead of the Solar Council. Anything you ask will be yours."

"You should know my answer," replied Chaan, getting to his feet.

"I expect a negative answer now," said Marl, also arising. "But when you think it over, remember that the Solar Council is just a government too, and its course may be wrong."

CHAPTER TEN

CHAAN LEFT THE little room feeling as though he had been taken to the mountaintop. Marl was perilously friendly, dangerously persuasive.

Jahr joined him outside. But when Chaan answered Jahr's greeting with an absent grunt, Jahr looked at him quizzically and said no more. The two men walked silently through the Volksheim building.

Of course, Marl's proposal was preposterous, and Chaan would have none of it. Yet the dictator had been correct when he said the idea was calculated to appeal to Chaan's psychology.

A daring plan, by which a tiny world of devil-may-care people hoped to conquer the massed might of the Sirius Quadrilateral! And a plan that would work, if Chaan would cooperate.

Chaan was accustomed to the heavy responsibility that rested on the shoulders of a Space Scout. But in this case he was a lone man holding in his hand the future of all the billions of humans in the universe.

He did like Volksweld and its people. Here in the cool atmosphere of this planet turning around its little red sun was an attitude of happy camaraderie, a sense of dedication to the present and the future that deeply appealed to him.

Chaan was too well trained to have overlooked the glint in Marl's eye. It was the age-old desire for power. But so far that power had been put to good use.

And was there not room in space for two interstellar governments? Would not the worlds of the Quadrilateral thrive better under a local regime than one imposed by faraway Earth?

As Marl had said, the Solar Council could be wrong. After all, it was an imperial government that imposed its will on other worlds, even if its aim—to enforce interstellar peace—was a good one.

They were in the cab on the way back to the hotel.

"Your leader is a very persuasive person, Jahr," said Chaan.

"He is a great man," said Jahr. "Some people of Volksweld think he is even greater than his father."

"But you don't?"

Jahr smiled a peculiar smile.

"I suppose it depends on the type of man you are," he answered. "I knew Adarl."

Chaan fell silent again, for a thought had struck him. There was Hildi! If ever he had met a woman he did not want to leave at the end of a brief year, Hildi was that woman. He wanted her with him always.

There was room in the scout ship for her, but he could not take, her, under Solar Council regulations, except in an emergency. But Marl unquestionably would agree to his taking Hildi with him.

No. What emergency could he plead, on arrival at Lalande? Furthermore, not even the dream of Hildi could turn him from his duty.

At the hotel, Oler had a message for him.

"Hildi Gretten asked that you come to her home at once, Captain," he said sourly.

Chaan frowned. He had told Hildi that he would get in touch with her when he wanted to see her again.

He attempted to call her, but received no answer. Beginning to get worried, he strapped on his heat-gun and took a cab to her suburban home. Could she be in some kind of trouble?

From the outside, the house was dark. Chaan strode swiftly through the gardens and pressed the door button. He waited. When there was no response, he pressed the button again. Still no response.

Carefully, he tried the latch. The door was unlocked. Chaan pushed the door open and stepped cautiously inside.

The hall was dark and there was no sound in the house. Chaan felt the wall until he found the light switch.

The lights came on, and with them an almost inaudible, rhythmic hum. The lights pulsed faintly, almost beyond the range of detection.

A hypno-trap! In Hildi's home!

Chaan suddenly was sick at heart. So Hildi had been one of the spies set against him all the time. He should have known it, their love affair had moved too swiftly. On any world but Volksweld he would have been suspicious at once.

All of her expressions of affection, then, had been false, just a build-up to lure him here when they wanted him. Chaan felt empty, as though he had suffered a great loss.

His hand was on the switch, to turn off the lights and sound, but he paused.

This was Marl's doing, but how could Marl be helped by the hypno-trap? Chaan's conditioning was rigid. There were no secrets of importance they could wring from him under hypnosis unless he consciously wished to reveal them. They could force him to do nothing under hypnosis, against his own volition.

And, under hypnosis, with the Volksweldvolken thinking him pliable, perhaps he could learn what Marl planned if he refused to cooperate.

Deliberately, he allowed the pulsating lights and throbbing sound to wash over him and conquer him.

Slowly the sound built up to the threshold of normal audibility, while at the same time the lights waxed alternately brighter and dimmer, with an increasing intensity. The sound gradually grew louder, humming and dying, humming and dying, and Chaan was vaguely aware that a voice now was speaking from the tape.

Against the throbbing background of the mechanical sound, the voice said:

"You are sleepy...very sleepy...you feel very relaxed...very happy...your eyes are heavy...heavier and heavier..."

He was floating pleasantly in a sea of light. Voices spoke to him, and faces passed before his eyes. Some of them, he realized he should know, but the effort to achieve definite recognition was beyond him. Others, he knew, were strange faces.

He was saying things and doing things in response to

commands that he did not take the trouble to interpret to his consciousness. Occasionally something—a voice, a question, a command—disturbed his peaceful acquiescence, brought a frown to his brow, sounded an alarm in his brain. Almost, each time, consciousness returned to him, but then the voices would soothe him and he would drift back into blissful relaxation.

Time seemed suspended. All sense of time left him. He did not know whether an incident that caught his drifting mind lasted seconds or days. At times it seemed to him that he was aware of the passage of day and night, but he could not be sure.

Once he snapped into complete, angry consciousness.

"No!" he shouted vehemently, to his own immediate surprise.

His surroundings were completely unfamiliar. He was sitting in a comfortable chair, in a well-lighted, well-furnished room. Through a window at his right, the blood-red rays of Wolf slanted into the room; it was obviously either early morning or late afternoon.

Standing in front of him were two men: Jahr, in the uniform of a Volksweld officer, and an older, blond-bearded man in the tights and cape of a civilian.

"I hope you gentlemen are enjoying yourselves as much as I am," said Chaan, managing a dazed smile.

"It's all right, Chaan," said Jahr, his eyes lighting. "You won't be harmed."

Jahr turned to the other man with an annoyed frown.

"I told you he wouldn't answer that question, Ramitz," he said.

"Who's the psychologist here?" snapped Ramitz. He fixed luminous eyes on Chaan. "You need not answer the question now. You may go to sleep again."

Chaan felt himself drifting back to semi-consciousness. Desperately, he fought his own mind. If he was to learn anything from the hypnotic sessions he was undergoing, he must be able to remember what they asked him and commanded him to do.

How long an eternity he fought that battle within himself he had no idea. But he knew he had failed when a new face swam into focus in his consciousness, peering anxiously into his, a face full of innocence, with round blue eyes and soft, trembling lips.

"Chaan, this is Hildi," she said. "I want you to know me and

142

understand me. Do you recognize me?"

"Yes," he said dully. The individual that was he fought for expression against the barriers that barred it within his mind, but he knew his voice was mechanical and dead.

"I love you, Chaan," she said, and there were tears in the blue eyes.

He made no response. He had been asked for none.

"Chaan, you must tell them what they want to know and do as Leader Marl asks," she said urgently. "I can't let you go away to Lalande and leave me, Chaan. I love you and want you with me. Do you hear me, Chaan?"

"Yes," he said mechanically.

"Please understand, Chaan," she begged. "You said you wanted the kind of love that will last a lifetime. I can give you that kind of love. Please do as they ask so we can be together."

Her face drifted away, and Chaan turned over her words in his mind with curious detachment, passing no judgment on them.

Then, somehow, there penetrated to the part of him that remained aware a great excitement. Somehow the contact Hildi had made had opened the path he sought. He knew that the memory of the things that happened to him under hypnosis now would remain with him.

CHAPTER ELEVEN

THE PSYCHOLOGIST, Ramitz, was Chaan's constant questioner. Others might be in the room from time to time-Jahr and Hildi frequently, occasionally Oler and a few times even Marl himself; but Ramitz was the inquisitor.

Chaan deduced that he was confined in a suite of the Regnal Hotel not far from his own quarters. He had a spacious, comfortable bedroom, in which his meals were served by Ingra.

The room in which he was questioned evidently was the converted living room of the suite. Now it was bare-floored and bare-walled, with a single straight chair in which Chaan sat while being questioned and a heavy sofa on which Ramitz half-reclined while questioning him. The only other objects in the room were light and sound equipment used in the hypnotic process.

Now that he retained connected consciousness under hypnosis, Chaan was puzzled at the general line of Ramitz's questioning. The Volksweld psychologist elicited from him every possible ounce of information about his past, systematically, from his childhood forward. Apparently Ramitz had covered his early childhood in previous questioning, but occasionally he returned to it, perhaps to clarify certain periods and incidents.

Once Ramitz asked him in detail, with questions that betrayed considerable familiarity with the incident, about Chaan's childhood contact with the alien that had given him the dodecahedron so many years ago on Earth.

"From his description, the creature sounds like one of the aborigines of Volksweld," said Ramitz in surprise to Jahr, who was present at the interview.

"I didn't know they ever achieved space travel," said Jahr.

"According to the archaeology I studied, they didn't," replied Ramitz. "With only one planet in the system, there never was any incentive for them to develop it. They may have done some traveling on human ships."

"He couldn't have seen a Volkswelder, as young as he is," said Jahr positively. "They've been extinct for years."

"That's where you're wrong," said Ramitz. "It's true that his subjective age is no more than your own, but don't forget he's been traveling between the stars most of his life since his early teens. They train them young in the Scout service. As near as I can figure it out, Chaan was born about seventy-five years ago, planetary time—perhaps even earlier."

"Well, seventy-five years!" said Jahr with a shrug. "The Volkswelder were extinct then, weren't they?"

"There were still thousands of them living in the mountains when you were a boy," answered Ramitz, smiling. "It was Adarl who conducted an extermination campaign against them because they were alien forms of life."

"My grandmother used to say they had strange powers," said Jahr. "Do you suppose that had anything to do with the experience in the attic he talks about?"

"Just a childish fantasy," said Ramitz indulgently. "They

frequently seem very real to children. I expect you'd find you've had just as vivid imaginary experiences as a youngster, if you could remember them."

His narration of that incident in his childhood provided Chaan with a fascinating subject for contemplation for a time. He had indeed forgotten about it until he recalled it under hypnosis, but had he not been chained to Ramitz's commands and unable to speak until told to do so, he would have disputed Ramitz's analysis of it. It seemed very vivid and real to him, not at all like a fantasy.

And there was one item Ramitz had overlooking in passing the matter off as of no importance. If it was not a real experience, what had happened to the dodecahedron?

Chaan was unable to understand Ramitz's objective in pumping him on minute details of his life. Logically, the psychologist could have been expected to hammer him with demands that he agree to Marl's proposal and betray the Solar Council. But there was not even a suggestion to this effect.

For a long time, the nearest Ramitz came to Chaan's inner core of resistance was exhaustive questioning about Space Scout training and procedure, and Chaan's own experience as a Scout. Chaan answered these questions without hesitation, for there was nothing secret about any of it.

At last, one day about two weeks after Chaan began counting consecutive time under hypnosis, came the question that set off the hidden alarm in his brain. In the midst of innocuous questions which had been answered several times before, Ramitz asked casually:

"What is the procedure for operating the stardrive?"

Chaan sat dumb.

He remembered now that this was the question that had brought him out of the hypnotic spell once before. This time, he remained under hypnosis, but he did not answer.

"What is the procedure for operating the stardrive?" demanded Ramitz, his voice quivering with the intensity of the question.

Chaan said nothing.

"ANSWER ME! WHAT IS THE PROCEDURE FOR OP-ERATING THE STARDRIVE?"

Chaan stared at him with entranced eyes and did not open his mouth.

"Why won't you answer that question?" asked Ramitz, his voice lapsing back to a controlled calm.

"I am forbidden to answer it," replied Chaan woodenly.

"Who forbids you?"

"The Solar Council."

"Under what circumstances would you answer that question?"

"None."

"Not even to an official of the Solar Council?"

"No."

"Another Space Scout?"

"No."

"What are your instructions regarding information as to operation of the stardrive?"

"As far as I am concerned, I am the only person in the universe who knows how to operate the stardrive and I am to explain its operation to no one else. I am aware, of course, that other Space Scouts and other Solar Council officials are familiar with its operation, but I am still not permitted to communicate any information about it to them."

"Well, we'll see about that," muttered Ramitz, pulling his blond beard. "Chaan, the next person who enters this room with me will be Victad."

He left the room and returned within five minutes. To Chaan's bemused surprise, the Solar Council agent was with him.

"Chaan," said Victad urgently, "I've just learned you are to be executed at Marl's orders, and I've got to get information on the situation here to the fleet at Lalande. Tell me how to operate the stardrive."

No, said Chaan.

Ramitz threw up his hands.

"It's no use," he said. "He won't tell."

With that, Victad's face and form shimmered and became Jahr. Ramitz's hypnotic command had imposed Victad's identity on him to Chaan's eyes.

Jahr grinned at Ramitz.

"Finding an incorruptible man is a new experience for you, isn't it, Ramitz?" he remarked.

"Nothing incorruptible about it," retorted Ramitz shortly. "His conditioning is just so strong it can't be broken down by direct attack."

The next day Marl entered while Ramitz was questioning Chaan about routine background, and Ramitz suspended the session to talk with the dictator. Briefly, Ramitz outlined what had happened the previous day, and played over the transcript of his attempt to question Chaan about the operation of the stardrive.

"Could the girl get the answer?" asked Marl.

"I doubt it," said Ramitz. "We'll try her, of course, but I'm almost sure he'll tell no one."

"Maybe there's a way around the problem," said Marl. "He's under hypnosis, and is supposed to follow hypnotic commands. Would it be effective to suggest to him that his loyalty to the Solar Council requires that he cooperate with us?"

"To a certain extent. His post-hypnotic cooperation with us would extend just as far as his cooperation under hypnosis. He still wouldn't tell us how to operate the stardrive."

"That wouldn't be necessary if we could be assured he'd give us a clean bill when he arrives at Lalande," said Marl.

"It won't work," said Ramitz, shaking his head. "Don't forget, any hypnosis or post-hypnotic suggestion would dissolve not more than two light-years away from Wolf."

"I know that," Marl said impatiently. "I propose to install a hypno-trap aboard his starship. To make sure he doesn't evade it as he did the one on Greyhound, you could command him to submit to it before the post-hypnotic suggestion wears off. Recorded commands could be installed in that hypno-trap to renew the hypnosis and carry him the rest of the way to Lalande under its influence."

"I'm sorry, sir," said Ramitz. "The factor of consent would be needed in that case, and it's absent."

"What do you mean by that?"

"No matter what post-hypnotic suggestion is given him, the hypnotic influence will wear off after two light-years in space and cannot be renewed by a repetition of the suggestion *unless he agrees to accept such a renewal voluntarily*. The reason for this is obscure, but we think it is connected with the peculiar liberating effect open space has on the mind and emotions."

"An agreement to accept such a renewal of hypnosis, gained from him while he is under hypnosis, wouldn't do any good?"

"No, sir. It would be useless."

"I see," said Marl thoughtfully. "Well, there's still considerable hope of getting such an agreement from him of his own free will. Meanwhile, we have to hedge against all possibilities. *Get that stardrive secret out of him, Ramitz!*"

"I'll try, sir."

For the next two weeks, Chaan was subjected to the most intense pressure to reveal the secret of the stardrive's operation. There were no more innocent questions about his background, his philosophy and his personal experiences. Every question, every command, led directly to the final order, repeated hour after hour, day after day:

"Tell me how the stardrive operates!"

At first Chaan sat in stony silence as the question was hurled at him again and again and again. But the constant, intense repetition began to penetrate even through the protective shell of his bemusement.

It was like the constant drip-drip of Chinese torture, beating inexorably at his resistance.

"Tell me how the stardrive operates!"

On his second day of questioning, the natural relaxation of the hypnotic state began to leave him. By the end of the day, he began to tense at the first words of the fatal question. By the time the end of the question struck him with its full impact, he sat rigid with shock.

"Tell me how the stardrive operates!"

On the third day, after the question had been pounded at him for the fiftieth time, Chaan's lips writhed and he groaned, "No!"

Ramitz redoubled his efforts.

"Tell me how the stardrive operates!"

"No!"

"TELL ME HOW THE STARDRIVE OPERATES!"

"No!"

During the days that followed, the incessant questioning and his incessant refusal reduced Chaan to a state of nervous frenzy. He could not shake off the hypnosis, and there was no emotional protection for him against Ramitz's merciless inquisition.

Chaan writhed, he wept, he shouted his refusal, but to no avail. Ramitz hammered him with the question, hour after grinding hour. Ramitz himself perspired with the sustained effort, and his voice grew hoarse, but he did not relent.

In his torment, Chaan wished earnestly that he could answer the question. He tried to answer it. He could not. The strength of his training on that one point formed a solid barrier that all the turbulence of his tortured emotions could not breach.

On the twelfth day they brought Hildi to him. She wept to see him sitting there, twisting and shivering, cringing in anticipation of the inevitable demand.

"Why won't you answer him, Chaan?" she cried. "They'll release you if you'll only answer."

"I can't answer," he whimpered, grateful for a different question. "I'm not permitted to answer."

She knelt before him and pressed his trembling hands to her bosom. She turned a tear-stained face up to him.

"Please, Chaan!" she begged. "I can't stand to see you like this. Won't you answer him for me? Won't you answer him, so we can be together again?"

"I can't answer," he repeated. "No one must know the answer but me."

At night he tossed in fitful sleep and awoke shouting, "No! No! I won't answer! No one must know but me!"

And in his broken dreams, as during the long days, the remorseless face of Ramitz loomed before him, shouting, demanding:

"Tell me how the stardrive operates!"

If only he could tell someone. At the end of the day, when he was released to the solitude of his bedroom, he would whisper the secret to himself, repeating it until the tension was relieved to some slight degree. Even in his bemused hypnotic state, he retired to bed each night in dire fear that he would speak the fatal instructions in his sleep. But apparently he did not, for it was

149

reasonable to assume that his room was wired and every word he spoke at night was recorded.

When the fifteenth day of his ordeal drew to a close, Chaan staggered to his room with the awful sensation that he had reached a crisis. He did not believe his belabored mind would stand another day of battering. He must either answer the question or slip helplessly into the refuge of insanity.

The choice lay before him, like a physical thing. As in a hypnagogic illusion, he saw the forked roads at his feet, one branch leading to light and freedom and the other turning downward into the misty and fearful realms of insanity. But to enter the upward branch he must answer The Question, and across its mouth stood a barrier stronger even than his fear of insanity or death. He knew the barrier was in his own mind, yet he could not break it down.

"No one must know the answer but me," he muttered.

Did his mind clear then, or did the hallucination change into another? The vision of the forked roads faded and he himself, Chaan Fritag, stood facing him just inside the door of the bedroom.

Chaan stared at himself. This was no mirror image, this was himself, as though he stood outside of himself and looked at himself.

"I'll not be taken in by a hypnotic suggestion that someone else is me," said Chaan aloud to Himself.

"You know that's not true in this case, don't you?" replied Himself to Chaan, looking somewhat disturbed.

"Yes," answered Chaan, looking at Himself closely.

He did. He examined his own mind closely. It was not just rationalization because he desperately needed a confidant. Somehow, he recognized a difference in this and in that appearance of Jahr as Victad and the many efforts they had made to fool him with illusions of his own superiors.

This might be a hallucination. It probably was. But the face and form were genuinely Chaan Fritag. It was not a hypnotic mask over someone else.

"Hallucination," he muttered. "You must be an hallucination. How do you justify yourself? Hallucination?"

"Why," said Himself, smiling, "are we not all many personalities in one? Should not each separate personality sometimes take on separate form?"

"A good argument," said Chaan dazedly. "As good as any other. What did I do with the dodecahedron?"

"I gave it to a big spaceman on a red world," said Himself, "Father thought I was imagining things, but if I was, what happened to the dodecahedron?"

"Ah, they missed that point," agreed Chaan, eyeing Himself cleverly. "They didn't think of that, did they?"

"They have us in a very bad fix," said Himself soberly. "If we don't answer The Question, they'll torment us until we die."

"That's true, but there's no way out," said Chaan, "No one must know the answer but me."

"Ah, but they overlooked this one thing," said Himself. It was Chaan, all right. Chaan's exact voice, his exact intonation. I am you. You are me. We are me.

"I understand now!" exclaimed Chaan joyously. "Now I know why I divided into us. I can confide in you, because you are only me!"

"That's exactly it," said Himself.

"Come close," said Chaan, looking around fearfully. "The room is wired, but of course you know that, don't you?"

"Certainly I know it, because you know it, and I am you," replied Himself, moving his ear close to Chaan's cheek. "You tell me, and I'll tell you."

"Now," said Chaan in a very low whisper, "the way to operate the stardrive is this... "

It wasn't the same as whispering the secret to himself, when he was alone in the room and Himself wasn't there. As he told it, eagerly, the heaviness lifted from his heart. And when Himself whispered the secret back in Chaan's ear, Chaan laughed aloud in flooding relief.

"Don't forget, they can't destroy us, because now we're two," said Himself then. "When you need me, I'll be back."

Himself turned and left the room, shutting the door behind him.

Chaan sat down on the edge of the bed, shaking with the

happiness of release, and slowly it dawned on him that now there was something different about the way he thought and felt. He was still tired, he was still dazed, but there was no longer a veil of compulsion before his eyes.

He was no longer under the hypnotic spell Ramitz bad imposed! He was fully conscious again. His will was free!

CHAPTER TWELVE

SLOWLY HIS INITIAL exultation left Chaan. He wasn't out of the woods yet.

The double of himself had been a hallucination. He had no doubt about that. It had seemed very real, but there was a conviction within him, which he trusted implicitly, that the double had not been someone else, his face appearing to Chaan to be his own only through hypnotic suggestion. Chaan was sure that his ingrained determination not to reveal the secret of the stardrive to anyone else would have prevented him from speaking, despite such a mask.

The double had seemed real enough—too real to be denied. But, now that he was free from the hypnotic spell, such an idea was patently impossible, so it must have been a hallucination.

The trouble with that was that, although he had relieved the pressure on his own mind and emotions by whispering the secret of the stardrive, Ramitz and Marl would be as eager as ever to worm it out of him. So, even though he was free of hypnosis now, Ramitz's first move would be to attempt to re-impose the hypnotic state on him.

Had Chaan been in peak condition, he knew he could resist such efforts. He had accepted the spell of the hypno-trap voluntarily before (and now he realized how foolish he had been). Had he not done so, he could have defied their every effort to gain any sort of control of his mind.

But he was weakened by his long battle with Ramitz now. The very fact that he had been under hypnosis weakened his resistance to any attempts to re-impose it.

Chaan was not sure how long he could hold out against a determined effort. There was only one thing to do.

He slept as well as he could, more peacefully than he had for more than a week, but he came awake at once in the dawn hours when his door opened. Through slitted lids, he watched Ramitz enter the room and come to the side of his bed.

Then Chaan sprang.

His hands clutched the surprised psychologist's throat and he bore Ramitz to the floor with the weight of his furious onslaught.

The struggle was brief. Chaan was too weak. Ramitz broke his strangling hold with strong hands, pushed him aside and rose to his feet. Chaan, panting, grasped Ramitz by the ankles, but had not the strength to bring him down.

"What are you trying to do?" demanded Ramitz indignantly.

"I won't go under hypnosis again!" gasped Chaan. "I'll find a way to kill myself first."

"Oh, that," said Ramitz. "You can stop fighting. I don't know how you broke the spell, but I have no intention of trying to put you under hypnosis again."

Chaan got to his feet with an effort and sank, exhausted, to the bed.

"I don't understand," he managed to say. "I told you nothing."

"Not all we wanted to know, no," conceded Ramitz. "But we couldn't get that out of you if you were driven to insanity, and I warned Marl yesterday that if we kept on badgering you that might happen. He decided it would be best to release you from the hypnosis and depend on getting your voluntary cooperation."

"Hell of a chance you have of getting it now," grunted Chaan, who promptly fell into a dreamless sleep.

When Chaan awoke, it was mid-afternoon and he was in bed in his own suite. He was alone. The rays of the great crimson sun slanted through the window, painting the furniture and hangings with rich hues of ruby.

Chaan felt fine. But when he rolled out of bed, he realized he was still weak from his long ordeal. He staggered a bit, as he moved across the room.

He looked down at his naked body. He was a little surprised that he was not actually emaciated, but he had lost some weight. The powerful muscles of arms, legs and chest stood out like ropes under stress, where they had moved smoothly under the flesh.

Chaan rubbed his face reflectively. The blond bristle scratched like sandpaper along his hollowed cheeks.

He was hungry.

Chaan opened the carved wardrobe door and took out a blue-and-silver Space Scout uniform. He had just climbed into it and was pulling on his boots when the bedroom door opened and Jahr entered.

"So you're awake at last," said Jahr cheerfully. "There's a meal prepared whenever you're ready for it."

"I'm starving," said Chaan. "I'll he out as soon as I shave."

"Glad you're back," said Jahr.

"There's something I want to say, Jahr," said Chaan. "I was aware of things enough during the last two weeks to know that you tried to ease things for me when you were there. I appreciate it."

"I don't care for the type of torture Ramitz calls 'psychological persuasion'," replied Jahr with a grimace of distaste. "Besides, I happen to like you, Chaan."

He went out of the room, but in a moment was back again.

"I have a pleasant surprise for you," he said, grinning.

"Hildi's here."

Chaan started, and frowned angrily.

"Send her away," he ordered. "'I don't want to see her!'"

Jahr looked puzzled, but turned to comply. But as he opened the door, Hildi herself came through it.

At the sight of her, Chaan's heart almost went soft. Round face framed in flaxen hair—round, round eyes full of anxiety—trembling full lips—slender white curves his arms remembered: he was almost overwhelmed by the vision of her.

"Chaan!" she cried, coming toward him with outstretched hands.

He turned from her.

"I told you, Jahr," he said steadily, "I don't want to see her.

"I'm sorry, Hildi," said Jahr. "You'd better go. Chaan's still very weak from what he's been through."

Chaan caught a glimpse of her face as Jahr escorted her out the door. His heart went sick at her forlorn, uncomprehending expression.

He was sorry he had seen her at all. Apparently it had been arranged from the start that Hildi would meet him and Jahr and strike up an acquaintance with him, in order to lure him to the hypno-trap at her home. Then for her to lend herself to their efforts to persuade him to reveal the secret of the stardrive! That she should pretend love for him for such a purpose infuriated him, and his having thought he had found in her something for which he had yearned: this made it all the worse.

Jahr was a different case entirely. He held no resentment against Jahr. He had known how Jahr stood all along, and Jahr had played a straight game of it.

It took Chaan several days to regain his strength and emotional balance completely. Then he went to see Victad.

"You look as though you've been ill," said Victad. The Solar Council agent was wearing a Sirian toga over his comfortable belly, for Chaan had come to his home to see him.

"I've been in a battle," said Chaan. "I almost lost it too."

He told Victad of the hypno-trap and Ramitz's efforts to elicit the secret of the stardrive from him.

"I don't know why they were so anxious to find out how to operate the stardrive," said Victad thoughtfully, when Chaan had finished. "It would do them no good to take your ship to Lalande to report, without you. And knowing how to operate it doesn't tell them how to build stardrives for their own ships—unless you know that secret, too."

"No, Space Scouts only know its operation. We don't know how they're built. They found out from me early that I didn't know anything about the stardrive's construction."

"Well, I'll report the matter to Sirius," said Victad. "To Lalande, too, if you say so. Would you interpret it as definite evidence of hostility?"

Chaan hesitated.

"No," he said, after a moment. "I want to investigate some more. A planetary government doesn't have to be hostile to want to find out about the stardrive, and Space Scouts expect to be imposed on occasionally."

"Whatever you say," said Victad. "You're taking the risks."

"There's an important facet of Volksweld I haven't investigated yet," said Chaan. "Didn't you say there is some sort of rebel organization on the planet, opposing Marl's rule?"

"The Wasser. I think I told you that it is said to exist, but I have never seen any actual evidence that it does exist. It has caused no trouble in Regn, so far as I know."

"It may not exist, of course, then," said Chaan. "Marl is smart enough to realize that he needs some opposition as an excuse for exercising strong military control, even if he has to make up that opposition out of whole cloth. But if it exists, I want to find it."

Victad put the tips of his fingers together and leaned back in his chair.

"The reports I've heard," he said, "have it that the Wasser's headquarters is located in the Harven Mountains, about a hundred miles north of Regn. It's a logical place, if the organization does exist, for that mountain range is about as effective a hiding place for any number of men as exists on the planet."

"Well, if that's the only lead you have, I suppose it's the one I'll follow," said Chaan.

"I'll show you the area in which you have the best chance of success," said Victad, getting out a map. "But if Marl hasn't been able to find the Wasser, I don't see how you expect to."

After Chaan had left Victad, he wondered why he hadn't allowed the Solar Council agent to report his experience under hypnosis as a hostile act by Volksweld. As far as he was concerned, it certainly was. There was also Marl's frank disclosure of Volksweld's imperialistic aims—something Chaan would expect to pass on to Victad under normal circumstances. Yet he had not.

His excuse to himself was that a Space Scout was an independent operator, and was bound by no routine. These circumstances justified unusual methods, Chaan told himself. Certainly Marl would not be so foolish as to let his objectives be known openly, and then allow Victad to communicate them to Lalande and Sirius by light-beam transmission. Any effort by Victad to do that would certainly be garbled, or blocked somehow. There was no point in getting Victad in trouble at this juncture.

One thing Chaan certainly would not concede to himself: that he was attracted at all by Marl's offer to him. After his experience with the hypno-trap, the very thought of it angered him.

Still, why hadn't he told Victad in confidence, instructing him not to attempt to transmit the information except in an emergency?

"Jahr," said Chaan that night, "pack me clothing and supplies for a couple of weeks. I'm going to do a bit of exploration, and I probably won't want to go into cities and towns en route."

"Fine," said Jahr, his eyes lighting. "I could use some country air myself."

"You'll get it by yourself, then," said Chaan. "This time I'm going alone. And Marl's at liberty to have me followed—if he can."

CHAPTER THIRTEEN

JAHR OBTAINED for Chaan the light plane he wanted: a hedgehopper. The jets could buzz through the sky all they wished, but he stayed close to the ground and they could sight him only for an instant at a time when they were lucky enough to see him at all. They could not travel at Chaan's slow pace.

Of course, there were other hedgehoppers on his trail, too. He wasn't followed openly, but there always just happened to be at least one light plane, or copter, or cross-country ground-car, somewhere in sight.

So Chaan's course was circuitous and leisurely. He landed frequently, in the midst of a farmer's field or on a wild moor, and spent hours just wandering around afoot, enjoying the puzzlement his followers must be undergoing as to his objective. During the first such stopover, he found and removed the tiny object aboard his plane that was a homing device for the Volksweld electronic finders. They could still track him by radar, but radar was very uncertain at low altitude over hilly terrain.

Chaan flew by manual control. At the end of the third day of fox-and-hounds tactics, he landed in the foothills of the Harven Mountains, in the general area which Victad had pointed out to him as being the most likely haunt of the Wasser.

At dusk, after he had puttered about for a few hours, Chaan set the plane on automatic, to fly southwest for twenty-five miles and then land. From the shelter of the scanty forest that covered these hills, he watched the plane take off and, with satisfaction, saw a copter streaking after it a few moments later.

During the night, Chaan made his way into the canyons and ravines of the Harven Mountains on foot. By dawn, he was well into the mountains, and could not have been found either by land or from the air except by the remotest accident.

The Harven Mountains were very old. Their peaks had been worn down and their deepest crevasses filled by long erosion. They were clothed in forests, dominated by a crooked, spreading tree with smooth black bark and pungent gray foliage. Chaan did not know the tree, as he had not seen it growing around Regn, and did not recall it from his previous stay on Volksweld.

He made his way deeper into the mountains that day, after a morning nap, his eyes open for sign. His Space Scout training had made him as expert at tracking as any ancient terrestrial savage. When he came into territory which humans had crossed recently, he would know it and could find them.

All that afternoon he followed wooded valleys, along which icy streams raced toward the plains far behind him. The little animals of Volksweld—there were no large ones still wild in this section—scurried across his path or barked at him from the trees. The great red orb of Wolf 359 swung westward above him, casting a pattern of sanguine light through the gray foliage.

That night Chaan stretched in a clearing on a mountainside and looked up at the stars for a long time before falling asleep. They were very bright in the clear, cold air of Volksweld. The constellations were, generally, the familiar ones of his boyhood on Earth, slightly distorted, for ten light-years were but a step in the vastness of the Galaxy. Sirius had moved into the constellation Aquilla to compete with a slightly displaced Altair, and Sol itself added a brilliant luster to the constellation Aquarius.

Chaan liked this world of bleak plains and ancient mountains, with its dying sun and its lonely stars. Volksweld was an island planet, not crowded by neighbors, as were the worlds in other systems. Here a man could commune with himself, he could pit himself against the planet's darkness and cold; here his relations with other men and women were not the busy unawareness of the social hive, but a joyous familiarity, sweetened by the zest of those who live on the edge of the great outer reaches.

The next morning Chaan found sign. But it was a trail that

puzzled him. No man broke a twig that high from the ground, no man left a tuft of hair that white and silky on an overhanging thorny bush. Yet the edge of that footprint in a spot of soft dirt was not the mark of claw or paw, and no animal had left that charred end of wood.

A man could be following a large animal, or a large animal could be following a man, except that there were no large animals in this region, that Chaan knew.

He followed the trail. In an hour, it led him into a cave in the side of a mountain. Here were evidences of continued existence on a primitive level: ashes, large stones worn smooth by sitting, charred bones and utensils, some of them broken. The sign was recent, yet there was something peculiarly non-human about it.

A shadow fell across the mouth of the cave, and Chaan turned quickly, drawing his heat-gun from its holster. Against the crimson-and-gray landscape outside was outlined a tall creature, white-furred and ghostlike. Its eyes were huge, dark and intelligent, and its mouth opened in a perpetual square across which fine strings of tissue hummed a musical cadence that pervaded the close confines of the cave.

A Volkswelder! One of the aborigines of Volksweld, now nearly extinct.

Chaan lowered his heat-gun. There was little likelihood of danger here. These creatures had been civilized for millennia.

The sight of the Volkswelder brought back a flood of memories. As though he was a child again, he could see Father talking with Kreel, using his stringed instrument to imitate the alien's musical language.

But Chaan had no stringed instrument, and he did not understand the Volkswelder language. To him it was a symphony of haunting beauty, but meaningless. The creature paused and looked at him expectantly, but Chaan shook his head.

Then the Volkswelder seemed to shimmer and go semi-transparent for an instant, and there was a large machine beside it in the cave mouth. The machine was very nearly cubical, about four feet to the side, and Chaan recognized it as an instrument used by Space Service exploration teams to imitate non-human tongues. It was actually a compact electronic computer with a sound mechanism, and many different kinds of languages could be stored in its tubes for intertranslation.

Now when the Volkswelder spoke in its musical tongue, the translator spoke hollowly in Volkswelden, the language of the human settlers of Volksweld.

"Why does one of the Wasser seek me?" asked the Volkswelder.

"I am not of the Wasser," replied Chaan, and his voice was symphonized by the machine into the Volkswelder's language. "I seek the Wasser."

"You are not of the Wasser, and yet you do not attempt to kill me?"

"I am not of Volksweld at all," answered Chaan. "I am from Sirius, and before that from Earth. I am a Space Scout."

The Volkswelder's eyes darkened thoughtfully. Again there was that blurring of its form, and when it had settled to stability again this time it said:

"You are the man on whom destiny hangs. I did not know our meeting was now."

"I don't understand," said Chaan.

"The pattern of the universe contains many motifs, and sometimes threads of different materials are interwoven," said the Volkswelder. "You have known my kind before."

"Yes. As a child. I know you are a very long-lived race. Are you the one who knew my father? Are you Kreel?"

"The name you use is not translated by the machine," said the Volkswelder. "But I am not the individual of my race you knew. His task was in one sector, mine in another."

"We were fated to meet here, then? There is some purpose in it?"

The chords of the Volkswelder's mouth hummed deeply.

"Who knows whether things happen by accident or because there is some hidden purpose to the pattern of the universe?" asked the Volkswelder. "I knew that we were to meet here and I was to say certain things to you. Whether there is any guidance behind that other than our own and the whim of circumstance, is knowledge not possessed by any living creature in this part of the universe."

Chaan realized his heat-gun was still dangling from his hand. He holstered it and sat down on a large rock. The Volkswelder moved farther into the cave, and Chaan could see it more clearly, now that it was not against the outside light.

The creature was tall and gaunt, with long white fur that probably protected it from the cold better than any garment. Chaan could not determine its sex, if it had any sex at all. Its eyes were very dark and very wise, but nothing akin to any human emotion could be read in them.

"What were you told to say to me?" asked Chaan.

"It is not that I was told to say anything. I do not know that what is said here has any purpose other than the meaning of the words, but I knew they would be said here and now."

"My father once said that you—the Volkswelder—know the future," said Chaan slowly. "That's true, then?"

"'Past' and 'future' are terms humans use," said the Volkswelder. "They have no meaning to my people. They are implicit in the translation of what I say to you, because they are required by the structure of your language. Because of some schizophrenic quality of the human mind, you use the incomplete concepts you term 'time' and 'space' for the same characteristic of the universe."

"I'm familiar with the theory of unified space-time," answered Chaan. "It is taken into consideration in all our interstellar travel. But the Volkswelder apparently have more control or at least more knowledge of the time factor."

"I have said they are the same," said the Volkswelder. "You know Earth and Sirius and the city of Regn, because you have been there. I know what you call 'the past' and 'the future' because I have been there. It is a difficult thing to state in your language. I move to 'the past' and 'the future' as you understand going from here to Regn. You could do the same if you could comprehend the concept fully."

"There's some difference, I think," said Chaan dryly. "I gather that you went either to the past or the future to bring that translator here?"

The Volkswelder hummed assent.

"It was a simple trip for you, apparently," said Chaan. "But were I to walk from here to Regn, it would be a long, difficult trip. And I couldn't walk from here to Sirius or Earth." To travel any distance, a human must have a machine.

"It is true that our capabilities are greater in covering the areas of the universe, for we are an older race," said the Volkswelder. "There are mechanical aids which humans can use, much simpler than your airplanes and starships. They are rare, however, and there is none on Volksweld now."

"If you can see the future," said Chaan, "tell me, will I find my starship and get away from Volksweld? Or maybe I can ask a neutral non-human...will Marl win me over to his side at last?"

"You do not know what is happening in Regn now, because you are not there," answered the Volkswelder. "Nor do I know what will happen in your future, because I am not there."

With that, its figure blurred again, and this time vanished entirely. The translator disappeared with it.

Chaan was alone in the cave, sitting amid the charred and broken-remnants of an alien habitation.

The next day he found what he sought, entirely by accident.

He found no trail, other than that left by the Volkswelder. He was moving deeper into the mountains when he came upon a ridge and saw three men around a campfire in a hollow below him.

They were clad in furs, and had heat-guns strapped around their waists. They were lunching on some sort of a small animal.

Chaan strode boldly down the slope toward them.

"Hello!" he called. "Are you members of the Wasser?" The three men jumped up and faced him, drawing their guns hurriedly.

"Who are you?" demanded one.

"What's Marl up to now?" asked another. "I haven't seen that uniform before."

"That's a Solar Council uniform!" exclaimed the third, lowering his gun. "You're the Space Scout, aren't you?"

"That's right," answered Chaan, coming up to them with outspread palms. "If you're the Wasser, you're the people I'm looking for."

"We're the Wasser all right," said the man who had recognized the uniform, holding out a welcoming hand.

CHAPTER FOURTEEN

THE THREE MEN led Chaan through a net of rocky ravines to a wide flat valley. The valley appeared to be just as wild and unsettled as the test of this mountainous country, but under the trees on one side of it was a tremendous cave mouth, concealed by overhanging bushes from all angles except that directly in front of it.

Several other men and a couple of women, all fur-clad, joined the group from various directions as they approached the cave. The newcomers talked in low tones among themselves, but asked the three men with Chaan no questions. Chaan rather got the impression they thought he was a prisoner.

Chaan's eyes opened wide when they entered the cave. It stretched upward into a spacious dome and reached far back into the mountain, as far as he could see. It was well lighted by electricity. Along the walls near the entrance were a score of copters: sleek, well kept, and well armed. Many people moved to and fro on the cave's floor, dwarfed by its expanse.

Beyond the line of copters, Chaan was escorted a short way down a side passage and into spacious offices carved into the rock. He passed through several outer offices populated by secretaries and underlings, and, after a bit of discussion between his escorts and dubious officials, was ushered into a large, comfortable private office.

There was one person in this office, a big man beginning to run to flesh. Like those in his outer offices, he had stripped off his furs and was clad in loose, flimsy undergarments. He was seated in an easy chair, crouching over a rather elaborate meal spread on a low table in front of him.

He raised cool blue eyes as Chaan came in with the other three, but went on eating.

"We found this man in the Third Sector, sir," said the one who had recognized Charm's uniform, "He's the Space Scout from Sirius, and he was looking for us."

The big man got to his feet, heavily, and advanced with outstretched hand.

"I'm glad to see you," he boomed in a voice that reverberated through the room. "I'm Horda. I didn't recognize that uniform at first, but I'm delighted that you've come to help us."

Chaan introduced himself, looking Horda over carefully. He had not known what to expect in the leader of the Wasser—if Horda was, indeed, the leader. His first impression was that he liked Marl better.

"I won't need you any more now," Horda said brusquely to the three men, and they filed out of the room, looking back over their shoulders at Chaan.

"Now," said Horda, turning back to Chaan, "will you have some lunch with me?"

"Thank you, no," refused Chaan, smiling slightly at the sumptuous spread Horda called "lunch." "I ate with the men on the way here."

"If you don't mind, I'll go on with mine, then," said Horda, sinking back into his chair and taking up his utensils without delay. "I'm glad you came, Fritag. Your advanced knowledge of modem weapons and warfare...and other talents as well...will be of considerable help in ending Marl's reign of terror. I've tried to get in touch with the Council agent, Victad, but Marl keeps the place too well guarded."

"Actually," said Chaan, sitting down uninvited in a nearby chair, "I'm here myself looking for some information, and probably some help."

"What helps one helps the other," said Horda, waving a meat bone casually. "We're both after Marl's scalp, after all."

Chaan resisted a strong impulse to make a clarifying statement. Instead, he said:

"Before we go any farther, Horda, you're top man in the Wasser, I trust. No insult intended, but I'm not here to deal with any underlings."

Horda stared at him in surprise, then laughed.

"No insult," he said. "I'm top man. Perhaps I'd better ask you for some credentials, too. For all I know...still no insult intended...you may be one of Marl's agents."

"No insult," Chaan gave him back his words. Chaan opened his sky-blue tunic to expose the left side of his chest, and tensed

164

certain muscles.

On the bare skin of his chest, above the left nipple, a luminous star-and-lightning diagram blazed like a diamond medallion. It was an insignia burned into the flesh of the Space Scouts, and the Space Scouts only.

"If you've had an elementary education, no doubt you recognize it," said Chaan dryly.

Horda flushed, but he spread his hands.

"No question about the credentials," he said. He appeared about to say more, but Chaan forestalled him.

"Before I ask for help from you," he said, "I'd like a little information. What's the strength of the Wasser?"

"That's one of our closely guarded secrets," said Horda, through a mouthful of meat.

Hot anger swept over Chaan, turning his face an angry red.

"I asked you a question, and I want an answer," he said bluntly. "I'm a representative of the Solar Council and I'm here in an official capacity. I didn't come here to dicker about your own schemes. I'm demanding assistance, if you want to put it that way."

Horda stopped chewing and glared at him.

"You're one man in a strange cave," he said ominously. "The people here follow my orders, even if they were to recognize that uniform of yours."

"The Council knows my whereabouts," said Chaan easily. "How do you think I found you, when Marl can't?"

"I didn't know Victad had that information," grunted Horda, taken aback. "Well, there are about two thousand of us at this base, and we have three others of the same size or a bit smaller."

"Not many to tackle a military organization the size of Marl's. But all I need is a task force. Do you have copters other than the ones here?"

"About fifty; all told."

"All right," said Chaan. "Now, what are your own plans for dealing with Marl?"

"Eliminate him, and the heart of his military organization with him. If we could ever get a hydrogen bomb over Regn, it could be done at a blow, and we'd take over in the confusion that followed.

But they've got good defenses, and of course it's impossible to take a bomb in by land or copter. We have one plane—at another base—big enough for the job."

"I'm surprised you haven't tried to use a guided missile."

Horda shrugged.

"A community of a few thousand, in hiding, isn't equipped technologically for such a task," he said. "We had to steal the copters, of course, and getting the plane with the bomb was quite a feat. Marl lives in constant dread of it."

"Is that the only plan you have: trying to get that plane through with an H-bomb?" asked Chaan, amazed. He had assumed the Wasser was a much more formidable organization than this.

"Oh, we have an alternate plan, but it will take some doing. If our agents in the city report conditions right, we expect to strike quickly, kill Marl and take over the government by using his own machinery."

"And what then? After you've taken over, I mean?"

"Why, we take over. What else is there to do?"

"You have no plans to dismantle Marl's totalitarian form of government…his military machine…his space fleet?"

"Well, in time those things could be done, of course," said Horda evasively. "We can't move too fast and disrupt the whole planet, you know. Marl built fairly well—he's just the wrong type of person to rule the planet."

Chaan scratched his head thoughtfully. Horda struck him as merely a would-be Marl.

"Well, those things are your local affairs," he said at last. "What I want is my starship. Marl says you have it."

Horda's eyes went wide with surprise.

"The Wasser?" he rumbled. "Marl would say that. Trying to put us in bad with the Solar Council!"

"Someone stole it the day I arrived."

"It was Marl, then," said Horda positively. "Space, man! Your starship's at the Regn spaceport. My agents have seen it there."

"I haven't. And I was at the spaceport a few days ago."

"Well, it's there. Of course they'd hide it when you come around, if they want to keep it from you. They know your every movement in the city, and what worries me is whether they trailed you here."

"They didn't," said Chaan. "I came here to get the Wasser to help me find the starship. Instead, I want you to help me get it back. Will you do it?"

Horda shrugged.

"The way you bulled in here and pulled your rank, I don't have much choice," he said resentfully. "It doesn't matter what we know of local conditions, or whether we think it's a good plan. We have to do what you want, if we ever hope for any recognition by the Solar Council."

Despite Horda's reluctance, he worked efficiently and swiftly to assemble the small task force Chaan wanted.

During the two days they were getting ready, Chaan spent a good deal of his time circulating through the underground headquarters, talking to various members of the Wasser. As few in numbers as they were, they represented a facet of Volksweld's current political organization on which he wanted to be able to report at Lalande.

The Wasser, he found, was a hodgepodge of disgruntled elements. There were criminals, idealists, crackpots and fiercely independent individualists, banded together in an explosive mixture. They were held together by the strong, sometimes ruthless, leadership of Horda and a small group of his companions.

Horda and the other leaders of the Wasser were men and women whose families had suffered direct losses through the rise of Adarl and Marl. They had been wealthy, some of the rising aristocracy of the nebulous society that had existed on Volksweld at that time. They had chosen to fight Adarl rather than turn over their assets and abilities to his cause, and eventually had had to flee. Around their wealth the Wasser had been built.

The trouble with these Wasser leaders, as Chaan saw it, was that if Marl were ousted it would be impossible now to reestablish the loosely knit, freewheeling society for which they once had been well adjusted. Nor did they have the imagination and altruism necessary to break Marl's pattern in favor of a more progressive society. They probably would prove an oligarchic substitute for Marl's dictatorship, if they succeeded.

But, as Chaan had told Horda, his immediate interest was not in local problems, but in regaining his starship. While he was recovering from his bout with the hypno-trap, he had gone to the spaceport unannounced to check on Marl's claim that the starship had not been recovered. He had looked around carefully, but had seen nothing.

But the spaceport was big and the starship was small. As Horda had said, Marl undoubtedly kept close watch on his movements in Regn.

Chaan had formed a low opinion of the gluttonous Horda's ability as a leader of men. He was surprised to discover that Horda intended to take personal charge of the Wasser forces in this operation.

"Since we are forced to commit some strength to accomplish your objective, I'm making it a dual operation," explained Horda. "Your only interest is in getting aboard the starship, and that will be our first task. But we have to get a well-armed force into the spaceport to do that, and it will be a good opportunity for us to capture a spaceship for our own use."

"What good will a spaceship do you?" asked Chaan, startled. "There's no other planet in this system."

"Plenty, if we can get it out of range of their radar network and hide it for a while," answered Horda with an unpleasant smile. "We can't get our plane through their defenses with the H-bomb, but we could get a spaceship above the atmosphere on a course that would take it over Regn at least once before they could intercept it."

"I don't approve of that sort of an operation at all," said Chaan. "There are a lot of innocent people in Regn, to say nothing of the Solar Council agency."

And there was Hildi, too. Chaan, disillusioned, wanted to see no more of her, but he didn't want to think of her being atomized with the city.

"Look," said Horda. "You said you weren't interested in how we handle our own affairs, as long as we help you get your starship. Let's leave it that way. The Solar Council has no right to interfere, unless it sends the fleet in and takes over the planet."

There was justice in Horda's position, and Chaan could say no more. Privately, he resolved that as soon as the starship cleared the planet he would warn Victad by radio, so the Solar Council agency—and Hildi—could be evacuated from Regn. It would be up to Victad to decide whether he wanted to warn Marl.

The Wasser task force was fifty men, outfitted in the crimson-and-black uniforms of Marl's forces to confuse the spaceport's defenders. They left the mountains in five copters at dusk. Chaan rode the flagship with Horda.

As they moved out of the mountains into the foothills, the copters scattered in different directions. The ship in which Chaan was riding flew low, straight toward the city, skimming ridges in a manner that indicated the pilot knew the terrain like the back of his hand.

About two miles out of Regn, the copter dropped suddenly into an open field, a few hundred yards away from a farmhouse and barn. The farmer, evidently a member of the Wasser, came out and helped them move the copter into the barn. Chaan, Horda, and the copter crew were served a meal in the farmer's spacious kitchen and all of them slept in the barn.

About two hours after midnight, the farmer aroused them. Chaan and Horda climbed into the seat of the farmer's truck with him, and the other men piled into the back, covering themselves with hay. The farmer drove off over a network of rough country roads that took them around the edge of the city.

Chaan's training had given him an unusual sense of orientation, but he had no idea where they were in relation to Regn and the spaceport when the truck pulled into a small patch of woods. Some of the men of the other copter crews were already there, checking their weapons, and the remainder of the task force arrived, on foot and in various vehicles, at intervals soon afterward

At the first gray streaks of dawn, the Wasser moved out in loosely grouped platoons. They had walked no more than a quarter of a mile over rough fields before Chaan saw the lights and parkways of the spaceport ahead of them, the giant spaceships silhouetted vaguely against the lightening sky.

The Wasser halted, and half a dozen men crawled forward to eliminate the spaceport sentries and put a sector of its warning network out of commission. In about fifteen minutes, a cautious

TWICE UPON A TIME

light signal flashed at the edge of "the spaceport and the task force moved forward again.

With the first platoon, Chaan and Horda stepped over the bodies of sentries killed silently by the advance scouts. Chaan tripped over a wire, but it was broken and no longer sent a warning to the spaceport defenses.

They emerged from the weed-grown field onto the hard-packed ground of the spaceport, and Horda held up his hand for a halt. Guarding a small light with his hand, he studied a map.

"The starship is near the edge of the field at this point," he said. "That's why we came in from this side. There are several spaceships parked close to it. As soon as we've gotten you inside the starship and you've closed the port, we'll make a bid for one of the spaceships. So if you'll delay blasting off until we've started our attack on the spaceship, it will help us considerably."

"Fair enough," agreed Chaan. "I'll delay blastoff for you, unless they start an attack to recover the starship."

He did not ask that the Wasser help him once he was inside the starship. He knew there probably would be only one or two guards inside and, with his knowledge of the ship, he could handle any number. Just inside the entrance port there was a secret compartment from which he could seal off every deck of the ship and Hood the vessel with paralyzing gas.

The platoon moved briskly into the spaceport. The supporting platoons followed it to the edge of the spaceport area, and there halted to await a call for reinforcements.

In this outer area of the spaceport, the giant spaceships were parked in concentric circles, about a hundred yards apart. Each was patrolled by two soldiers walking in opposite directions around it. The system provided an effective line-of-sight network of guards, as each sentry was to watch for the passage of sentries around adjacent ships each time he made his rounds, and the failure of guards at anyone ship to make their rounds would be reported quickly.

The area was lighted too brightly for passage between two ships without being seen. Horda took the course of marching his men boldly up to one of the ships. They came up swiftly as one guard was disappearing around the hull of the ship and his alternate was approaching around the other side.

"Halt!" cried the guard, throwing up the muzzle of his heat-gun. "Who approaches?"

"Patrol around the spaceport periphery," replied Horda, continuing to move toward him with the platoon behind him. "Is everything in order?"

"What's the password?" demanded the guard, aiming his gun at Horda. But he hesitated at the sight of the Volksweld uniforms.

His hesitation was fatal. An expertly thrown knife by one of the Wasser soldiers caught him in the throat. One of the Wasser ran to the fallen man, scooped up his communicator and fell into his interrupted beat around the ship.

The platoon moved into the shadows at the side of the ship, and when the second guard came around he was cut down before he knew what had struck him. Another Wasser took up his beat.

"We could take this ship now, without any trouble," said Horda wistfully.

"You get me to my starship first," replied Chaan firmly.

"All right," surrendered Horda. "It's just beyond the next circle of spaceships. I can't break radio silence now, but I'm going to send a runner back to the other platoons and tell them to move in on this ship."

"Suit yourself about that," said Chaan.

The messenger was sent out and the remainder of the platoon moved across the intervening ground to the next spaceship. But when they approached it, there was no challenge. Instead, the guard opened up with his heat-gun and ran for cover around the ship.

"Damn trigger-happy sentry!" bawled Horda. "They'll detect that radiation and have reinforcements out here. Attack!"

Spreading out, the platoon rushed the ship. Two of the Wasser fell, their clothing ablaze, but the guards were outflanked and cut down within minutes.

Suddenly a tremendous clangor of alarm bells burst out all over the spaceport, and distant sirens began to wail. From somewhere down the line of spaceships a body of men appeared in the distance, approaching at a run.

Right in front of Chaan, less than a hundred yards away, the needle nose of the starship pointed to the sky.

"There it is!" he shouted at Horda. "We can make it!"

"Make it yourself!" roared Horda. "I'm going to get that spaceship! Back, men!"

The platoon milled about, turned and headed back for the spaceship they had just left. An armed copter dropped from the darkness above the spaceport lights, spewing forth men to block their path. The whirring blades of other copters sounded loud in the air, and the sirens of armored cars were drawing nearer.

Chaan raced for the starship. Surprisingly, no one appeared to interfere with him. Behind him, the Wasser and the constantly reinforced spaceport forces were engaged in heavy fighting.

Two guards were on the ramp of the starship, but the sight of a single man in a Volksweld uniform evidently confused them. They stood with drawn guns until Chaan, his own heat-gun in his hand, ran up the ramp. One raised his gun to fire; Chaan cut him down. The other dropped his weapon in fright. Chaan pushed him roughly to the ground and ran into the ship. In the airlock, he pushed the button that slammed the heavy entrance port shut behind him.

Now, he exulted, let them fight it out among themselves. He was off to Lalande!

CHAPTER FIFTEEN

THERE WAS something wrong here. Chaan peered around into the silent dimness of the storage deck. He could see nothing out of place. But his starship was like a part of himself, and the feeling of this ship was not quite right to him.

On the lower control deck above he heard the clump of booted feet, and the sound of voices drifted down the open companionway. There were more than two guards up there!

Chaan turned to the wall, and his fingers sought the concealed button that would open the secret compartment. From it, he could immobilize these guards easily.

There was no button there.

172

Frantically his fingers raced over the wall. There was no button. There was no secret compartment.

This was not his starship!

"Turn around, slow, and keep your hands away from your heat-gun," said a voice behind him.

Chaan obeyed. A Volksweld soldier was standing on the ladder, just below the hatch to the deck above, pointing a heat-gun steadily at him.

"It's one man, sir," said the soldier to someone above him. "I'll cover him while you come down."

A pair of boots appeared through the hatch, followed by the uniformed back of an officer. The officer climbed down past the wary soldier, leaped lightly to the deck and turned to face Chaan.

Chaan's eyes widened in surprise. The officer was Jahr!

"Well, Chaan! I didn't expect this trap to catch you!" exclaimed Jahr. He looked up at the soldier on the ladder and commanded: "Put away your gun, man. This is the Space Scout."

The man did so, sheepishly, and descended the ladder. He was followed by half a dozen other Volksweld soldiers.

"Jahr, this isn't my starship," said Chaan flatly.

"No, it's a dummy," admitted Jahr. "There's nothing above decks but a hollow shell. The fleet hasn't located your starship yet."

"It's a pretty good fake," said Chaan ruefully. "It fooled me, from the outside. But what's the purpose of it?"

"Well, Marl felt your starship would be natural bait for the Wasser. I don't know whether it's true, but the general belief here is that a scout ship can defeat a battleship on even terms."

"It's true," said Chaan.

"Of course, the Wasser would go to great lengths to get a ship like that," said Jahr, "There's also the angle that, by stealing your ship and hiding it on the planet somewhere, you wouldn't appear at Lalande on schedule and that would bring the fleet down on us. It's still our theory that they stole it when you arrived, but in case they didn't we put up this dummy in an attempt to trap a force of them here."

"They may very well have stolen it, although they claim they didn't," said Chaan thoughtfully. "They didn't come here after my starship, though that could be because I was along. They were interested in capturing one of your spaceships. But, Jahr, if you didn't expect me to come to your dummy starship, how do you happen to be here?"

"Oh, when you disappeared on your own private business, Marl returned me to active duty until you should come back, and assigned me to stake out the dummy ship. Of course, Marl may have suspected it would draw you as well as the Wasser, and had me on hand to make sure you weren't shot by mistake."

Leaving Jahr's soldiers inside the fake starship, Chaan and Jahr opened the airlock and went out onto the spaceport.

The fighting Chaan left had ended. Horda and the survivors of his three platoons—about half of them—were lined up with their hands up, surrounded by armed soldiers. Dead bodies in the crimson-and-black uniforms were scattered over the area, and ambulances were removing a number of wounded.

"A nice haul," said Jahr with satisfaction. "By the way, Chaan, Marl issued standing orders to everyone that if you showed up he'd like to talk with you at your earliest convenience."

"In view of what's happened here, I expect that should be as soon as possible," said Chaan, watching the Volksweld soldiers march their prisoners away. "Let's have some breakfast on our way uptown, and go by Marl's office."

"All right," agreed Jahr. "Let me turn over this detachment to my second in command and tell him to notify Marl we're on our way to see him."

The crimson rim of Wolf 359 was setting the eastern horizon ablaze as the two of them left the spaceport in a military car. They enjoyed a leisurely meal at the clubhouse of an officers' organization to which Jahr belonged, and arrived at the Volksheim building before mid-morning.

Chaan and Jahr entered Marl's office together. Marl greeted them with the air of a man who already had put in several hours work. He waved them to seats and leaned back in his own chair, removing his spectacles.

"You're an elusive man, Chaan," said Marl. "We thought we were keeping pretty close tabs on you until your plane came down in the middle of a lake."

"A lake?" Chaan laughed. "Is that where it landed?"

"It gave us quite a turn," said Marl. "We thought you were downed till we brought it up and found it empty, with the controls on automatic."

"Part of my job is to be elusive when necessary," said Chaan. "Was there something you wanted to talk to me about, Marl?"

"Mostly, I wanted to know when you returned," said Marl. "But the events of this morning raise some interesting questions in my mind. You've been with the Wasser these last few days, haven't you?"

"A remarkable bit of deduction," said Chaan dryly. "That raises an interesting question in my mind, too. What do you plan to do with Horda and the Wasser you captured at the spaceport?"

"I'm not sure yet. Probably execute them."

"Turn them loose," said Chaan.

"What!" For, the first time, Chaan caught Marl genuinely surprised.

"Turn them loose. They were on Solar Council business. They were helping me get back to my starship—or so we thought."

"I could refuse on the ground that you know my objectives with respect to the Solar Council, and unless I can persuade you to cooperate with me you're a dead duck anyhow," said Marl with a peculiar smile. "It's too late for me to worry about the Solar Council's displeasure, you see. But I have justice on my side, as I think you'll agree. Horda admitted to me that he and his men were trying to capture one of my spaceships to haul their hydrogen bomb over Regn.

Chaan could not argue that point. The slender technicality of his having enlisted Horda's aid would hardly outweigh Horda's own admission to Marl. He said nothing.

"I don't suppose you'd tell me where the Wasser are?" suggested Marl.

"You're right, I wouldn't," answered Chaan.

"Ah, well." Marl sighed. "Now that you've become acquainted with the Wasser, what do you think of them?"

"I don't like them," said Chaan honestly. "They have good men among them, like almost any group, but I don't like their leadership or their leaders' aims."

"I didn't think you would. Now don't you agree that, at worst, my regime is the lesser of two evils for Volksweld?"

"That's precisely the term I'd use, except that I doubt Horda and the other Wasser leaders have your ability," said Chaan. "Thus, from the standpoint of the Solar Council, they probably would be less of a threat to the peace of the Galaxy."

"Nothing is more vicious than a war started by stupid people," said Marl. "But I won't argue with you the comparative merits of Marl and the Wasser. Suffice it to say that I do not consider myself an evil, either lesser or greater, and I'd like to persuade you to the same attitude."

"If you're asking me again for my cooperation in your plans..."

"I am."

"...The answer is no."

Marl shrugged.

"I'm in no hurry," he said. "You have a year on Volksweld, and a great deal can happen in a year to change your mind."

"You seemed in a hell of a hurry when you turned Ramitz loose on me," remarked Chaan.

"One tries all avenues to attain one's goal," answered Marl with a smile. "There may be other pleasant surprises in store for you, if I think up any new approaches, but I'd much rather have you join me of your own free will."

"I'll discuss nothing further with you, Marl, until I get my starship back," said Chaan, getting to his feet.

"We still haven't recovered your starship," said Marl. "When we do, perhaps we can deal on that basis."

Chaan and Jahr left Marl and returned to the Regnal Hotel. That last remark of Marl's disturbed Chaan. Marl might be telling the truth about not having recovered the starship—the fact of the dummy ship at the spaceport possibly was evidence in support of it—but even when he did recover it, Chaan would face some difficulty getting it back.

Chaan was thoroughly puzzled over the identity of the starship thieves. He had watched Marl's face closely, and he had watched

Horda's face closely. Both had seemed to be telling the truth when they denied they were responsible for it. The dummy starship was an indication Marl was telling the truth; for why would they build a dummy starship as bait for the Wasser if they had the real one? On the other hand, Horda's leading his men into such a trap was an indication that Horda was telling the truth; for if the Wasser had the starship, they would have known the one at the spaceport was a fake. Was it possible that someone had stolen it without the knowledge of either Marl or the Wasser?

Marl obviously intended to use the starship to bargain with him, when and if he could produce it, and he could hide it anywhere on Volksweld. But, as Marl had said, a year was a long time. Once Chaan had reason to believe the ship was back on the planet, he had some tricks for ferreting it out that he doubted Marl could match.

Oler admitted them to Chaan's suite at the hotel. He showed no surprise at Chaan's return, favoring them both with his customary sour look.

"You have a visitor, Captain," said Oler unhappily.

"Who?" asked Chaan.

"Miss Gretten. She's waiting in the reception room."

"Space! What does a man have to do to get rid of a woman?" growled Chaan.

Jahr went into the kitchen with Oler; Chaan pushed open the door to the parlor.

Hildi was sitting on a low chair with her bare back to the door. Her shoulders drooped. At the sound of his entry, she turned and rose to her feet in a joyous How of motion, her face lighting.

"Chaan!" she cried. "One of Jahr's officers told me you had come back. I was afraid something had happened to you."

"Jahr should mind his own business," said Chaan sternly. "Hildi, I told you I didn't want to see you again."

She came up to him and put a timid hand on his arm. She turned up round blue eyes in which tears shone.

"Doesn't the condemned criminal have the right to know the charge?" she asked. "Even Marl's courts don't deny us that."

"Hildi," said Chaan sorrowfully, "my experiences in many different cultures have made me tolerant. But it still goes against my nature for a woman to pretend love for a man with the deliberate intention of betraying him to his enemies."

"Betraying?" she repeated with wide eyes. "How did I betray you, Chaan? How could I help what happened?"

"'I was twice betrayed," he said bitterly. "Do you deny that your meeting me was pre-arranged so I'd be lured into the hypno-trap at your house? And do you deny that you tried to persuade me to surrender to Marl's demands while I was under hypnosis?"

"There wasn't anything pre-arranged about our meeting!" she cried, "I met you and I loved you and I still love you, Chaan! I knew nothing about the hypno-trap until they brought me to the hotel and I found you already under its spell, being questioned by Ramitz."

"Is this true?"

"I swear it. They did order me to try to persuade you to answer their questions, but I didn't do it because they told me to. If you could only remember what I said to you then—it was true, every word of it—I wanted you to do as they asked so they'd free you without harming you. Chaan, I don't know anything about politics and interstellar diplomacy or whether Marl's right or wrong, and I don't care to know. I just know that I love you, and I'd do anything to protect you from harm."

Chaan's heart melted. He took her in his arms. She clung to him tightly sobbing against his shoulder.

"Hildi, Hildi," he murmured. "There's no woman I've ever wanted with me so much as I want you. But you must remember I have a duty, and I must be true to it. It's not just a question of whether Marl is bad or good for Volksweld. I have the peace of this whole section of the Galaxy in my hands, and I'm stranded on a world where everyone is against me. I don't want you against me too."

"I'll never be against you, in anything," she said against his chest. "Oh, please believe me, Chaan! I'll work with you, I'll help you, I'll do anything you ask. Whatever you do is right to me. If you're against Marl, I'm against Marl, and if you become a traitor to the Solar Council, I'll become a traitor too, without a qualm. I just want to be with you."

"You shall be," he said gently. "And if the time comes when I must leave you—but we won't think about that now. I'm not going to turn traitor to the Solar Council, in spite of all Marl can do. He's failed so far. He did his best to get the secret of the stardrive's operation from me under hypnosis, and failed

She leaned back against his confining arms, her eyes round with alarm.

"You did tell him the secret of the stardrive's operation!" she whispered. "Didn't you know?"

"What!" he gasped, a terrible fear sweeping over him. "I couldn't have, Hildi! I couldn't have! I whispered it only to a hallucination of myself, so low that even their recorders couldn't have picked it up."

"Hallucination? Oh, darling, did you think it was a hallucination? That man was a double of yourself, built up by surgery to look like you even to the fingerprints, his mind and emotions impregnated with your own background from the information you yourself gave them under hypnosis!"

CHAPTER SIXTEEN

IN CHAAN'S peculiar shock reaction to Hildi's words, the big room seemed to expand enormously. It arched over them and around them like the great bowl of the universe. The walls and ceiling seemed infinitely distant; he could almost see the powdered stars before them. Tiny figures isolated in the center of this vastness, Chaan and Hildi stood in loose embrace, their horrified stares meeting in the still air between them.

"Hildi, what do you know about this?" demanded Chaan in a low, urgent voice.

"What I've told you. I pieced together bits of information I overheard, and they don't know that I know about it. I wanted to tell you right after you were released from hypnosis, but I was afraid to tell you in front of Jahr and you sent me away."

"I can see why they'd go to all that trouble to get the secret," said Chaan reflectively. "It's worth it, to them or anyone else. But I didn't know they had time to build a double of me in the short period I was under hypnosis."

"Do you know how long you were under hypnosis?" asked

Hildi. "One hundred and twenty-five days!"

"Great space!" exclaimed Chaan. "I thought it was only about five weeks. Marl was misleading me today, then—my year on Volksweld is more than a third gone. I hadn't thought of it before, but I haven't looked at a calendar since I broke free from Ramitz."

He looked at one now, a small one that sat on a table against the wall. The date was the sixth day of the Volksweld month Amwit. Chaan mentally translated that into Earth Standard: Sept. 11, 3503.

"You should have noticed the colder weather," said Hildi. "It's mid-autumn now."

"Volksweld is just a cold planet to me, anyhow," said Chaan with a shrug. "But what more do you know about this double business?"

"Well," said Hildi, "they didn't make over the man as your double just to get the secret of the stardrive's operation from you. Marl's plan is if you refuse to cooperate and give a favorable report on Volksweld at Lalande, he'll send the double in your place. They'll think the double is you, and he'll report anything Marl tells him to."

"Hmm. He'll have to have more information about procedure than they got out of me to pass for me at Lalande—I think. That's probably why Marl is so anxious to get my cooperation."

"That's why I urged you to tell them what they wanted to know," said Hildi. "I thought if they would send a double, you'd stay on Volksweld with me. I still don't want you to go, Chaan, but if you think you must, why don't you agree to give the sort of report Marl asks and then report the truth when you get there?"

"It won't work. If I agree to cooperate with Marl, they'll give me hypnotic treatment to be sure I don't betray them. They can't force that treatment on me, but it will be effective if I agree to help them. Do you know this double's name, Hildi?"

"No."

"I must find him. It they ask certain questions at Lalande, they would uncover the fraud, but they might not become suspicious enough of him to ask those questions."

He patted her shoulder, smiled down at her and added:

"But for the rest of the day, nothing's going to spoil our

reunion."

Hildi moved her clothing and other effects into Chaan's suite at the hotel that night.

The next day, Chaan visited Victad again, and told of the loss of the stardrive secret.

"That's bad," said Victad, pulling, at his lower lip with chubby fingers. "I hope you didn't give away the principle of the stardrive, too."

"Fortunately, that's one Space Scouts don't know," said Chaan. "They won't be able to build any stardrive ships from anything I told them, but they'll be able to operate mine."

"I'll do my best to get word to Sirius," said Victad.

"You should, and right away. They'll want to change the combinations and circuits in stardrives all over the Galaxy after this."

"I'll do my best," repeated Victad slowly. "But there's a situation here you don't know about. I suspected it before, but I just had confirmation of it while you were in the Harven Mountains. I can't communicate directly with Sirius and the other systems any more. I haven't been doing it for months."

"You mean they're censoring the light-beam transmission? I didn't think it could be done."

"They found a way. I found out the circuits had been detoured so I don't either send or receive directly. They've been operating the light-beam transmitter themselves for months, and relaying to and from me."

"It doesn't surprise me too much," said Chaan. "Marl's got Volksweld thoroughly sealed off now. But even if you could get that message through, I can't alter the stardrive circuits on my ship unless I can get hold of it. Do you have any contacts with the Wasser, Victad?"

"I'm afraid not. Just reports."

"Make contact with them. If necessary, send a man to the Harven Mountains. I can tell you where to find them. I want them to help find a man who looks, talks and acts exactly like me."

And he told Victad about the double.

"I'll try," said Victad again. "From what you tell me of your last escapade with the Wasser, though, I doubt they'll be enthusiastic about helping you again."

"They may not be, but they'll help if they want any consideration at all when the fleet moves in here."

Chaan began a citywide search for the man with his face. He could only hope that the double was still, in Regn, and not somewhere else on the planet.

The course he adopted was to cover as much of the city, block by block, as possible. He wore the crimson-and-black uniform of a Volksweld officer, and he made inquiries at strategic stores, shops and residential buildings.

"I'm searching for my brother," he would say. "He's a twin and looks exactly like me. My name is Hann Dittow and my brother's name is Mann, but he has been going under an assumed name and I don't know what he calls himself now. Have you seen him?"

Many of those he contacted were sympathetic, but none helpful. To those who asked additional questions, he explained that their father had died and he needed to find his brother to help, settle the estate.

Chaan watched faces, too, for the slightest sign of recognition when he entered a building or passed people on the street. The reactions he did get in this respect were of no value to him, however. They were people who recognized him as Chaan Fritag, the Space Scout.

He did not, of course, tell Jahr, Oler, or Ingra of his mission. Jahr was considerably disgruntled at being left out of so many of Chaan's daily reconnaissances into the city and often Chaan was virtually forced to take the big fellow along. At such times, he made no inquiries, but relied on the recognition factor alone.

Hildi did accompany him, frequently. Chaan spent most of every day and a good part of most nights in his search, and he was not willing to be separated from her constantly. Some of the time they worked separately, Hildi armed with a picture of Chaan to check some places while he inquired at others. Each night they returned to the hotel suite, footsore and bone-weary.

It was a disheartening search. Day after day, in every section of the city, in every type of store and building, often through chill rain or biting snow flurries and always through the increasing cold of the approaching Volksweld winter, they plodded through the streets of Regn without success. Chaan began to believe that the double he sought certainly must have been sent away to some other section of the planet.

"I realize I'm not supposed to know the mysterious ways of a Space Scout," said Jahr one day when he was touring with them, "but all this wandering you've been doing the last few weeks seems aimless to me. If you're trying to survey Regn on foot, it's been done."

"Let's just say I'm out for exercise," replied Chaan with a smile.

"All right. But if you ever care to take me into your confidence, I'll be glad to help you do whatever you're trying to do."

Chaan received regular reports from the Wasser, through Victad, but all were negative.

The first glimmer of hope in the search came after about six weeks.

He was alone, late one afternoon, in a section of Regn where all the buildings were old and weatherworn. The heaviest snow of the season was coming down, great flakes falling slowly. A blanket of white was building up on the streets and sidewalks, its smooth surface occasionally scarred temporarily by passing vehicles.

Streetlights already were on, and illumination from the windows of buildings and the infrequent storefronts struggled dimly through the falling snow. Chaan trudged along, shivering and cursing the hardiness of the Volksweldvolken. The uniform he wore was not tropical garb, but it was too thin to protect him against this biting cold. He was thankful he had not chosen the shirtless civilian garb.

Hildi was searching another section of the city that day. In an hour, they were to meet for supper, and would search together that evening.

His shoulders hunched and his hands in the pockets of his tunic, Chaan came even with a closed door above which was the sign: *Norvad's Restaurant.* Light streamed thinly from small windows on either side of the door. It opened, throwing a rectangle of light momentarily on the snow, and a customer in civilian dress emerged, picking his teeth. He glanced at Chaan standing there, turned and walked down the street.

Restaurants were good places to look. A double who was

expected to take a starship ride would hardly be a family man. Chaan took his hands out of his pockets, pushed the door open and went in.

He stopped just inside to stamp his feet and brush the snow from his shoulders. The place was small but well lighted. It contained a dozen tables, four of them occupied. Food was spread out in covered dishes on a low bar that stretched along one side of the room. Behind the bar was a door that evidently led to the kitchen.

A big man, bald as an egg, with huge handlebar mustache, stood behind the bar, stirring soup in a large tureen. Looking up at Chaan's entrance, he smiled a greeting and raised one hand casually.

"Hello, Augang," he said. "You're early tonight."

With difficulty, Chaan repressed an exclamation of surprise and exultation. The man mistook him for his double!

"I'm hungry tonight," he answered calmly, walking up to the bar. If his double could pass for him, certainly he could pass for his double, with proper precautions. "What's good tonight?"

"Everything," retorted the mustached one with a smile. "Want to start out with hot soup?"

"Might as well," replied Chaan. "It's cold out today."

He accepted a bowl of steaming soup and went over to one of the tables.

It was good soup. Chaan sipped it thoughtfully. He kept his eyes and ears open. One of the other customers, going to the bar to get a second helping of some dish, addressed the mustached man as "Norvad," so Chaan gathered he was the owner.

Evidently "Augang" ate here regularly, and Chaan had just happened to come in at an earlier hour than Augang was accustomed to eat. If that was true, all he had to do was wait, and the chances were that his double would walk through the door into his hands.

He did not worry about Norvad suspecting him unless he allowed himself to be drawn into conversation about daily trivialities. Ramitz and his colleagues would have been careful to coach this double in Chaan's exact manner of speaking, his exact vocabulary and gestures, even his personality and philosophy. All Chaan had to do was act natural and wait.

The customers at one of the tables finished their meal, paid the bill and left. New customers came in, selected their dishes and occupied two other tables.

Chaan finished his soup. He looked at the battered clock on the wall over the food counter. He had been in the restaurant fifteen minutes. The soup and the warmth of the restaurant had driven the chill from his body; he felt snug and comfortable now.

He took his empty soup bowl over to the bar and studied the varied dishes by lifting the covers and sniffing. Whether the Volksweld psychologists had been able to go so far as to inculcate his tastes in food into Augang, he didn't know.

"What do you recommend, Norvad?" he asked.

"Stew's good tonight."

"Who knows what's in stew?" countered Chaan, and at Norvad's knowing grin, added: "Especially your stew. How about some of this meat?"

"The roast gumbel? All right."

Norvad served some of the meat on a plate, while Chaan selected several vegetables.

"Where's the girl friend tonight?" asked Norvad.

"Oh, she'll be along later," answered Chaan cautiously.

But that reminded him. Hildi!

He took the food back to his table and sat chewing thoughtfully. He was due to meet Hildi in little more than half an hour now at the Crimson Star Restaurant halfway across Regn. If he failed to appear, she would be frantic. Hildi was convinced that Chaan was exposing himself to great danger by searching for his double and attempting to thwart Marl's plans.

Chaan hoped Augang would come into the restaurant by that time. He could settle the matter Quickly, and get in touch with Hildi. He ate slowly, dawdling over his food.

"Thought you were hungry," said Norvad, when Chaan went back to refill his ale glass.

"I am," said Chaan, adding with a wink: "I'm waiting for company."

"Never seen a woman yet who got anywhere on time," agreed Norvad.

Chaan went back to his table. The hands of the clock moved with disconcerting swiftness, and still Augang did not come through the front door.

The hour arrived at which he was to meet Hildi. Chaan finished the remnants of his meal and arose from the table.

"Where's your communicator?" he asked Norvad.

"Are you joking? You know I don't have a communicator."

"That's right, I'd forgotten," said Chaan hastily. "Where's the nearest one? I think I'd better do some checking if I'm not to spend an evening alone."

Norvad looked at him peculiarly.

"If there's one any closer than your own place, it would be at the police substation," he replied.

"Yes, I'll try there or just run home," said Chaan, not daring to ask where the substation was. Obviously, Augang lived very near and was familiar with the neighborhood. It was probable that the woman to whom Norvad referred lived with Augang, and Norvad was wondering why he needed a communicator to call such a short distance.

Chaan paid his bill and left the restaurant. He paused outside the door. He had approached it from the left and had not seen the substation, so it probably was a short distance up the street to the right.

He found it at the end of the block, at the intersection of one of the moving streets. One of the three policemen playing some sort of a card game inside pointed out the communicator booth to him in a comer. Chaan went in and dialed the call letters of the Crimson Star.

The employee who answered at the Crimson Star called Hildi to the communicator. Chaan gave her the address of Norvad's.

"Go back to the hotel and pick up Jahr," he instructed. "Then meet me there. I think Norvad's beginning to suspect me, and Augang may be well supplied with friends around here. Jahr will be a good man to have along in an emergency."

Chaan went back to Norvad's to wait.

As he entered, a man in uniform was standing at the bar, talking to Norvad, his back to Chaan.

"You're crazy, Norvad," the man was saying in a loud voice that was like an echo of Chaan's own. "I haven't eaten in here tonight."

"By space, Augang, am I to doubt the evidence of my own eyes?" demanded Norvad angrily.

Norvad glanced over Augang's shoulders and caught sight of Chaan at the door. His eyes widened. In three swift strides, Chaan came up to the bar, drawing his heat-gun from inside his tunic.

"I've been looking for you, Augang," he said.

The man turned and Chaan looked at his own face, as in a mirror. The blue eyes were surprised but not frightened, the mouth twisted slightly in a defiant smile and the firm jaw jutted with the desperation of the trapped.

Norvad moved like lightning. With both hands he raised the tureen in a quick, pitching motion, and hot soup splashed over Chaan's face and hands, soaking the front of his uniform.

With a cry of pain and surprise, Chaan dropped his heat-gun and dashed his hands to his stinging eyes. Half-blinded, he saw Augang leap for the door.

In a single motion, he scooped his heat-gun from the floor and fired.

The beam caught Augang in the middle of the back. He pitched forward to the floor, his burning flesh smoking through a great hole in his tunic.

Chaan whirled to cover Norvad, who was vaulting over the bar.

"There'll be no more tricks," Chaan warned, brushing meat and vegetables from his soaked tunic with his free hand. "Until my friends get here, no one leaves."

He backed over by the door, and turned the dead man over with his booted toe.

"Now, let's see what sort of terms Marl talks!" he muttered grimly.

CHAPTER SEVENTEEN

CHAAN STRODE into Marl's office like a conquering prince. It was early morning, but again Marl gave the impression of having been at work for quite a while.

Chaan tossed Augang's identification papers on Marl's desk, so that they spread out like a fan.

"You've probably heard about this from your police, Marl," he said. "I just want you to know who did it. I think you know why."

Marl did not appear disconcerted.

"You are a very talented man, Chaan," he said, blinking at Chaan through his spectacles. "You found the Wasser, when I haven't been able to track them down with all my forces. Now, you found this man, whom I thought as securely hidden in the city as a needle in a haystack."

"There isn't any use in your keeping my starship hidden now, is there, Marl?" suggested Chaan, "You may know how to operate the stardrive, but now you don't have anyone who can pass for me. And you can be sure I'm not going to fall for any more hypno-traps."

"I have told you we don't have your starship," replied Marl patiently. "We're still looking for it in space."

"After half a year? Man, you expect me to believe that? Even on anti-gravity, it would be more than a billion miles out by now.

"Do you think I don't realize that? My ships have been going farther and farther out, covering a bigger and bigger sphere of space, at maximum speed, and we haven't gotten a trace of it in our detectors. Trying to find your starship is an expensive proposition for Volksweld. But you yourself said no one else could have thrown it into stardrive."

"That's true," said Chaan, "No one else could have until you twisted the secret out of me weeks later. That's what makes me wonder if you haven't recovered the ship and hidden it here on the planet."

"Chaan," said Marl soberly, "I'm as anxious to get your ship back as you are. I'll let you look over the records of the entire search operation if you want to. I'll let you interview every officer in my space service, and order them to tell you the whole truth about everything you ask."

Chaan smiled triumphantly. Now that he had covered Marl's trump card by disposing of Augang, Marl evidently was trying to get back in his good graces. But Marl's next action dispelled this illusion.

"Perhaps, first," said Marl, "you'd better see something."

He arose and went to the window, beckoning Chaan to follow. Chaan went to his side.

Below them in the courtyard, a man was walking, his hands clasped behind him, his head bowed in thought. He wore a blue-and-silver uniform like Chaan's own.

Marl opened the window and called:

"Carvel!"

The man below turned his face up to them.

For one shocked instant, Chaan thought Augang had come back to life through some Volksweld super science. Then he realized that Carvel was another, different Augang—another double of himself.

He whipped out his heat-gun.

"Go ahead and shoot," said Marl heartlessly. "There are enough of them to be expendable."

Chaan lowered the gun.

"Just how many doubles of me did you construct, Marl?" he asked.

"Twelve, I believe. Perhaps thirteen. All of them are oriented to your manner of acting and speaking, and all have been hypno-impressed with your knowledge and background. The others are scattered around Volksweld, in safe hiding places."

"Damn you, Marl, I ought to shoot you down here and now!"

"I even considered that possibility," said Marl. "Besides the fact that it isn't in the cards for a Space Scout to assassinate the head of a planetary government, you must know that I've arranged for my work to be carried on in the event of my death."

The man meant it. There was the gleam of fanaticism in his eyes. Whatever others might think about his methods and his threat to the peace of the Galaxy, Marl believed absolutely in his own objectives.

"You see, Chaan," said Marl softly, "I am offering you a key role in one of the great moments of human history. Even you, a Space Scout, can't halt the tide of destiny in its flooding—and you have tried, with great cleverness and courage. I'm not trying to betray you—I'm trying to enlist your help, freely and willingly, as an ally in a noble cause."

Suddenly Chaan remembered words the mysterious Volks-welder had spoken to him in a mountain cave:

"You are the man on whom destiny hangs."

Was this what the Volkswelder meant? Destiny could hang on him either way—it did hang on him, he realized fully. But Marl had said he could not halt the tide of destiny, and was that not true?

"Why do you need me now?" he asked Marl bitterly. "You have doubles who can play my part on Lalande. I'm surprised you haven't disposed of me before now."

"There are always people who can distinguish the artificial rose from the real one," answered Marl. "Is it not likely that the Space Service would be careful in recognizing its own Scouts? No matter how well we indoctrinate a double, he cannot play the role of Chaan Fritag as well as Chaan Fritag can play it."

"That's true," admitted Chaan, thinking of the identification badge burned into the skin of his chest.

Why hadn't Marl thought of that? It was generally known as the surest credentials of the Space Scout. Perhaps Marl had, and perhaps that was why Chaan was still alive. No one could duplicate that mark, brought to view by tension of certain muscles, except the surgeons of the Space Service on faraway Earth.

"What do you ask me to do?" asked Chaan, knowing the answer.

"I've told you," said Marl. "Report that things are in good shape on Volksweld when you reach Lalande. Report troubles, of course, but not serious enough to justify investigation by the fleet."

"And if I refuse, you take the chance of sending a double anyhow?"

"Exactly."

"You tempt me, Marl," said Chaan, and he told himself he was dissembling. He told himself he was trying to elicit more information from Marl, to find out how watertight were Marl's plans for deceiving the Solar Council.

"I hope you mean that," said Marl, his mouth twisting with the ghost of a smile. "If you agree, you'll have to prove your willingness to cooperate by more than words, you know. "You'll have to submit to a hypnoprobe of your own free will.

"Why didn't you try to re-hypnotize me when you had my back against the wall before?"

"Ramitz said any further assaults on your integrity at that time would drive you insane, and you would be of no more value to us. But if you submit freely to a hypnoprobe, we can assure ourselves you actually are cooperating and that you will continue to accept hypnotic commands when you have reached Lalande. Without your own acceptance of hypnosis, its effects would dissipate two light-years out, and you know that as well as I do."

All at once, Chaan found his mind in a state of utter confusion. One impulse told him to fling Marl's offer back in the dictator's face as he had done before, and yet he did not. Another unsuspected urge, creeping up from some dim recess of his brain, painted a picture he had thrust aside before: Chaan as one of the respected leaders of a militant new empire. This picture, with its many hidden implications, spread through his mind a sneaking, guilty thrill.

"You could, of course, take your woman," Hildi, with you to Lalande," Marl went on inexorably. "On leaving Lalande, you could return here instead of going to Procyon, and help us take care of the other Scout you say is coming by the reverse route. When you fail to arrive at Procyon, they will think you are lost in space, but they won't have any reason to suspect Volksweld."

Blindly, Chaan turned and fled from Marl's presence, without answering.

He had to think, he had to think.

He liked Volksweld. He liked the carefree, reckless air of the planet and its people. He liked the sensation that hung like an aura about them all: men with a purpose, men marching with heads high toward a sure and glorious destiny. Nothing had ever appealed to him so much, not even the great empty freedom of space, not even the feeling that he rode high above the mundane affairs of men, above destiny itself.

Would he forever ride the stairways, while life and the companionship of men and women ran their courses below him, touched by him only when he descended for a brief year at a time, each time to a different world? Would he make friends, would he know love, time and again, only to have these intimate things pass from him forever as he moved on his endless rounds?

He thought of Hildi, slim and virginal as only a woman can be who has surrendered to love without reservation. The vision of her blue eyes and bright hair rose before him as though she walked with him and smiled at him now. If ever there had been a woman out among the stars for him, if ever there had been an aeon-lost companion found at last, that woman, that companion, was Hildi.

If he left her now and followed the call of duty to Lalande—assuming, of course, that he found his starship he could resign from the service and return from Lalande with the fleet. He might even be able to hitch a ride with the other Scout and get back ahead of the fleet. But then it would be too late. Hildi would be years older than he, and the life they wanted together would have passed them by.

Even so, he believed that were he still young and Hildi entering her middle years, he would still love her. He believed he would come back, if that were the course he took.

He found himself walking aimlessly, somewhere in Regn. He realized with a start that several hours had passed while he wandered, wrestling with his soul. It was nearing noon.

He stopped in a merchant's shop and put in a communicator call to Marl. He had some difficulty getting through the network of underlings at the Volksheim building, but by leaning heavily on his authority as a Space Scout he finally got Marl on the other end.

"Marl," he said, "taking you at your word, what happens if you don't recover my starship? What good would my cooperation be then?"

"In that case, I've lost," answered Marl simply. "When no Scout arrives at Lalande, the fleet will come in. But I promise you that I won't betray your cooperation to the fleet. As far as they're concerned, you'll be a Space Scout who did your best."

Chaan went back to his wandering. Marl was making him the kind of offer with which it was difficult to find any fault. Marl was taking desperate risks, but he proposed that Chaan could not lose, no matter which way the dice fell.

Chaan realized now that finding the Wasser had been a greater disappointment to him than he had known at the time. He realized now that he had portrayed the Wasser hopefully to himself as a patriotic underground organization with whom he might conceivably cooperate against Marl. There had been the chance—perhaps even an unadmitted hope—that, failing to gain his starship and get away to Lalande, he and Hildi could flee to the Wasser and await the coming of the fleet.

But the Wasser would be no better in control of Volksweld than Marl, and might be worse. And he could no longer sit back complacently in hiding, knowing that without him Marl could not stop the fleet from coming to Volksweld.

No, that was the key to the whole situation. Marl could do without him in a pinch now. Marl had him beaten now. If there was no hope of blocking Marl any more, was it not wiser to surrender and accept the many satisfactions that went with being Marl's ally?

And if Marl told the truth, and the starship still was missing—well, if it hadn't been recovered in this time, didn't the prospect that Marl wasn't likely to recover it now make it easier for him? Get in Marl's good graces and await the automatic arrival of the fleet, with nothing to lose—it was foolish to fight Marl over a starship out of reach of them both.

What had Marl said? *"Even you can't halt the tide of destiny in its flooding."* Perhaps the tide of destiny was running, and Marl was riding its crest.

Late in the afternoon, Chaan returned to the hotel, to be greeted by Jahr and an anxious Hildi. He took Hildi tenderly in his arms.

"I love you, Hildi," he told her softly. "I love you so much I'm going to sell the universe for you."

He turned to Jahr.

"Jahr, go to Marl in the morning," he instructed. "Tell him I think I'm going to agree to his terms, but I must have another day to argue the matter out with my conscience."

"Are you sure that's what you want to do?" asked Jahr. At Chaan's look of surprise, he grinned sheepishly and added: "I know that's what we've all been working for here, but somehow I didn't expect you to ever give up."

"It looks as though there's nothing else I can do," said Chaan, managing a smile with some difficulty. "But tell Marl I'm going out of the city to think, away from his crowds and soldiers, and this time I don't want to be followed."

CHAPTER EIGHTEEN

AT DAWN Chaan awoke. He lay for a few minutes on his back, staring up into the dimness of the big bedroom, trying to recall disturbing dreams.

Hildi lay on the other side of the bed in her favorite sleeping position: on her stomach, her face turned to one side and cradled on a forearm. The heavy blanket, slipping a bit off her shoulders, blurred the humps and hollows of her sprawled body.

This was the day of decision. Chaan pulled the edge of the blanket gently up to the pale, tousled hair and kissed her softly just in front of the ear lobe. Then he threw the blanket aside on his side of the bed and sat up. The chill morning air struck his naked skin and he shivered.

Hildi stirred, turned over and opened her eyes. The long lashes fluttered open and she gazed up into his face with enormous eyes, still dark with sleep and bemused with dreaming. Recognition lighted them, and she held up her arms to him, the blanket sliding from her bare shoulders and bosom.

He took her in his arms and they snuggled together, the blanket forming a single warm cocoon for their two bodies.

"It's very early," she murmured.

He laughed lightly.

"On Proteus, the major planet of Procyon," he related "there's a village near the principal spaceport. The authorities were unable to understand why it had a much higher birthrate than other towns in the area, until someone pointed out that a ground-to-space rocket blasted off at a certain hour each morning to carry supplies to the space station. It made an ear-shattering noise—and the hour was a little too early to get up and a little too late to go back to sleep."

She laughed with him, and her soft lips punctuated the joke.

Some time later, Chaan heaved himself out of bed with a sigh and began to dress. Hildi got up too.

"I'll fix you some breakfast," she said. "There's no use in disturbing the others."

"All right," he said. "But I'm going to wake Jahr anyhow. I want him to carry my message to Marl."

The three of them were silent through breakfast. At last Jahr said:

"Chaan, there's something I should tell you."

"What is it, Jahr?"

Jahr hesitated.

"Nothing," he said then, gloomily. "When you look at it realistically, we're enemies, aren't we?"

"Yes," said Chaan, smiling, "but that may be changed before sunset."

"Chaan, I hate to see you go under hypnosis again," said Hildi apprehensively. "It was such an ordeal for you. I could hardly bear seeing you struggle against Ramitz's torment."

"It will be different this time, Hildi," he said. "I'll be cooperating willingly, and there won't be any conflict between us. I'll come out of it fresh as a daisy."

Chaan left Hildi at the hotel. While Jahr went to the Volksheim building, Chaan went to the nearest heliport and took a copter. He lifted it above the city's buildings and set it on a course westward.

In this direction, the wooded hills came in fairly close to Regn. The produce farms that ringed the city were left behind him about seven miles out. At a distance of about ten miles from Regn, Chaan set the copter down in a clearing on the slope of a ridge, and stepped out of it.

It was one of those days that would have been called "Indian summer" in that part of Earth where Chaan had spent his boyhood. A violet morning haze hung over the distant city, against the sun, veiling it with wisps of magic. The air was crisp, but warming to the day. The snowfall of two nights earlier had melted, leaving only rearguard pockets in shady hollows. The hardy grass and tree foliage had not yet fled before approaching winter, but had turned from their summer blue-gray to a rich bluish-purple hue. The sky was deep blue, like the depths of a wide ocean into which the glowing crimson orb of Wolf 359 pushed its morning way.

Chaan hitched up his gun-belt, loosened the heat-gun in its

holster and walked away from the copter into the sparse woods. The dew shone from his boots, and brushed from the bushes onto his blue-and-silver uniform. In the space between the trees, the sun's rays clung to his yellow hair and caressed his cheeks.

Chaan took in the woodland peace with thoughtful blue eyes, and wondered why he had taken a day of grace. It seemed to him now that his decision had been made yesterday. He did not want to belabor his brain with the same old arguments again today.

"Today," he said aloud, "I am a traitor."

The first traitor in the long and noble history of the Space Scouts: Chaan Fritag of Earth. The first break in that shining shield that so long had protected the star-flung ramparts of humanity against the whims of adventurers and imperialists. His blackened name would be an epithet across the Galaxy.

But what could he do? He had been willing to die here, as often before on other worlds. But death was bearable only for a cause. Of what value would his death be to the Galaxy, pinned to the slender chance that Marl's doubles of him might make a slip?

The identification mark on his chest? He knew the surgeons who had built up doubles of him from other men, though they could not duplicate that insignia, could lift the flesh from his chest and graft it smoothly to the chest of Carvel or one of the others. There were a few other secrets he still held, such as the knowledge of the compartment by the starship's airlock. It was for these secrets that Marl sought his cooperation, but Chaan knew a Space Scout arriving at Lalande would not be questioned on such detailed matters unless suspicion was aroused.

No, Marl could do without him very well, and yet Marl offered him alliance.

And was not Marl right, after all? Could Chaan be this powerfully attracted to a world and its people, as fiercely as he loved freedom, if Marl's dictatorship were so onerous? It would mean war, if Marl succeeded. But Chaan himself had not hesitated to kill, often, in the name of the Solar Council. Was there not some justification in Marl's plea for an autonomous Sirius Quadrilateral, freed from the protective custody of distant Earth?

Thus Chaan meditated, and after a while he stretched out and slept in a sun-touched patch of forked grass.

He awoke to the alarming sense that danger was imminent, and was on his feet in a single move, his hand on the butt of his heat-gun. It was late morning. At the edge of the little clearing, the bushes rustled and moved. This noise had awakened him.

Chaan stood still, crouching slightly, and watched. There was a sudden rush of movement and a large animal leaped across a break in the underbrush and vanished again. Chaan brought the gun up quickly, but it was too late to fire.

From the glimpse, he recognized the animal. It was a carnivorous *bethom*, a beast that normally ranged far north of these parts. Evidently cold weather had forced it this far south.

The *bethom* was a weird-looking furry beast, with stripes of blue and black and three pairs of tentacles on the sides of its head to hold its living prey while it fed. It could easily do a great deal of damage by raiding farms around Regn and, besides, Chaan was in a hunting mood. He drew his heat-gun and stepped warily into the bushes.

The *bethom's* trail was not hard to follow, by the branches and twigs its bulky body had broken and crushed. Chaan had only to beware of its doubling back and ambushing him.

He moved swiftly through the brush-grown woods and presently came to the edge of a glade. Cautiously, he parted the bushes and looked out.

The *bethom,* moving faster than he realized, already had encircled the glade and emerged from the undergrowth at its other side. It was crouched for a charge, the tips of its six tentacles waving.

And between Chaan and the *bethom* stood a sturdy, defiant little figure—a boy in a close-fitting black suit and a transparent helmet. The boy was facing the *bethom,* two useless toy guns in his hands.

Even as the *bethom* roared and leaped, Chaan fired. The *bethom* burst into smoking flame in mid-air and fell writhing in its death agony at the boy's very feet.

Chaan came up behind the boy, who was holstering the toy guns with a puzzled air, and laid his hands on the youngster's shoulder. The boy turned.

"That was a narrow escape," said Chaan.

"Yes, sir," agreed the boy. "I'm afraid my guns weren't strong enough for such an animal. It's lucky you came along.

Chaan looked down at him, and amazed recognition dawned on him.

"You're Chaan, aren't you?" he asked, his voice trembling a little as he, remembered a long-past experience.

"Yes, sir," said the boy. "Captain Chaan of the Centaurus Patrol. I'm here trying to run down a space pirate, but I've got to get back in time for supper."

Chaan smiled, a vision before him of the house in Memfis, and Mother and Father seated around the supper table.

"Do you think I'll have time to take a look at the city?" asked the boy. "The pirate may be hiding out there."

"The city's pretty far away," said Chaan gravely. "I think we'd better just go to the top of the hill and look down on the city from there."

Together they walked to the top of the slope that overlooked Regn. As they walked, Chaan explained to the boy that this was Volksweld, the planet of the star Wolf 359. He was wondering if he had studied about Wolf yet, at that age.

"I hope I can come here again some day," said the boy eagerly, looking down at Regn. "On a spaceship I mean, not through the attic. I want to be a spaceman when I grow up. A spaceman like you."

"Why, Chaan?" asked Chaan.

"I study history in school," answered the boy. "People are always fighting in the history books because some people want things one way and some people want them another way. They don't have to do that any more."

"And what does that have to do with being a spaceman?"

"Why, there's plenty of room out there for everybody. If people don't like the way things are on one world, they can move on to another one. There are lots of worlds—that's what they teach us in school, you know—and there won't be any reason for fighting when people who think one thing can have "a world all to themselves."

A different memory came to Chaan: a memory of a gray-headed man with sad eyes in which had yet burned the spark of a visionary hope. He had been one of Chaan's instructors at the Space Scout school on Luna, and he had said...

"You're right," said Chaan softly to the boy. "There won't be any fighting. Now, I think we'd better go back if you're going to make it to supper on time."

The tremendous disc of Wolf had just passed the zenith as Chaan accompanied the boy back to the glade, past the scorched body of the *bethom* and to a tree that stirred Chaan's memory. There was a hollow between its roots, just big enough for a boy like this one to negotiate.

"I wish I could go back with you," said Chaan.

"I wish you could, too," said the boy. "I'm sure my mother and father would be glad to meet you."

"Perhaps," said Chaan. "But, then, it might not work for me now."

The boy started to climb down in the hole, then hesitated. He put his hand in his pocket and pulled out a small object that flashed in the crimson rays of Wolf.

"You should have something for saving my life," he said gravely to Chaan. "I don't carry any medals on my spaceship, but maybe this will do."

He laid the little shining object in Chaan's hand and vanished through the hole among the roots.

Chaan stood there for a time, looking longingly at that door to a world he once had known. He tried to remember just how Mother and Father had reacted when he had gone downstairs, dirty and sweaty, with a marvelous tale about the attic.

Chaan looked down at the object the boy had put into his hand. It was a dodecahedron.

It was very small, about two inches in diameter, and it was transparent. Looking into it, he could see not only its twelve facets, but apparently many, many more. He fancied it shone with a light that was more than the crimson reflection of Wolf.

Bedazzled by reminiscent wonder, Chaan made his way slowly back toward the clearing where he had left his copter. On the way, he was startled to realize he had come to a decision—a decision just the reverse of that to which he had committed himself that morning.

Now there swept over him the memory of all the star-thoughts, the bright sense of goodness and justice that had possessed him as a boy. Now he remembered why he had chosen the stern way of the Space Scout: "to give a part of yourself to man," had said that long-dead teacher, "until you find your own place and happiness, and step aside to grow old in a world you have helped to make."

In his self-deception, he had thought he had found his place upon Volksweld and his happiness in Hildi alone. But that place and that happiness could not be complete as long as Marl hurled Volksweld recklessly toward the destruction of the Galaxy.

The boy, whom Chaan once had been, was right. There was a world for those who wanted such a world. No one, not Marl or himself, had the right to impose on someone else the world he and his people wanted.

Marl's comparison of his own plans with the Solar Council's trusteeship of the inhabited worlds was not valid. The Council did not rule. Each planet might govern itself as it wished—a dictatorship, a monarchy, a theocracy, a democracy, even anarchy if it so desired. The Council sought only to guarantee that no planet commit suicide or threaten the integrity of other worlds.

Chaan knew now he would lend himself to none of Marl's devilry. He would fight, if it meant death, if it mean loss of Hildi, if it meant sure defeat. He would stall Marl off for the remainder of his year on Volksweld.

He was a Space Scout, a man trained to deception and danger, a man whose nerves and senses made possible for him what was impossible for others. Perhaps he could find the light-beam transmitter, which Marl had cut off from Victad, and get a message to Lalande to send the fleet.

He emerged into the clearing just as another copter swept in from the direction of Regn and landed beside his own. Chaan stopped, warily, prepared to draw his heat-gun and, leap back into the protection of the bushes.

But the two people who stepped from the copter were Jahr and Hildi.

CHAPTER NINETEEN

CHAAN WENT ACROSS the grass to meet them.
"How did you find me?" he asked.

"Well, Marl didn't obey your wishes, entirely," answered Jahr. "He didn't send ships to follow you, but he tracked your copter by radar, as you might have expected. As a Volksweld officer, I have a certain amount of authority, and I used it to look at the radar records."

He looked down at Chaan's hand.

"What's that?" he asked.

Chaan realized he was still carrying the dodecahedron in his left hand.

"A bauble," said Chaan, and slipped it into the pocket of his tunic. "But why did you and Hildi come here?"

"To save your life," said Jahr grimly. "To tell you that you must not ally yourself with Marl and accept the hypnoprobe."

"Everybody's a traitor these days," commented Chaan pleasantly. "It must be the fashion."

Jahr grinned.

"'I don't look at it quite that way," he replied. "When you came to Volksweld, Marl assigned me to stay with you and protect you. I'm fulfilling that duty, although he might not appreciate the way I'm doing it. Besides, like you, Chaan. We've been good friends, and I've never been too fond of Marl."

"Well, you'll be happy to know that I had decided already not to cooperate with Marl. But I'd like to know why you think I shouldn't."

"I told you once that I knew Adarl, Marl's father," said Jahr in a low voice. "Adarl was my kind of man. He was a warrior. He accepted the risks of the game. If it had been Adarl, when he got the secret of the stardrive's operation out of you, he'd have killed you clean and sent a double to Lalande in your place without further ado.

"But Marl is a perfectionist. I suppose he's as brilliant as Adarl was, but he doesn't like to take the slightest chance of things going wrong. He wants to wring the last small secret out of you and then kill you under the hypnoprobe, because he's afraid he couldn't trust you, even with your willing cooperation and under hypnotic control. If you were to accept the hypnoprobe, you'd be handing Marl the gun with which he'd shoot you down."

"Carefully avoiding mutilation of the chest," remarked Chaan wryly.

"Certainly," answered Jahr with a flash of his teeth. "He plans to cut the identification mark out of you to graft to one of your doubles."

"Nice fellow. But, as I told you, I'm not going to cooperate with Marl. I'm going to stall him some more."

"It won't work now," Jahr warned. "Marl is desperately afraid you'll get word to Lalande somehow. And after that sortie with the Wasser, he's not sure you can't snatch the starship from under his very nose if he ever recovers it. I've known for several weeks now that if you refused him this time he's made plans to go ahead and dispose of you, and depend on a double. I've just been hard put to it to decide whether I ought to tell you or be blindly loyal to Marl."

"I appreciate what you've done, Jahr," said Chaan, laying a hand affectionately on his friend's arm, "you don't think I ought to go back into Regn, then?"

"No, that's why I brought Hildi to you. Marl was certain you'd come back to her, and that's why he didn't interfere with your coming up here."

Chaan put an arm around Hildi's waist. The flowing cape that hung from her bare shoulder drifted in the breeze to envelop both of them.

"What do you suggest we do, Jahr?" he asked.

"Get to space out of here. Hide in the hills. Go back to the Wasser. Anything to stay out of Marl's clutches. There are supplies for a couple of weeks in my copter, and I'll take yours back to Regn."

"But what about you?"

"I'll manage," replied Jahr confidently. "I won't go with you, because Volksweld is still my world and its people are still my people. And don't worry about Marl punishing me. I'm a higher-ranking officer than you know, Chaan, and a large part of the forces in Regn are loyal to me personally. Marl may exile me and demote me, hut he won't harm me for fear of disturbances that could disrupt his carefully laid plans."

Chaan took his hand.

"Thank you again, Jahr," he said. "I hope we'll meet again."

"I hope so, too, when this business has been settled," said Jahr, grinning and gripping his hand tightly. If we meet before then, remember we're still technically enemies, and may the best man come out alive!"

He turned and strode swiftly toward the copters. Halfway there, he stopped and faced them.

"And hurry, damn it!" he called. "Oler will have reported my leaving with Hildi—the sneaking spy! When Marl finds I've checked the radar reports and taken off in a copter, he'll put the pieces of the puzzle together."

He waved and ran to the copters. He climbed into Chaan's craft and took off recklessly, with whirring blades. He streaked straight for Regn, but in a moment veered off sharply southward and the copter dwindled swiftly, climbing and vanishing into the deep blue sky.

Almost instantly, Chaan saw the reason for the maneuver. He and Hildi had taken two steps toward the remaining copter when suddenly the sky toward Regn was black with aircraft. Jet planes burst from the sky and flashed low over them before they could turn, and the other ships were approaching the hills at terrifying speed.

"Great space!" cried Chaan. "We can't make it!"

Seizing Hildi's hand, he turned and ran for the woods. Even as they ducked into the underbrush, the first contingent of copters was swarming down into the clearing.

Chaan plunged straight westward through the light forest, and Hildi paced him like a deer. They ran for a long time, keeping as much under the shelter of the blue-purple trees as possible. The whole atmosphere above them vibrated with the roar of aircraft.

Twice they detoured hurriedly to give a wide berth to clearings in which copters were descending. Marl evidently had thrown a great force into the search, and landings were being made all through the hills.

At last they had to stop for breath. Under a big tree, they leaned against each other, panting. Chaan took Hildi's hand in his.

"We'll have to find some sort of shelter," he gasped. "We can get through them if we can, hide until night. Then we'd better move on as far as we can. If Marl doesn't find us in a day or two, I wouldn't be surprised to see him saturate this whole range of hills with A-bombs."

"Why not here?" asked Hildi, pointing upward.

Chaan shook his head.

"Didn't you see the smoke rising behind us when we passed around that last clearing?" he asked. "They're burning the foliage out of all the trees as they search."

After a while, they went on, more slowly. They crossed the summit of the first ridge and moved westward on a downward slope. Through breaks in the foliage, they could see higher hills at a distance ahead of them.

Occasionally they heard the shouting of men. They did not dare stop and attempt to hide. They moved on, steadily.

They came unexpectedly into a small clearing, almost colliding with three Volksweld soldiers who were peering up into the trees and blasting the foliage with heat-beams.

Chaan drew and fired like lightning. The beam of his heat-gun sizzled across the shoulders of one soldier arid caught another in the back of the neck. Chaan ducked, pushing Hildi to the ground, as the third man's beam swept over them in a vicious arc; then his own beam took the man gruesomely in the face.

Chaan helped Hildi to her feet and they went over to the fallen soldiers.

"Two of these uniforms are still wearable," he said practically. "If we put them on, we'll have a better chance of getting through them."

They sat down on the ground and removed their boots. Chaan took off the blue-and-silver uniform, and Hildi threw away the flowing cape and slid out of the tight trousers. Chaan was desperately afraid some of the other Volksweld soldiers would come up on them while they were naked, but they got into the crimson-and-black uniforms without incident. Chaan's was a little tight and Hildi's too loose, but they would pass.

As they started off, armed with two heat-guns each, Chaan remembered something. He went back and took the bright little dodecahedron from the pocket of his Space Scout tunic. He looked at it thoughtfully, a half-formed idea in his mind, and dropped it into the pocket of the jacket he wore.

He burned their discarded clothing, as an afterthought.

He and Hildi moved with more confidence, for now they would have a moment or two of grace if they met any Volksweld soldiers, before they were recognized as the fugitives.

They reached the edge of a ravine, and stopped. It was flat-bottomed, at the foot of a short, steep slope, and it stretched out of sight in both directions. There were no trees in the ravine, but copters were grounded in it and Volksweld soldiers swarmed all over it.

"We can't go through that," said Chaan. "They'd spot us, sure. If only we had some way to cut off that hair of yours, we might make it, but we'll have to go around."

"How about a hear-gun?" suggested Hildi.

"Might work," he agreed. "But you'd sure better not move your head."

They sat down, hidden by the bushes from the edge of the ravine, and Chaan drew one of the heat-guns. He adjusted it to a pencil-narrow beam, took Hildi's bright, shoulder-length hair in his left hand and amputated it carefully.

It took a while, because he had to avoid setting her head ablaze and he had to stop constantly to put out little fires the beam set in the foliage around them. At last, however, he had burned it off as closely as he dared, and he brushed away the ashes and charred ends. It was not a neat trim, but she could pass at a slight distance as an unusually shaggy-haired soldier with a soft-lipped, big-eyed boyish face.

"That tunic doesn't entirely, hide the width of your hips, but there are certain of your feminine characteristics I'd like to save for myself," he said with a smile. "Maybe if we wait till dusk without being discovered, we can pass through that gang."

They relaxed against the bole of the bush, and Chaan pulled out the dodecahedron.

"I wonder about this," he said to Hildi.

"What is it?" she asked curiously, taking it from him and examining it.

"It's a souvenir of a marvelous experience," he said, and told her of meeting the boy.

"You say you dreamed you were that boy, when you were a child?" she asked, handing him back the dodecahedron.

"It wasn't a dream," he said solemnly, gazing down into her wide eyes. "It happened. I'm convinced that I came through a time-fault as a boy, and crossed decades of time and light-years of space to meet myself as the man I am now. The question is, what brought me through that time-fault?"

"The fault must have been in the way the rafters of the attic were twisted, and in the hole in the tree roots," she suggested.

"I don't think so. I tried to go back through that 'door' in the attic, and never could. And I almost didn't get back through the tree roots after I gave the dodecahedron away to myself. I think it's the dodecahedron."

"That little thing?" she asked, glancing down curiously at the bright, faceted object.

"Yes," said Chaan. "You know, I told you about meeting the Volkswelder when I was searching for the Wasser. It was a Volkswelder who gave me this dodecahedron when I was a child on Earth. The Volkswelder can travel through time as well as space, you know, and the one I met in the mountains said there are mechanical aids that humans can use to do the same thing. I think this dodecahedron is one of those."

"But there are no buttons or levers on it," she protested. "It's just a bright stone, like a big diamond."

"As a child," he said dreamily, "I looked into it and thought I saw great vistas. An artifact of the Volkswelder would not be so crude as to have buttons and levers. It would be attuned to the currents of the mind."

Together, fascinated, they gazed into the dodecahedron. The light within it seemed to writhe, and its reflected facets formed alien angles. The starry universe, the plains and mountains of every world in every age and time, seemed to reach out from it to envelop them.

"If I understood the Volkswelder," said Chaan in a bemused voice, "you can only go to a place and time where you have been or will be. If we could only go back to an earlier time on Sirius, so I could warn them to dispatch the fleet to Volksweld..."

There was no darkening of the day about them. But they were, all at once, no longer sitting under a bush in the wooded hills. They were sitting on, the landing area of a spaceport, in the shade of a spaceship's huge fin. It was still late afternoon, and the sun in the sky was still the crimson disc of Wolf 359.

"We're at the Regn spaceport!" exclaimed Chaan, disappointed, "We must have traveled just in space, not in time."

"But how could that be?" asked Hildi, hugging his arm closely and fearfully.

"Of course! You were never in the Sirius system, so we couldn't go back to Sirius. So we must not have moved in time at all. The Volkswelder told me time and space were the same, so it would be logical that this dodecahedron could take us through space without altering the time."

There was a great crowd of people at the spaceport, in a cleared area in front of them. Chaan and Hildi were far enough back from the crowd to he taken for two Volksweld soldiers. Beyond the fringes of the crowd was some sort of a military formation.

And then there was a sound as of an approaching artillery shell, and a-needle-like ship dropped from the sky. It settled gently to the ground, just beyond the crowd.

"My starship!" cried Chaan, getting to his feet. "Marl lied to me! They're bringing back my starship!"

CHAPTER TWENTY

CHAAN AND HILDI pushed their way up through the fringes of the crowd, toward the starship. The entry port of the starship opened, and a man emerged: a man in the blue-and-silver uniform of the Space Scout, a man with Chaan's sober face and alert blue eyes.

"One of those accursed doubles!" exclaimed Chaan in a low tone. "Marl's had that starship all the time. This fellow must have just gotten back from a test flight."

He laid his hand on the butt of his heat-gun.

"Well, he'll regret not heading straight for Lalande," he muttered. "I can get him from here."

"No!" whispered Hildi desperately, catching his wrist, "they'd just burn you down!"

"That's right," admitted Chaan. "Hildi, we've got to take a

desperate chance. Come along."

With Hildi at his side, he moved closer to the starship, as near as the line of uniformed guards would permit. To the people around them, he and Hildi were just two Volksweld soldiers on free time, joining the crowd to watch the starship come in.

The man with Chaan's face stepped firmly down the ramp. Clutching a thick briefcase under his arm, he strode down the lane formed by uniformed guards with hardly a sidelong glance. His expression was grim.

Chaan waited until the man was past them, and all eyes were following him to the group of people waiting to welcome him.

"Now, Hildi!" he said.

Together they burst through the line of guards and raced up the ramp to the starship's open port. They made it inside.

Orders were being shouted, and heat-beams splashed around the edge of the port behind them. Chaan pushed a button frantically and the port swung shut. As it closed, he could see half a dozen soldiers falling to the ground from the ramp as it was pulled into the ship below the port.

Chaan climbed the ladder in breathless haste to the lower control deck. The heat-guns could not harm the metal hull of the starship, but he could not give them time to bring up artillery or to get to an interceptor ship.

He flung himself into the control chair and threw the ship into anti-gravity. Looking out the port, he saw the ground receding below, soldiers and civilians scurrying like frantic ants.

A few moments later, Hildi came up.

"Their only chance to intercept us would be with some ship already aspace that is close enough to change course and cross our line of flight," said Chaan, "and this ship can blast one of Marl's battleships out of space if necessary. As soon as we're far enough out of range of Volksweld, I'll throw it into stardrive."

"But Chaan," she objected, "this is a scout ship. You can't take me aboard it to Lalande, can you?"

"I don't think the Solar Council would disagree that this is an emergency situation," he answered happily. "I just hope Marl has this ship stocked up for the trip."

He turned to the control board to check the supply indicators.

His glance fell on the chronometer.

It read April 23, 35031

"Hildi!" he cried. "Look at that!"

"That can't be right," she said in a puzzled tone. "Today is the 10th day of Wilmar…" She paused and figured briefly in her mind, then added: "That would be November 6, 3503, Earth Standard."

"Exactly!" said Chaan exultantly. "But April 23rd was the day I landed on Volksweld."

"You mean the chronometer's stopped?"

"Hildi, this chronometer doesn't stop, as long as the stars shine. It's right. Don't you see what's happened? The dodecahedron did take us back through time, back to the spaceport just as I was landing this ship on Volksweld!"

"But I was in the crowd watching the ship land that day," she protested.

"That's exactly why we went back to that time and spot. I was concentrating on some time in the past when I'd be able to warn the Solar Council, but we were both looking into the dodecahedron together, and it took us both back to the only place and time where both of us were close and yet there was still a chance of doing anything."

"But I don't understand," she said. "If you landed the starship…"

She stopped. Her eyes grew big and round and she clapped her fingers over her open mouth.

"Now, do you see?" he exclaimed. "We doubled back in time. That man who left the starship, whom I would have shot: he was no double, he was me, landing on Volksweld seven months ago.

"Those two soldiers I saw steal my ship that day: Hildi, *they were you and I!* No wonder Marl couldn't recover my starship. I had stolen it myself, and the stardrive explosion he saw was not a fake explosion, as I told him; it was the explosion he'll see when I put the ship into stardrive in a few hours."

Chaan leaned back and laughed. Hildi crept into his arms.

"I'm not sure I understand how it happened," she said quietly, "but the important thing to me is that I'm still with you, and we're going to Lalande together."

"Well, the ship wasn't restocked, but it carries a certain reserve," said Chaan. "We'll have to go on tight rations, but it isn't as far to Lalande as to Sirius, and we'll make it all right."

"And then," said Hildi in a very small voice, looking up into his face, "will you leave me after your year on Lalande?"

He smiled down at her and held her close.

"I shall not," he said firmly. "In the words of an old teacher, I have helped make my world, and I have found my place and my happiness. I'm leaving the service at Lalande, Hildi. Maybe we'll take a ship to Greyhound, or come back with the fleet to Volksweld, or even return to Earth, if we should care to spend a few years traveling; but we'll always be together now."

A few hours later they sat, two citizens of the Sirius Quadrilateral clad comfortably in Sirian togas, and watched the rearward screens. They were very sleepy, for it was far past midnight in that area of a little planet they had left so recently.

That planet was now nothing but a small dark blot that dimmed the baleful light of the receding star, Wolf 359. A tiny planet revolving around a tiny star: and a tiny man on it had threatened the peace of the Galaxy.

It seemed to Chaan that he should feel very big and powerful, but he did not. He felt very small in the big universe, and he was proud it was so: for only a tiny man could block the star-spread ambitions of another tiny man.

He hefted the dodecahedron, and watched it sparkle in the red rays of Wolf.

"I'll give this to our son when he's old enough," he told Hildi dreamily. "Perhaps it will take him, too, through a hole in some attic on some world. And perhaps some day it will help him, too, to turn the tide of destiny."

THE END

If you've enjoyed this book, you will not want to miss these terrific titles…

ARMCHAIR SCI-FI & HORROR DOUBLE NOVELS, $12.95 each

D-11 **PERIL OF THE STARMEN** by Kris Neville
       THE STRANGE INVASION by Murray Leinster

D-12 **THE STAR LORD** by Boyd Ellanby
       CAPTIVES OF THE FLAME by Samuel R. Delany

D-13 **MEN OF THE MORNING STAR** by Edmond Hamilton
       PLANET FOR PLUNDER by Hal Clement and Sam Merwin, Jr.

D-14 **ICE CITY OF THE GORGON** by Chester S. Geier and Richard Shaver
       WHEN THE WORLD TOTTERED by Lester del Rey

D-15 **WORLDS WITHOUT END** by Clifford D. Simak
       THE LAVENDER VINE OF DEATH by Don Wilcox

D-16 **SHADOW ON THE MOON** by Joe Gibson
       ARMAGEDDON EARTH by Geoff St. Reynard

D-17 **THE GIRL WHO LOVED DEATH** by Paul W. Fairman
       SLAVE PLANET by Laurence M. Janifer

D-18 **SECOND CHANCE** by J. F. Bone
       MISSION TO A DISTANT STAR by Frank Belknap Long

D-19 **THE SYNDIC** by C. M. Kornbluth
       FLIGHT TO FOREVER by Poul Anderson

D-20 **SOMEWHERE I'LL FIND YOU** by Milton Lesser
       THE TIME ARMADA by Fox B. Holden

ARMCHAIR SCIENCE FICTION CLASSICS, $12.95 each

C-4 **CORPUS EARTHLING**
      by Louis Charbonneau

C-5 **THE TIME DISSOLVER**
      by Jerry Sohl

C-6 **WEST OF THE SUN**
      by Edgar Pangborn

ARMCHAIR SCI-FI & HORROR GEMS SERIES, $12.95 each

G-1 **SCIENCE FICTION GEMS, Vol. One**
      Isaac Asimov and others

G-2 **HORROR GEMS, Vol. One**
      Carl Jacobi and others

If you've enjoyed this book, you will not want to miss these terrific titles…

ARMCHAIR SCI-FI & HORROR DOUBLE NOVELS, $12.95 each

D-21   **EMPIRE OF EVIL** by Robert Arnette
THE SIGN OF THE TIGER by Alan E. Nourse & J. A. Meyer

D-22   **OPERATION SQUARE PEG** by Frank Belknap Long
ENCHANTRESS OF VENUS by Leigh Brackett

D-23   **THE LIFE WATCH** by Lester del Rey
CREATURES OF THE ABYSS by Murray Leinster

D-24   **LEGION OF LAZARUS** by Edmond Hamilton
STAR HUNTER by Andre Norton

D-25   **EMPIRE OF WOMEN** by John Fletcher
ONE OF OUR CITIES IS MISSING by Irving Cox

D-26   **THE WRONG SIDE OF PARADISE** by Raymond F. Jones
THE INVOLUNTARY IMMORTALS by Rog Phillips

D-27   **EARTH QUARTER** by Damon Knight
ENVOY TO NEW WORLDS by Keith Laumer

D-28   **SLAVES TO THE METAL HORDE** by Milton Lesser
HUNTERS OUT OF TIME by Joseph E. Kelleam

D-29   **RX JUPITER SAVE US** by Ward Moore
BEWARE THE USURPERS by Geoff St. Reynard

D-30   **SECRET OF THE SERPENT** by Don Wilcox
CRUSADE ACROSS THE VOID by Dwight V. Swain

ARMCHAIR SCIENCE FICTION CLASSICS, $12.95 each

C-7   **THE SHAVER MYSTERY, Book One**
by Richard S. Shaver

C-8   **THE SHAVER MYSTERY, Book Two**
by Richard S. Shaver

C-9   **MURDER IN SPACE** by David V. Reed
by David V. Reed

ARMCHAIR MASTERS OF SCIENCE FICTION SERIES, $16.95 each

M-3   **MASTERS OF SCIENCE FICTION, Vol. Three**
Robert Sheckley, "The Perfect Woman" and other tales

M-4   **MASTERS OF SCIENCE FICTION, Vol. Four**
Mack Reynolds, "Stowaway" and other tales

If you've enjoyed this book, you will not want to miss these terrific titles…

ARMCHAIR SCI-FI & HORROR DOUBLE NOVELS, $12.95 each

D-31 **A HOAX IN TIME** by Keith Laumer
INSIDE EARTH by Poul Anderson

D-32 **TERROR STATION** by Dwight V. Swain
THE WEAPON FROM ETERNITY by Dwight V. Swain

D-33 **THE SHIP FROM INFINITY** by Edmond Hamilton
TAKEOFF by C. M. Kornbluth

D-34 **THE METAL DOOM** by David H. Keller
TWELVE TIMES ZERO by Howard Browne

D-35 **HUNTERS OUT OF SPACE** by Joseph Kelleam
INVASION FROM THE DEEP by Paul W. Fairman,

D-36 **THE BEES OF DEATH** by Robert Moore Williams
A PLAGUE OF PYTHONS by Frederik Pohl

D-37 **THE LORDS OF QUARMALL** by Fritz Leiber and Harry Fischer
BEACON TO ELSEWHERE by James H. Schmitz

D-38 **BEYOND PLUTO** by John S. Campbell
ARTERY OF FIRE by Thomas N. Scortia

D-39 **SPECIAL DELIVERY** by Kris Neville
NO TIME FOR TOFFEE by Charles F. Meyers

D-40 **RECALLED TO LIFE** by Robert Silverberg
JUNGLE IN THE SKY by Milton Lesser

ARMCHAIR SCIENCE FICTION CLASSICS, $12.95 each

C-10 **MARS IS MY DESTINATION**
by Frank Belknap Long

C-11 **SPACE PLAGUE**
by George O. Smith

C-12 **SO SHALL YE REAP**
by Rog Phillips

ARMCHAIR SCI-FI & HORROR GEMS SERIES, $12.95 each

G-3 **SCIENCE FICTION GEMS, Vol. Two**
James Blish and others

G-4 **HORROR GEMS, Vol. Two**
Joseph Payne Brennan and others

If you've enjoyed this book, you will not want to miss these terrific titles…

ARMCHAIR SCI-FI & HORROR DOUBLE NOVELS, $12.95 each

D-41   **FULL CYCLE** by Clifford D. Simak
            IT WAS THE DAY OF THE ROBOT by Frank Belknap Long

D-42   **THIS CROWDED EARTH** by Robert Bloch
            REIGN OF THE TELEPUPPETS by Daniel Galouye

D-43   **THE CRISPIN AFFAIR** by Jack Sharkey
            THE RED HELL OF JUPITER by Paul Ernst

D-44   **PLANET OF DREAD** by Dwight V. Swain
            WE THE MACHINE by Gerald Vance

D-45   **THE STAR HUNTER** by Edmond Hamilton
            THE ALIEN by Raymond F. Jones

D-46   **WORLD OF IF** by Rog Phillips
            SLAVE RAIDERS FROM MERCURY by Don Wilcox

D-47   **THE ULTIMATE PERIL** by Robert Abernathy
            PLANET OF SHAME by Bruce Elliot

D-48   **THE FLYING EYES** by J. Hunter Holly
            SOME FABULOUS YONDER by Phillip Jose Farmer

D-49   **THE COSMIC BUNGLARS** by Geoff St. Reynard
            THE BUTTONED SKY by Geoff St. Reynard

D-50   **TYRANTS OF TIME** by Milton Lesser
            PARIAH PLANET by Murray Leinster

ARMCHAIR SCIENCE FICTION CLASSICS, $12.95 each

C-13   **SUNKEN WORLD**
            by Stanton A. Coblentz

C-14   **THE LAST VIAL**
            by Sam McClatchie, M. D.

C-15   **WE WHO SURVIVED (THE FIFTH ICE AGE)**
            by Sterling Noel

ARMCHAIR MASTERS OF SCIENCE FICTION SERIES, $16.95 each

MS-5   **MASTERS OF SCIENCE FICTION, Vol. Five**
            Winston K. Marks—Test Colony and other tales

MS-6   **MASTERS OF SCIENCE FICTION, Vol. Six**
            Fritz Leiber—Deadly Moon and other tales

If you've enjoyed this book, you will not want to miss these terrific titles…

ARMCHAIR SCI-FI & HORROR DOUBLE NOVELS, $12.95 each

D-51   **A GOD NAMED SMITH** by Henry Slesar
            WORLDS OF THE IMPERIUM by Keith Laumer

D-52   **CRAIG'S BOOK** by Don Wilcox
            EDGE OF THE KNIFE by H. Beam Piper

D-53   **THE SHINING CITY** by Rena M. Vale
            THE RED PLANET by Russ Winterbotham

D-54   **THE MAN WHO LIVED TWICE** by Rog Phillips
            VALLEY OF THE CROEN by Lee Tarbell

D-55   **OPERATION DISASTER** by Milton Lesser
            LAND OF THE DAMNED by Berkeley Livingston

D-56   **CAPTIVE OF THE CENTAURIANESS** by Poul Anderson
            A PRINCESS OF MARS by Edgar Rice Burroughs

D-57   **THE NON-STATISTICAL MAN** by Raymond F. Jones
            MISSION FROM MARS by Rick Conroy

D-58   **INTRUDERS FROM THE STARS** by Ross Rocklynne
            FLIGHT OF THE STARLING by Chester S. Geier

D-59   **COSMIC SABOTEUR** by Frank M. Robinson
            LOOK TO THE STARS by Willard Hawkins

D-60   **THE MOON IS HELL!** by John W. Campbell, Jr.
            THE GREEN WORLD by Hal Clement

ARMCHAIR SCIENCE FICTION CLASSICS, $12.95 each

C-16   **THE SHAVER MYSTERY, Book Three**
            by Richard S. Shaver

C-17   **THE PLANET STRAPPERS**
            by Raymond Z. Gallun

C-18   **THE FOURTH "R"**
            by George O. Smith

ARMCHAIR SCI-FI & HORROR GEMS SERIES, $12.95 each

G-5   **SCIENCE FICTION GEMS, Vol. Three**
           C. M. Kornbluth and others

G-6   **HORROR GEMS, Vol. Three**
           August Derleth and others

If you've enjoyed this book, you will not want to miss these terrific titles…

ARMCHAIR SCI-FI & HORROR DOUBLE NOVELS, $12.95 each

D-61 **THE MAN WHO STOPPED AT NOTHING** by Paul W. Fairman
TEN FROM INFINITY by Ivar Jorgensen

D-62 **WORLDS WITHIN** by Rog Phillips
THE SLAVE by C.M. Kornbluth

D-63 **SECRET OF THE BLACK PLANET** by Milton Lesser
THE OUTCASTS OF SOLAR III by Emmett McDowell

D-64 **WEB OF THE WORLDS** by Harry Harrison and Katherine MacLean
RULE GOLDEN by Damon Knight

D-65 **TEN TO THE STARS** by Raymond Z. Gallun
THE CONQUERORS by David H. Keller, M. D.

D-66 **THE HORDE FROM INFINITY** by Dwight V. Swain
THE DAY THE EARTH FROZE by Gerald Hatch

D-67 **THE WAR OF THE WORLDS** by H. G. Wells
THE TIME MACHINE by H. G. Wells

D-68 **STARCOMBERS** by Edmond Hamilton
THE YEAR WHEN STARDUST FELL by Raymond F. Jones

D-69 **HOCUS-POCUS UNIVERSE** by Jack Williamson
QUEEN OF THE PANTHER WORLD by Berkeley Livingston

D-70 **BATTERING RAMS OF SPACE** by Don Wilcox
DOOMSDAY WING by George H. Smith

ARMCHAIR SCIENCE FICTION CLASSICS, $12.95 each

C-19 **EMPIRE OF JEGGA**
by David V. Reed

C-20 **THE TOMORROW PEOPLE**
by Judith Merril

C-21 **THE MAN FROM YESTERDAY**
by Howard Browne as by Lee Francis

C-22 **THE TIME TRADERS**
by Andre Norton

C-23 **ISLANDS OF SPACE**
by John W. Campbell

C-24 **THE GALAXY PRIMES**
by E. E. "Doc" Smith

Made in the USA
Middletown, DE
28 July 2022

70157477R00130